"You thought you had beaten me, you sonofabitch," grated Steel Hand. He had lost a lot of blood. His face was pale beneath the tan. The heavy LeMat shook slightly as he steadied it while aiming at Dave. That fistful of firepower made Dave sick.

Dave had made the mistake of leaning too far over the rim so that his outspread hands held most of his weight on the rock bulge. If he raised his hands to push himself backward he might very well slide down into the pool, a perfect target for his Colt without falling.

"You'll die down there unless you get help," Dave bluffed.

Steel Hand nodded. "That's right. And I'll take you with me."

THE
WALKING
SANDS

Gordon D. Shirreffs

FAWCETT GOLD MEDAL • NEW YORK

A Fawcett Gold Medal Book
Published by Ballantine Books
Copyright © 1990 by Gordon D. Shirreffs

Library of Congress Catalog Card Number: 89-92447

ISBN 0-449-14680-4

Manufactured in the United States of America

First Editon: May 1990

The Walking Sands

There's gold, and it's haunting and haunting;
It's luring me on as of old;
Yet it isn't the gold that I'm wanting
So much as just finding the gold. . . .

Robert Service
"The Spell of the Yukon"

CHAPTER 1

THE REDDISH-BROWN GLOW OF THE RISING NEW MOON made it look as though it was lit from within like a Japanese lantern. Its eerie light cast upon the dimly seen, leaden-hued humps of the Growler Mountains sixty miles to the east across the Lechuguilla Desert from the Tinajas Altas Mountains. The Tinajas Altas Mountains usually held the only reliable source of water from Quitabaquito Springs sixty miles to the east along the fearful Camino del Diablo, or the Devil's Road. The camino crossed the border into Arizona Territory about thirteen miles west-northwest of Agua Salado on the Rio Sonoyta and remained on the American side all the way to Tinajas Altas. East of the Tinajas Altas Mountains the road turned northwest to reach Yuma on the Colorado River. The road was so named because of the hundreds of travelers who had perished along the way from thirst, hunger, and fatigue; of these three, thirst was paramount. A traveler could hardly miss his way on the camino. It was marked at various intervals with faded crosses, mounded graves, or by the sun-bleached human bones scattered by desert predators.

The higher slopes of the Tinajas Altas Mountains were marked by a huge studding of massive granite boulders. High among them were eight natural hollows deeply eroded into the granite that filled with rainwater in the downpours of summer cloudbursts. The term *tinaja* translated into "large earthen jar," but the Americans had dubbed the deep hollows "tanks," and so it was called the High Tanks. It was a difficult climb to reach them and get the water, but one either

1

did so or died of thirst. The nearest other water supplies were at Yuma, twenty-five miles away across the dry Lechuguilla Desert, or at the Colorado River some fifty miles to the west.

Dave Hunter stood guard while his partner Ash Mawson and their prisoner, the Jack of Spades, slept. They had reached Tinajas Altas before dawn that day after a murderous, sixty-mile trip from Quitabaquito Springs. They had meant to go on to Yuma that day, but their horses and the pack mule were exhausted. They had allowed the animals a day of rest. Bounty hunting for escaped prisoners from Yuma Penitentiary was a tough-enough business under ordinary circumstances, but to hunt two escaped prisoners down in the area of the Camino del Diablo was hell itself.

Dave was about six-feet-plus tall, a lean, sinewy, narrow-waisted, broad-shouldered lath of a man, all rawhide and spring steel without an ounce of fat anywhere on him. His saddle-hued face was angular and big of nose. He had been nicknamed Hawk-Face by the Chiricahua Apaches with whom he had once served as an army scout. His hard-looking, light-blue eyes stood out in rather startling contrast to the tanned skin of his face. They were a *hard* blue, likened to high mountain water tumbling down snowy slopes under a film of transparent ice during a spring thaw. Glacial blue an intellectual might term their color, perhaps like the terrible frozen Norse hell.

His eyes were one of his natural weapons. His sight was almost eaglelike. It had a psychological effect on any man who challenged him. It could be a stare that stopped most challenges. A few women had managed to penetrate beyond those eyes of his, at least partway, to find a warm, caring man of infinite tenderness. Still, there was always something hidden from them. Something no man or woman, with perhaps a few exceptions, had ever even partly understood, and even then they were not at all sure about that which they thought they had learned.

Dave and Ash had been working out of Yuma for three months on call to deliver hard-case prisoners to Yuma Pen or to track down and recapture escaped prisoners. To escape from Yuma Pen was an almost impossible feat. One might get free of the penitentiary itself, but to avoid death out on the waterless desert or recapture by Yuman, Cocopah, or Apache trackers was quite another story. This trip had been in pursuit of two prisoners who had escaped. Somehow they had managed to elude the Indian trackers and survive the lack of water and the killing heat of the desert country north, east, and south of Yuma. In time they had been seen by a prospector at Growler Wash between the Growler Mountains to the east and the Granite Mountains to the west, evidently heading southeast for Quitabaquito Springs.

Dave and Ash had taken a pair of horses each and a pack mule. They traveled by stagecoach from Yuma to Mohawk with the horses and mule trotting along behind. By changing horses at intervals and walking a good part of the way, they had reached the Springs five days after the prison break. In Mexico they had caught the man known in the United States as Jack Spade. His alias in Mexico was Juan Espada, and he was known on both sides of the border as the Jack of Spades. The other escapee, a certain Jesus Valencia, had simply vanished, possibly to his death by exhaustion and thirst south and west, in the environs of the Gran Desierto de Altar of Sonora. The Gran Desierto was a vast and merciless area, one of the most remote, mysterious, and least-known areas of the world. Uninhabited, it was practically waterless, a sunbeaten wasteland that broiled in the summer months with an average temperature of 120 degrees. It stretched over three hundred miles south of the border diagonally from northwest to southeast. Its southern limit for a considerable stretch was the Gulf of California. Dave Hunter thought there was a deadly, frightening quality about the Gran Desierto. It bred eerie tales and mysterious legends about strange goings-on and lost treasures of the early Spaniards and the secretive Jesuits, the powerful Soldiers of Christ.

Dave leaned on his long-barreled Sharps Old Reliable rifle and looked out across the desert country to the south. Once crossed by man, the soul-searing experience of the Gran Desierto was never to be forgotten. The penalty for those who foolishly dared its challenge was either an agonizingly cruel and horrible death or fearful, haunting nightmares for the tortured survivors who lived to tell about it. Those survivors were few in number. Dave was one of them.

There was an uneasiness about the night. The moon was casting its pale clear light over the windless desert. Nothing moved, and yet *something* seemed to be there, just out of sight, watching and waiting.

Dave peered through his powerful German field glasses. They were the very best made by the master Vollmer of Jena. The clear lenses magnified the distance, bringing out in sharp detail the items upon which they were focused. They enlarged the creosote bushes, the cacti, ironwood trees, and the low graves covered by mounded stones with here and there a weathered cross tilted by the strong furnace winds of that country. The area of the graves was known as the Mesita de los Muertos, the Little Mesa of the Dead. It was not a place of the living; the living stayed in that area just long enough to get their fill of water from the High Tanks and then get on with their traveling. It was truly a place of the dead, victims of the Camino del Diablo.

Dave lowered his field glasses. It was always the same. Nothing moved. It was like a sombre painting by a melancholy artist. There was nothing living out there, *and yet* . . . He sniffed the air like a hunting wolf. All he smelled was the odor of his body and clothing, the stale perspiration aroused by that of the fresh tobacco, and the freshly tarred roof odor of the resinous creosote bush. *Hedondilla* the Mexicans called it—little stinker.

Dave cased his field glasses and picked up his rifle. It was about time for him to be relieved by Ash. He climbed to one of the tanks and drank from it. The water was so clear he could see the algae growing on the bottom. Bird feathers floated on the surface, and nocturnal, four-footed drinkers sometimes left their droppings and voidings on the brink or in the water itself. One got used to it. It was either drink it or die of thirst. "Coyote tea," Ash whimsically called it.

Dave heard the faint musical jingling of Ash's spur rowels

as the other man came to the tank. Ash knelt and cupped water in his hands to drink. He looked sideways at Dave. An unspoken thought seemed to pass between them. It was a way they had with each other. There was no accounting for it, but it was there. "You should have wakened me earlier," Ash said. He squatted beside the tank. He tilted his head to one side and studied Dave with those damnable green eyes of his. "Something bothering you?" he asked quietly.

Ash was tall and lean with a beak of a nose. His hair was black and straight, and his cheekbones were high. The Indian showed in him. His mother had been a Sac Indian. His eyes were green like bottle glass. He was not quite as tall as Dave. He was a past master with the long gun and the six-shooter, but his particular pride and greatest skill was with the bowie knife. If any man could be called a genius in the handling of the heavy-bladed and downright deadly knife originally named after Jim Bowie, that man was Ash Mawson. He and Dave were partners and as deadly a duo as could be conjured up by a necromancer from the smoky, flame-shot depths of hell itself.

Dave shrugged. "What the hell are we doing out here anyway? We chased Spade and Valencia for about one-hundred-and-twenty-five-miles. We lost two good horses. They cost us fifty dollars apiece. We had to outfit ourselves in Yuma which maybe ran one-hundred-and-fifty dollars. We were offered five hundred dollars apiece for Spade and Valencia, and we never did find Valencia. So, now we end up with two-hundred-and-fifty dollars. Split two ways that's *one-hundred-and-twenty-five apiece*! Gawd dammit! You can spend that much in a weekend in Yuma drinking, playing faro, and frolicking in the feathers with a whore or two."

Ash shrugged. "Ain't nothing to stop you from doing the same."

Dave slapped his right hand against the side of his hat. "Certainly! But what about Monday morning?"

Ash eyed him thoughtfully. "That's true. On top of all that you mentioned I've never quite been able to figure out this deal of bringing in Spade and Valencia for five hundred dollars apiece. And how in hell did they get out of Yuma Pen in

the first place?'' Ash shook his head. ''The prison superintendent ever tell you how?''

''No, but then I didn't talk with him. He just put up the
reward. Actually, it was Deputy-Sheriff Bull Andrews who
closed the deal. The super was off on leave right after I spoke
with him.''

Ash spat to one side. ''Bull Andrews? That crooked son
of a bitch!''

Dave nodded. ''There was nothing I could do. We needed
the money. I don't trust him any more than you do, but we
can depend on the superintendent for payment.''

Ash shrugged. ''All five hundred of it,'' he said in disgust.
He leaned closer to Dave and then looked back over both
shoulders as though someone might be listening. ''Davie,''
he said in a low voice, ''that son of a bitch Spade was talking
in his sleep while you were on guard. He was repeating some
words over and over again. I was half-asleep myself, and at
first I didn't pay any attention to him talking. Then I began
to listen. Suddenly he sat up straight and looked all about
him kinda wild-like, about like he didn't know where he was.
Then he said one word real clear-like while he was looking
right at me, but it was as though he was looking right *through*
me. Then he lay back and went right to sleep. He didn't talk
any more after that. He had said something about a 'lost
mission,' then gold and treasure. Then he said something
about the Grand Desierto of Altar. Then he added the one
word.'' He looked carefully about. *''Jesuit,''* he whispered.

It was very quiet. Some nocturnal creature scuttled about
in the brush. There was a sharp squeak as though whatever
it was had caught its prey—a lizard, perhaps, or maybe a
kangaroo rat who had left its thorny daytime habitat for a
little night foraging. Hunt and kill; be hunted and killed. It
was the unwritten law of the desert night.

''Well?'' asked Ash.

''Jack Spade is said to be loco. At least, that's about what
everyone says on both sides of the border. He's got a record
as long as your arm both in Mexico and the United States.

Well, anyway, they finally caught up with him and slammed him into Yuma for ten years. And he *escaped*. How?''

''I've been wondering about that.''

''Then there's this little man who calls himself Jesus Valencia.'' Dave took out his sweat-damp wallet and withdrew a cracked and faded photograph. The moonlight revealed a thin-faced man with narrow shoulders and an intent, almost mystical kind of gaze; it seemed as though he was looking into the camera and beyond it to some unseen goal of his own. His thin hands held a prison badge as round as a saucer pinned to his striped prison jacket. His number had been painted on the badge. Dave handed the photo to Ash.

Ash studied the picture. ''They said he was an educated man with fine manners. Hardly the type to end up in Yuma Pen.''

''Or make an escape with the Jack of Spades,'' added Dave. ''What does he look like to you?''

Ash shrugged. ''A doctor maybe, or a lawyer; maybe a college professor. Some kind of professional man maybe. Certainly not the type to be in Yuma Pen.''

''Like a . . .'' Ash started to say.

Dave nodded. ''A priest. Possibly a Jesuit . . .''

Something moved quietly higher up the slope. Ash drew and cocked his Colt. Dave cocked the hammer and set the firing trigger of his Sharps. The men faded into the shadow of a huge boulder. It was quiet again; a tense sort of quietness.

Suddenly, so suddenly it made both men jump a little nervously, the quick, sharp howl of a coyote broke the stillness. A few seconds later another one howled. An eerie chorus of many more followed the second howler. It was difficult to tell how many of them there were, as the noise drew out the echoes from the rocks and sent them tumbling downslope in all directions to die away in the distance.

Dave grinned uneasily. ''They're after their evening drink,'' he commented.

Ash nodded. ''Let's let them have it. It's their country anyway.''

They passed between huge boulders and clambered up the heights to their sparse camp and the sleeping Jack of Spades.

CHAPTER 2

ASH TOOK THE LEAD. GRIPPING HIS COLT, HE STOPPED and quickly raised his right hand to halt Dave. They were within fifty feet of the place where they had made their camp. Ash faded into the shadow of a towering boulder with Dave close behind him, rifle slung over his shoulder, knife in his left hand, and half-cocked Colt in his right. Dave could see over Ash's shoulder to where Jack Spade had been sleeping in his Spanish bed—lying on his belly on the hard ground with his back drawn up over him for a cover. He wasn't there now. He was nowhere in sight. The only reminder of his late presence was the worn leather hobble thong that Ash had used to tie his wrists behind his back. It lay now in two pieces on the ground.

Ash turned his head a little. "Be careful. My Winchester is missing. He's likely got it. He'll be after the horses! *Andale!*"

It was Ash's usual way—don't stop to think too long. Move fast to the scene and go into action!

"*Wait,*" Dave hissed. "Maybe he wouldn't take that chance until he made sure of us. If he got away with the horses, he'd know damned well we'd track him right into hell itself if we had to."

Ash grinned. "Besides, he's worth five hundred eagles to us."

They distinctly heard the dry click of a sear, like a cricket rubbing his hind legs together, as a gun hammer was cocked higher up the slope beyond the camp. Dave looked to where he and Ash had picketed the two horses and the mule. He could see their heads as they looked down toward the camp. He pointed up the slope and nodded to Ash. "They're still there," he whispered.

Ash cupped his hands about his mouth. "You baldheaded bastard! If you aimed to get away from here with those horses, why didn't you go when you had the chance?" Both he and Dave moved as soon as he spoke.

Jack took up the challenge. "You beak-nosed son of a bitch!" he rasped. He had a voice like a rusty file cutting through metal. "What say we lay down these guns and meet out in the open? I'll show you some real and fancy ass kickin'!"

"Come on down, manure mouth!" returned Ash. "You just ain't got the guts! Come on! Tell you what! I'll throw out my bowie, and we'll race for it, you ugly lizard!"

Jack let loose with a broadside of curses that would have put a mule skinner to shame.

Dave grinned. "Let him alone, Ash," he pleaded mockingly. "You know he's not in his right mind. Maybe we can dicker with him."

"You're another, Hunter!" yelled Jack. "I'll kick in your ribs and mess up that big nose of yours so you look less like an anteater and more like a damned bullfrog."

"There ain't anything in our contract says we've got to bring you in alive!" Ash called out.

"The Indian trackers usually get paid if they just bring in the heads. Jack is so ugly we'd have no problem proving it was him," added Dave. "Besides, we wouldn't have to listen to his bullshit all the way to Yuma."

There was a long silence.

Jack broke the quiet. "Them Indian trackers are Gawd damned heathens! What the hell can you expect from them gut-eatin' bastards? Now, you're *white* men. You wouldn't do a thing like that, would you?" He paused uncertainly. "Or would you?" he asked in a low voice. It was faintly heard by the two-legged, blue-eyed cougar and the green-eyed wolf hidden from his sight.

Dave leaned against the boulder. He looked at his big Sharps. It fired a .44/90-caliber, paper-patched, 500-grain bullet. The soft lead would make a .44-caliber hole going in and then come out the other side with a hole the size of a doubled fist. The shock of a wound in the arm or leg might very well kill a man. Dave knew it wouldn't make any difference to Ash. Ash was more practical, some would say more cold-blooded, than his partner.

"I know what you're thinkin', Dave!" Ash called out, making sure Jack could hear. "He makes a break for the horses, and you've got him cold with Old Satan there."

Jack felt a chill. He knew about Dave Hunter and that big Sharps Model 1874. Hunter was known as a deadly marksman and was rarely seen without his gun. He became a little reckless in his fear. "You cold-blooded bastards!" he yelled. "The moonlight won't last forever! Hawwww!"

Ash gave it back to him, "Maybe you're right, *cabron*! But then, if *we* can't see you, then *you* can't see *us* either. Two against one in the dark and the devil takes the hindmost—*you*, certainly. . . ."

Jack hunkered down. As a rule he wasn't scared of anything wearing hide, fur, fins, or feathers, but he knew about these two manhunters. Dave Hunter, the man with the icy blue eyes—some said like the devil himself—was known to the Mexicans and many Americans as El Buscadero, the Seeker or Searcher. He was always looking for something: treasures and lost mines for the most part, which he didn't seem to be too successful at finding, and wanted men, which he was eminently successful at finding. He was like the *leon fantasma*, the phantom mountain lion who killed quietly and unseen. Then there was his partner Ash Mawson. The man with the flinty green eyes and the murderous, heavy-bladed bowie knife that was rumored to have taken more than one man's head off at the shoulders with one stroke. No phantom lion he, but rather a two-legged wolf howling in his mad quest for blood.

Jack shifted his position. "Hey, you two buzzards! Looks like we've got a Mexican standoff here. A draw. Supposin' you just let me walk away, like good fellas. What the hell is five hundred bucks to you?''

Ash grinned. ''Sure thing, Jack! We'll let you go, but we'll keep your head as security.''

''There's always *ley del fuego*,'' added Dave.

Ash wiggled a dirty little finger tip in his off ear. His gravelly voice carried clearly to the Jack of Spades. ''We'll give you a hundred-yard start downhill under the bright moonlight, Jack.''

Ley del fuego—the Mexican law of fire. Let a condemned prisoner run loose with, say, a fifty- to one-hundred-yard start depending on how many good marksmen one might have, then open fire. It saved the bother and expense of a trial, incarceration, and eventual formal execution. If a mistake was made, such as the dead man being found innocent, or perhaps the wrong person had been summarily executed, there was always the pseudo-pious saying, ''God will sort the souls.''

There was no reply from Jack.

Dave leaned close to Ash. ''What now? Maybe it is a Mexican standoff.''

''We're between him and the water,'' Ash replied.

''You forgot we refilled the water kegs. All he's got to do is load them on the mule and take off with the two horses.''

''Not if we get to him first.''

Dave nodded. ''But he's still got your Winchester.''

Ash reached inside his shirt and brought out a pint earthen flask of Baconora. It was real firewater—distilled from cactus juice to form a clear fluid that could be judiciously tinted a pleasing amber color by either soaking orange peel or, at times, a piece of raw chicken in it. Clear or tinted it had the wonderful quality of temporarily erasing one's troubles and was not known to raise the agonizing torment of a morning hangover. It could make an outright hero out of a dyed-in-the-wool coward. ''Baconora is the drink for heroes,'' the Mexicans said, usually with complacency and conviction. Dave and Ash had never heard one of them say how long the effect of heroism might last. The two men drank thought-fully, passing the flask back and forth a few times.

Ash cupped his hands about his mouth. "Hey, Jack! You give me back my Winchester, and we'll give you a full can-teen of water and that hundred-yard start I promised you!"

"You let me loose with a full canteen, an empty Colt and a handful of cartridges for it, and a two-hundred-yard start, and I'm ready to do business. They say you two are mean like a pair of tomcats tied in a sack, but at least you will give a man a fair shake. That's what *they* say."

Dave drank again. "You sure you want to do that?" he called out. "A canteen might help you make it to Yuma. That's the closest water. Quitabaquito Springs is sixty miles back east. The Colorado River is fifty miles. You'd have to try for Yuma, and when you got there you'd end up right back in Yuma Pen."

"You'll never get me back in that hellhole! I made a deal to get out of there! I *got* out of there! I ain't goin' back for the devil himself!"

Ash and Dave looked at each other. They each nodded.

"Who got you out of there, Jack?" asked Dave.

There was a moment or two of silence.

"Someone who swore they'd track me down and kill me if I talked too much," Jack said slowly.

Dave poked his head around the side of the boulder. "You come down out of there and lay the Winchester on the ground in plain sight and then raise your hands in the air and step back. Then we'll talk business."

"Who's to be the judge of whether I'm telling the truth or not?" demanded Jack.

Dave stepped out in the open with his hands in the air. "Why, *we* are, of course."

Jack hesitated. "I've heard you're a man of your word, Hunter. But I don't trust that beak-nosed bastard Mawson, and by God, I ain't never heard of anyone *else* who trusted him."

Ash stuck his head around the side of the boulder opposite

from Dave. "Well now, Jack my boy, it's right handsome of you to say that about me." He grinned widely.

"He's got you pegged all right," Dave said out of the side of his mouth. He raised his voice, "Are you coming down or not?"

Jack stood and held the Winchester up over his head. He made his way down the slope to where the sparse camp had been made. He placed it carefully on the ground and stepped back slowly with his hands still raised. His dark eyes nervously darted back and forth as he withdrew to stand with his back against a boulder.

Ash catfooted out and picked up his rifle.

"It's loaded," said Jack.

Ash nodded. *"Gracias."*

Jack shrugged. *"Por nada."*

Ash turned. "Put the irons on him, Dave."

"They're in my saddlebags." Dave looked at Jack. He tipped his hat. "Be patient, Mr. Spade. I'll be right back."

"This wasn't in the deal," Jack grunted.

Ash smiled. "It is now."

John "Jack" Spade was about three inches short of being six feet tall. He was almost as wide as maybe a single seat outhouse, with a barrel chest, virtually no neck, and powerful arms so long they seemed almost deformed on a human. His legs were disproportionally short and slightly bowed from many years in the saddle. His egg-shaped head was completely bald. His eyes were Yaqui, black with a hint of deep red in the pupils while the whites were the color of a pickled egg. His background was curious. His father, John Spade, had been Irish and deserted the United States Army to fight in the San Patricio Battalion formed of Irishmen who fought with the Mexican Army during the War with Mexico. He then deserted from the San Patricio Battalion and made his way westward to the Gulf of California, where he had gotten work as a skilled seaman and had become the skipper of a nondescript cargo steamer on the Gulf. He had married a Yaqui woman and Mexicanized his name to Juan Espada. Jack was a product of that unusual union. He had been raised in the seedy *barrios* of the Gulf of California coastline ports. He had gone to sea with his father and for a time had worked on the steamers of the Colorado River. A charge of murder had driven him from Mexico to the United States where a similar charge, never quite proven, had sent him back to Mexico. Always in trouble on one side of the border or the other he had, in time, become a legend among his own people. His name had been easily coined into the Jack of Spades. He was said to be simpleminded, some said loco, but he had a native shrewdness about him. Loco or not, he was dangerous when his anger was aroused.

Dave climbed up to where the horses and the mule were picketed. Ulysses, his *bayo coyote* dun nuzzled him. Dave had named him and his predecessors after his favorite hero— General Ulysses S. Grant. Dave kept a wary eye on Ash's sorrel, Dearly Beloved, one of many horses he had christened with that same name. The name evidently came from someone, a woman certainly, in Ash's checkered and somewhat mystifying past, but he had never divulged the reason for the name. Dearly Beloved raised his head from cropping the dry coarse grasses. He drew back his lips, showing his yellowed teeth, and laid back his ears. He watched Dave out of the corners of his eyes.

"Waiting for your chance, eh?" murmured Dave.

Dearly Beloved had a tendency to nip with his teeth or kick like a 12-pounder muzzle-loading Napoleon cannon. "Never take your eyes off him," Ash had warned. "Keep away from both ends of him. They're lethal! *Never* walk too closely behind him. This one liked to have killed me once. Well, he's never let me down when I needed him most. I guess I owe him something."

Dave eyed the sorrel. "Like a trip to the glue factory," he said. He quickly laid his hand on the butt of his Colt as he noticed what he assumed was a flicker of hate in Dearly Beloved's squinty eyes. "Go on! I dare you!"

Jughead the mule suddenly raised his head and looked toward the southeast. The mule seemed to have a sixth sense about him. A mule was better than a watchdog when it came to spotting Indians. "A horse or mule talks with his ears," an old New Mexican vaquero had once told Dave.

Dave looked down toward the Camino del Diablo. Then he saw, or *thought* he saw, the faintest of movements just beyond the foot of the slopes leading up to the High Tanks. Then it was gone as quickly as it had appeared. He waited. Nothing moved. He looked at the mule. Jughead had not resumed his grazing. The animal stood stock still. Only his ears moved a little. There *was* something out there!

Dave focused his field glasses on the area where he thought he had seen something. Nothing moved. He closed his eyes and then opened them quickly. For a fraction of a second he was certain, or almost certain, he had seen something in among the desert growths. It was gone again. *Yaquis?* The feared name seemed to form a ball of ice in the pit of his stomach.

Dave took out the heavy Mattatuck wrist irons and their key. He slid down the steep slope to reach the camp. He handed the irons to Ash.

Ash snapped the irons about Jack's thick wrists. "There, you ugly bastard. Let me see you work your way out of those!" He turned to Dave. "What the hell took you so long?"

Dave pointed to Jack. "Look at him" he said quietly.

Ash turned. Jack was like Jughead the mule. His bald head was tilted back, his eyes were half-closed, while he looked to the southeast.

"He senses something out there," Dave explained. "The mule was like that, too. I think I might have seen something."

"Like what?"

Dave shrugged. "*Yaquis* maybe?"

Ash whistled softly. "*This* far north? Hardly possible."

"I'll take a look."

Dave walked to a place where he could see the vastness of the desert terrain, which seemed to lap against the lower slopes of the Tinajas Altas like a great sandy sea. He scanned the area with his field glasses. Then he picked out something that seemed foreign to the dull texture and tone of the gravelly soil and sand stippled thickly with scraggly desert growths. It was as yet indistinguishable and was motionless, at least most of the time, any movement being hardly perceptible.

He sat there for a time. Had it really moved? Perhaps it was an optical illusion compounded by moonbeams. Was it a mirage? There was no blazing sun to create one.

Dave well knew the desert had a powerful identity of its own carefully disguised and sometimes hidden from the casual or careless observer who was usually always in haste to get to a more salubrious clime. Not so with Dave. To him the desert had an attraction, especially the hidden and unsolved mysteries within its vast and lonely areas. Dave himself had seen things for which there had been no explanation. He had heard sounds which had seemed to have no known source, on this planet at least.

Dave rubbed his eyes. "You've been out here too long," he murmured.

He turned to go.

From somewhere on that vast, moonlit expanse he heard, or perhaps *thought* he heard, a faint gutteral sound followed by a subdued roaring tone. He whirled, letting the field glasses fall to be held suspended by the strap about his neck. He snatched up his Sharps and cocked it. He narrowed his eyes and watched the lower slopes. Nothing moved.

Ash came quickly down the long slope with his Winchester held ready for a snap shot. "What the hell was that noise?" he asked.

Dave shook his head. "I don't know. I thought I might have imagined it."

Ash shook his head. "I heard it and so did Jack. You know, Dave, I've always heard that this damned place might be haunted."

Dave nodded. "It *is* haunted."

"You want to pull out of here before dawn?"

"We should, but there may be someone or *something* out there."

"That's what Spade says, too."

"Did he say what he thought it was?"

Ash shrugged. "He clammed up when I started asking questions. Well, I'll take over guard now. Go on and get some sleep."

Dave shook his head. "I can't sleep now. I'll stay on guard. If I get sleepy I'll wake you up."

Ash turned and started up the slope. "Make sure Brother Jack is well tied up about the legs," Dave called after him.

Ash nodded. "Keep your ears open for that sound again, hey?"

Dave sat down with his back against a boulder. He kept his cocked rifle across his thighs. Now and again he looked out across the desert. There was nothing unusual to be seen.

CHAPTER 3

DAVE SUDDENLY OPENED HIS EYES. THE MOON WAS FAR-
ther west. How long had he slept? He looked about himself,
and his attention became riveted on what looked like a human figure standing fifty yards from him. It was a small
naked man with long white hair and a tangled beard. The
slanting moonlight glistened from his eyes and shone dully
on something that lay against his chest. Was it an illusion?
Was it a phantom composed of moonbeams? Perhaps it was
a ghost who had emerged from one of the unmarked graves
on The Little Mesa of the Dead.

Dave stood up with his Sharps rifle in his hands. "Who
are you? *Quien va?* Speak, damn you!"

The ghostlike figure did not speak. He held out his thin
arms with palms upward as though cupping something in
them. His lips moved, but no sound came from them. Then
there came the faint gutteral sound followed by the subdued
roaring that Dave had heard before. The figure started staggering up the slope. As he drew closer Dave saw the scrawny,
dried-out-looking arms and legs. His abdomen seemed to be
drawn in almost to the vertebral column. His ribs stood out
like those of a starving horse. When he drew closer his facial
features appeared grotesque. It was as though his lips had
been amputated, leaving low ridges of blackened tissue. The
eyes were sunken and yet seemed to glitter in the dying
moonlight. The skin clung to the frame and limbs in a way
suggesting the shrunken rawhide used to repair a broken

18

wagon wheel. It was like tanned leather in appearance, with cuts and scratches from the thorned desert growths.

The man stopped twenty feet from Dave while swaying on his feet. His breathing was slow and spasmodic. The faint gutteral sound followed by the subdued roaring came from his open mouth.

Dave recognized the obvious signs on this tortured relic of a human being. They indicated thirst to an almost absolute extremity. The man was certainly within a hairbreadth of death.

The blackened lips moved soundlessly repeating one word over and over again. Dave read the lips. The man was saying, *"Agua . . . agua . . . agua . . ."*

Then the man fell forward awkwardly as though he was a mannequin manipulated by the strings of a master puppeteer. His face struck the hard ground. He lay still while his scrawny, clawlike hands opened and closed spasmodically.

Dave slung his Sharps. He picked up the little man and was surprised at the extreme lightness of the body. He started up the slope. "Ash! Ash! Ash!" he shouted.

When Ash came they carried the man to the tank where they had their camp. They placed him on a blanket. He lay on his back with his mouth squared like that of a Greek mask of tragedy. His tongue was a mere nub of blackened integument. Ash thumb-snapped a lucifer into flame. The faint flickering light revealed that the mucous membrane lining the mouth was cracked, shriveled, and blackened like the tongue.

Ash blew out the match. "He'll never make it, Davie. I've never seen one as bad as this. He should be dead."

Dave looked up at him. "*Something* kept him alive." He dribbled a little water into the desiccated hole that once had been a warm and moist pulsing membrane. The man coughed. He stared up at Dave. His lips moved in the repetitive, *"Agua . . . agua . . . agua . . ."*

"He's a Mexican," said Ash.

Dave looked down into the blue eyes. "Perhaps."

"What's this?" Ash asked. A silver chain hung about his

neck, and whatever had hung from it had slid down between his left arm and side. Ash drew up the chain and then whistled softly. The dying moonlight shone dully on a six-inch gold cross of heavy construction. It was what Dave had seen earlier against the man's chest.

Dave passed his hands over the man's shrunken extremities. They were cold, as though death had already claimed the body. He could detect no pulse at the wrists. There was apparently little circulation beyond the knees and elbows.

"By God," breathed Ash. "This cross is pure gold!"

"Give me a hand," ordered Dave. "Forget about the damned cross. This man is as close to death as I've ever seen."

They slopped water from the canteen over the dried-out flesh. They rubbed it into his limbs. The man's skin seemed to have the absorption of a sponge. They rationed his water to a small mouthful at a time.

Ash studied him. "He should be dead. What's keeping him alive?"

"Maybe the cross," Dave dryly suggested.

"What'll we do with him? It'd be too risky to move him this way. He might live a few more days. We can't stay here with him."

"We'll gamble on it," said Dave.

"We can leave him here beside a tank. Get Spade to Yuma and maybe come back to see if he survived."

Dave stood up. He shook his head. "If you want to get Spade to Yuma and then come back, go ahead. I'm staying with him until he lives or dies."

Ash squatted on his heels, teetering back and forth, looking from Dave to the man, or rather the cross, thought Dave.

"Are you figuring on how much that cross will bring in Yuma?" asked Dave.

Ash hefted the cross. Slowly a shrunken hand came up and weakly pushed Ash's hand away from the cross. There was almost a menacing look in the man's eyes. Dave noticed how blue they were. Odds were he wasn't a Mexican at all, although Dave had seen many Mexicans who did have blue eyes.

"The cross stays with him until he dies, if it comes to that," added Dave.

Ash looked up at Dave, holding him with those damnable green eyes. "And if he dies are you plannin' to bury the cross with him? You know, partner—symbolic and sentimental-like?"

Dave shrugged. "I hadn't thought of that."

Ash stood up. "Well, *think* about it. And while you're thinking about it, think about where it came from. Where did he get it? That cross is important to him. It's not only the value of the cross itself but what it might stand for. A naked man, almost dead from heat and thirst stumbles into our lives. You know as well as I do that a man without water in this damned country will throw away anything he's carrying no matter how valuable it is. Next he'll strip off his clothing." He paused and looked down at the man. "So this one must have thrown away anything he was carrying and then stripped off his clothing, but *he did not throw away that cross*, Davie."

"I've thought of that, Ash," agreed Dave.

They stood there looking at each other. Two rawhide-tough Middlewesterners who had often shared their last drink, frijole, and two bits with each other. They had been hungry, thirsty, and drunk together. They had fought side by side, sometimes against seemingly impossible odds. Neither of them had any certain recollection as to how many times they had saved each other's lives. They never spoke of it, nor did they keep a tally, but they *remembered*.

Ash turned away. "I'll stick it out with you, Davie. It's not that damned cross neither. Every time I let you strike out alone you get yourself in a mess—salt, pepper, and gravel in the grease."

Dave grinned. "I don't know what I'd do without you, you big-nosed bastard." He had known all along that Ash would never take Jack Spade into Yuma without Dave siding him.

Dave looked down at the stranger. "He *knows* something,

Ash. Something has kept him alive under circumstances that would have killed any ordinary man.''

"Maybe he ain't a man at all," mused Ash. He looked quickly about himself. There were times when Ash's Indian blood was predominant.

Dave shook his head. "He is a man of flesh and blood, Ash. That's what is so damned strange about this." He looked down at the stranger, who was now asleep. "One thing, old wolf: Don't fool with that cross of his. You saw how he pushed your hand away from it. By God, Ash, I saw *menace* in his eyes."

"Well, anyway, I hope he lives long enough to talk about that cross. I'm going to take a look-see around. Maybe he dropped something else out there." He grinned, picked up his Winchester, and left the camp.

While the stranger slept, Dave examined the gold cross more closely. It could have been a casting, but was probably cut out of a solid chunk of gold. It had been shaped with fine craftsmanship but had suffered somewhat from rough handling, as there were dents, nicks, and scratches in the soft metal. He looked at some of the scratches and then took out his magnifying glass, which he always carried for use in identifying mineral specimens. He placed more wood on the fire. When it flared up he examined the shaft, or longer part of the cross. Dave saw the letter "t," then a gap, and the letters "io," "s," and "u." He could not make out the first letter. It was perhaps a capital "B," or part of it anyway, or possibly a "C" or even a "Q." He replaced the cross on the man's chest and then stood up to study his face. The features, despite the changes wrought by heat and extreme thirst, looked vaguely familiar, almost as though Dave was looking at them through a veil of water or drifting smoke. He started to turn away, and just as he did so he was almost certain the man's eyelids raised a fraction or so and then immediately closed again.

Dave looked at Jack. He sat back in the shadows, but the firelight reflected in his eyes. "Do you know him?" asked Dave quietly.

There was no reply from Jack.

"You can tell me now or wait until my partner gets back," suggested Dave. "He's not as patient as I am, but you've noticed that already." He waited for a few moments. "Is he Jesus Valencia?"

"I don't know," grunted Jack. He turned his head away from Dave's direct gaze.

Dave took out the photograph of Jesus Valencia and walked back to the stranger.

Ash came back to the camp. "Found nothing," he reported. "But then I didn't expect to find anything. What are you doing?"

"Comparing the picture of Jesus Valencia with this man."

Ash looked at the photograph. He nodded. "There's some resemblance." He turned and looked toward Jack. "He ought'a know," he added.

"I asked him twice if he knew who it was. He said he didn't know."

Ash eyed Jack. "Is that so?"

Jack shifted a little under Ash's steady gaze. His iron chain jingled.

"He doesn't want to talk," said Dave. He walked over to Jack and squatted in front of him. "I warned you about my partner. You can talk now."

Jack was silent.

Dave looked back at Ash. "Maybe you can get some satisfaction from him."

Ash nodded. "I'll try." He drew out his bowie knife and then withdrew a slim hone from his shirt pocket. He began to whet the edge of the blade.

It seemed to get quieter about the camp except for the soft, whining sound of the stone against the highly tempered steel.

"Who is he?" Dave asked Jack.

Jack did not answer.

Wheet . . . wheet . . . wheet . . . went the sound of the hone on the blade.

Dave jerked a thumb at the stranger. "You know him, don't you, Jack?" he repeated.

There was no response, but Dave seemed to sense more fully that Jack did know the stranger.

Wheet . . . wheet . . . wheet . . .

Jack looked sideways at the bowie blade, now reflecting the last light from the fire—a dull reddish glowing like the stain of fresh wet blood on the steel. He seemed almost mesmerized by the steady, sweeping motion of the hone on the knife edge. He looked up and suddenly realized that Ash's hard green eyes were not on the knife but on him, with a steady and penetrating gaze. Maybe they aren't bluffing, Jack thought dully.

"Talk, damn you!" snapped Dave.

Jack jerked a little at the harsh sound of the voice. He couldn't fight back and he couldn't run. There was a deep sinking feeling in his gut.

Ash stopped honing the blade. He put away the stone and then spat on the palm of his left hand and slapped the blade back and forth on the callused flesh, as good as any piece of whetting leather.

It was now very quiet, very quiet indeed, except for the tiny snapping sounds of the firewood.

Ash looked at Dave. Dave nodded.

Ash stalked toward Jack. The silver in his fine Mexican spurs jingled musically. The jingling stopped. Jack peered sideways and saw Ash's thighs. He did not want to look up into those icy green eyes. Ash moved swiftly. He gripped Jack's right ear with his left hand and viciously twisted it, forcing the head back so that the thick throat with its distended blood vessels was wide open to the razor edge of the bowie blade, which he now rested firm on the throat. Ash looked down over the bald head and into the wide-open eyes clouded with agonizing fear. A sudden foul odor came from Jack.

Ash wrinkled his beak of a nose. "Jesus," he said in disgust. "He's filled his drawers."

Jack rolled his eyes sideways. He knew about these two hard-case hombres, or at least he *thought* he did. The wolf-like man with the adamantine eyes and the soul to match them could and would kill without the slightest trace of compunction. It was all a day's work for him. It was the other one, the tall, lean man with the dark reddish hair and beard and the cold blue eyes who might, just *might*, mind you, have a trace of pity.

Dave smiled thinly. "You can talk, *bazofa*," he suggested. "That is, while you still have a closed throat to talk through. . . ."

"For the love of Christ!" gasped Jack. It wasn't easy to talk with his throat muscles forcing the flesh up under that damned razor-edged bowie held by a homicidal maniac. "I'll talk! Just get this madman away from me!"

Dave nodded. Ash withdrew the knife, gave the ear one last savage twist, and released it. He stepped back a few feet but he did not sheath the knife. He was always ready for the killing slash or stroke. He moved around behind Jack so that he could not be seen, but his presence was made obvious by the combined rank odors of stale sweat and horse shit, and another, indefinable odor, one that wasn't too palpable. Perhaps it was only in Jack's fearful mind, but it was there all the same—the cold, slime-green odor of sudden death.

CHAPTER 4

DAVE TOOK A FLASK OF BACONORA FROM ONE OF HIS SAD-
dlebags. He pulled out the cork, squatted in front of Jack,
and held out the flask. "Have a *copita*, Jack," he gently
offered. Something Bull Andrews had told him about Jack
had come back to him. "Jack Spade is a mean, tough son of
a bitch who could hunt grizzly bears with a willow switch.
He's outfought any man who challenged him. He can eat
enough for two or three men at a sitting. *But* he can't drink
worth a damn! That's probably one of the reasons he got
caught so many times by the law. Sober he's as crafty as a
fox and slick as goose grease. Get a few drinks into him, and
he'll shoot off his big mouth about everything he knows,
which ain't too much, and a helluva lot more about things he
doesn't know. By God, Hunter, he's one of these men who
can tell you the God's honest truth, and you'll swear on a
stack of bibles he's lying like Ananias. On the other hand,
he can lie *like* Ananias, and you'd swear he was telling the
truth. I had an uncle like that, Hunter. I tell you . . ."

Jack felt the tiny trickle of blood running down his chest
from where the bowie knife had nicked the skin just over his
jugular vein. He took the flask and downed a good one. He
coughed hard. "Jesus," he gasped.

"Is it that bad?" Dave asked solicitously. He felt like a
damned hypocrite. "Have another, Jack."

Jack drank again and then once more. He seemed oblivi-
ous to the two lean men silently watching him.

Ash drew out his bowie knife and began to whet the edge of the blade.

Jack drank once more. He watched Ash out of the corner of his eye.

"It's about time," Dave suggested.

Jack nodded. "That's Jesus Valencia, or what's left of him. He's like me, worth five hundred dollars on the hoof if you're stupid enough to take him back to Yuma Pen."

"Why didn't you tell us that before Ash got a little careless with his knife?" asked Dave.

Ash grunted. "I *never* get careless."

Jack shrugged. "Look at him, hombre. His own mother wouldn't have known him the way he looks now." He hiccupped. "Besides, I wanted to protect him against people like you."

Ash shook his head. "Listen to him! That son of a bitch never protected anything or anyone in his life unless there was something in it for him."

Dave looked sideways at Ash. "Exactly!"

"What the hell do you mean?" demanded Jack.

"We're asking the questions," Dave said.

Ash nodded. "Just how in hell did you manage to escape with him from the Pen and why *him*?"

"Have another drink, Jack," urged Dave.

Jack had another drink. In fact, he had two big ones. "I can't tell you how we escaped. I told you that before. I can tell you about him though. He's well educated. Speaks three or four languages. Speaks English with an accent. Knows a couple of Indian languages—Yuma, Cocopah, and Chiricahua Apache. I tried Yaqui on him, and he seemed to know a little of it. Sometimes he worked as a clerk for some of the businesses in Yuma. Worked in Tucson, too. I think someone was trying to get him to talk in Yuma Pen. They even locked him up in the Crazy Hole for a time." His voice died away.

Dave knew of the Crazy Hole. It was a narrow cavity hewn out of solid rock. It was about five feet by four. It had no headroom for a tall man. It was almost impossible to stand up inside, and one couldn't lie down at full length. It was usually kept as a cell for the violently insane until they quieted down—if ever.

Jack looked at Valencia. "My God," he murmured. "To put a man like *him* in the Crazy Hole." There was an unaccustomed note of pity in his hoarse voice.

"You thought a lot of him, eh, Jack?" asked Dave. "Why?"

For the first time since he and Ash had caught Jack, Dave noticed a different light in his dark eyes. A look of pity, perhaps even of reverence.

It was Ash who took the bull by the horns. "They say despite your criminal record that you are a devoted son of the Church, Jack. Is that true?"

Jack quickly crossed himself with his manacled hands. "My mother should have been a saint," he murmured. "She taught me."

Dave felt that Ash might have hit upon the curious paradox of why Jack had agreed to *someone* that he would help Jesus in his rigged escape from Yuma Pen.

"You spoke in your sleep," Ash said quietly. "You spoke of a lost mission, gold and treasure, and the Gran Desierto de Altar." He paused. "Then you spoke the word Jesuit."

Jack closed his eyes for a moment.

"Is Jesus Valencia a Jesuit?" asked Dave.

Jack opened his eyes. "I don't really know but I think so. Or, he *was* a Jesuit."

"Come back to find the Jesuit church treasures said to be hidden before they were expelled from Mexico by King Carlos III in the Jesuit Expulsion of 1767," said Dave. "*All* Jesuits were expelled."

"Why?" asked Ash.

Dave shrugged. "They had gained too much power and wealth to suit Carlos, or so it is said. No other organization ever held as much power over their converts as did the Jesuits over the Indians. They were said to have vast treasures hidden away before they were expelled, and none were ever found, or at least no one seems to know *if* they were ever found. They had mines of incredible richness worked by

Indians under their control. Before they were expelled they imposed a terrible binding oath on the Indians, perhaps with threats of eternal damnation on whoever breathed a word of the hidden treasures. Whether they did or did not impose this oath is open to question, but it is a known fact that no Indians have ever revealed the sites of these hidden treasures and sealed mines.''

Jack nodded. ''And if Jesuits or anyone else have ever found those hidden treasures and sealed mines, they never talked about it.''

Dave looked at the sleeping Jesus. ''How did a learned little man like him ever get put into Yuma Pen?''

Jack shrugged. ''He never talked about it. I heard he had committed fraud in Tucson or somewhere. Some said he had murdered a man, some said it was a woman. No one really knew. He was kept away from the other prisoners pretty much. They sometimes kept him in a cell by himself in the place where they kept the tuberculosis prisoners. Most of them were Indians. They couldn't stand prison life. Died off like flies. Far as I know, Jesus Valencia did not have tuberculosis.''

''Why do you think they kept him off by himself?'' asked Dave. ''Was it because someone might have wanted to kill him?''

Jack shook his head. ''It was something he *knew*. I think he was kept in the Pen because he knew something that someone didn't want him to talk about until they were ready, maybe, to have him reveal it to *them*.''

Ash drew closer. ''Like who?'' he asked quietly. ''Maybe the same people who rigged your escape for you from Yuma and had horses ready for you when you did escape? They figured you knew that country down there somewhere south of Quitabaquito Springs, like maybe the Gran Desierto?''

Dave nodded. ''You said we'd be stupid to take him back to Yuma Pen for five hundred dollars, Jack. Why?''

Jack took another drink, wiped his mouth, and handed the flask to Dave. ''I've had enough both of this coffin varnish and the two of you. I ain't goin' to tell you a Gawd damned thing about who sprung us from Yuma Pen. I will tell you *one* thing, hombres. You're about as stupid a pair of man-hunters as I've ever seen, and I've had a few run-ins with some of the best, I tell you!''

Ash scratched inside his shirt. ''I hope that's the real beloved Jack of Spades who's talking and not that coffin varnish you mentioned.'' He drew out his bowie knife and spat on his left palm. He began to whet the blade edge.

Dave studied Jack. ''What we have here, partner, is a rather wild tale of a confirmed outlaw wanted on both sides of the border. He knows Sonora and Arizona. He knows the Gulf and the Colorado River. He gets imprisoned in Yuma Pen to serve ten years. Then one day they bring in a little man, obviously well educated. He's serving a sentence for fraud and murder. He's kept away from the other prisoners. He's not allowed to talk with any of them. Perhaps he's a Jesuit or maybe a defrocked priest. Maybe he still *is* a Jesuit or a priest. Then suddenly Jack Spade is allowed to escape, providing he will take Jesus Valencia with him.''

Jack shook his head. ''I never said that!''

Dave shrugged. ''It's obvious, Jack. If you had managed an escape by yourself you sure as hell wouldn't have taken along a little weak man and take the risk of having him hold you back on your would-be dash for Mexico. No! There was no way you could have escaped from Yuma Pen other than the way I've just said.''

Ash looked at Jesus. ''He couldn't have been so weak. Look how he survived the desert.''

Jack crossed himself. ''He has a *power*, hombres. He is not an ordinary man.''

''Bullshit!'' cried Ash. ''There ain't no such thing!''

Dave sipped at the flask of Baconora and then handed it to Ash. ''There might be. Indians believe in it. I've seen proof of it. How else can you explain Valencia surviving that damned desert for days without water and still being alive? Let me go on with my story. Jack and Jesus somehow make it to the Sonoyta area across about 180 miles of almost waterless desert country. Somewhere south of the border they part company. Jesus vanishes, at least for the time being. Two intrepid manhunters track down and capture the Jack of Spades. Now, Jack, my bucko, how does that tally with you?''

Jack was eyeing Ash's blade. He wiped the sweat from his forehead. ''You're right about the escape. I *had* to take him with me. I had nine and a half years more to serve. I knew I'd never make it. I woulda done anything to get out of there. I took my chances. I knew I might get killed once I got him out of the pen and delivered him to where I was supposed to. You know the unwritten law: *Los muertos no hablan*. The dead do not talk. Seems like I was damned if I didn't take him with me from Yuma Pen and still damned if I did. I took that chance. . . .''

''Where were you supposed to deliver him?'' asked Dave.

Jack half grinned. ''*Here*, at Tinajas Altas. There was supposed to be someone here to meet me and take charge of Valencia. Valencia himself told me I would be killed as soon as I delivered him.''

Dave nodded. ''So, you took him instead to Quitabaquito Springs, where he wanted to go?''

''That's right,'' replied Jack. He grinned. ''I ain't no fool. I had a good horse and some guns. I could have dumped Valencia and taken off for Mexico. You woulda never caught me then.''

It was quiet for a time. The only sound was the occasional snapping of wood in the fire and the soft breathing coming from Jesus as he slept.

Ash studied Jack. ''Then why didn't you dump him?''

Jack looked at Jesus and then up at the sky. He crossed himself. ''Something told me to take care of him.''

''Like that gold cross?'' Ash dryly asked.

Jack shook his head. ''I never saw that cross before tonight. He didn't have it in Yuma Pen. He didn't have it on our ride down to Quitabaquito Springs and across the border to Agua Salado on the Rio Sonoyta.''

Ash nodded. ''I see what you mean. If he *had* had it with

him when you made that ride, you would have taken it from him and probably slipped a knife into him in the bargain.''

Jack was horrified. His eyes opened wide. His mouth was agape. ''Before God! *No!* Maybe for money or jewelry, or even a good horse I might have done it. But as for that cross, I would not touch it if I was dying of hunger without a centavo to my name. Now hear this! I believe that man is or was a Jesuit priest come to this country to find hidden and long-lost Jesuit treasures. And I tell you hombres, that whoever touches any Jesuit treasure other than a Jesuit or Jesuits will surely die a horrible death and will end up in the everlasting flames of hell!'' His hoarse voice rang out like a prophecy of doom while the chain between his irons jangled as he vigorously crossed himself.

Dave studied the big man. There was a strong base within Jack for such superstition. His father had been an Irish Catholic, a people rife with superstition. His mother had been Yaqui. To them superstition was a powerful factor in their everyday lives. The odd thought came to Dave that perhaps that might have been the reason or one of the reasons ''they,'' whoever *they* were, had selected this bear of a man to carry out the escape from Yuma Pen and allow Jesus Valencia to pursue his quest for the supposed treasures of the Jesuits. Jack had said Jesus had a ''power.'' Perhaps it was so. Ash might have unwittingly put his finger on the problem. He had said Valencia had followed the pattern of men in the desert without water, first throwing away anything they had been carrying, then stripping off their clothing; but he had not thrown away the heavy cross suspended about his thin neck. Something beyond most men's comprehension had prevented him from so doing. Jack Spade had understood why. Some Indians, particularly the Chiricahua Apaches, believed the gods gave certain powers to chosen people. When Dave had served with the Apache Scouts he had participated in some of their mysteries and had witnessed a spectacular and eerie Ghost Dance wherein he had seen certain things, ''powers'' perhaps, that he had never forgotten. The Chiricahuas had called him Hawk-Face and believed that he had great powers with his uncanny eyesight and his great skill with his Sharps rifle.

Jack had been watching Dave closely. "*You* believe me," he said quietly.

Dave looked away. Jack Spade was no fool. He *knew*. . . .

Ash studied the two of them. He was quite sure that Dave believed, at least partly, that there were such things. He had to admit that he himself had seen certain things and incidents for which there had been no explanation.

Dave broke the silence. "What is Jesus Valencia looking for?" he asked. It was as though he was talking to himself.

"I've heard it said that he had been searching around near where the Gila and the Colorado join. Some say there was a 'lost mission' in that area," said Jack.

Ash grinned. "The Lost San Ysabel?" he asked slyly.

"There never was a San Ysabel Mission in the Yuma area," said Dave.

Ash nodded. "And there *never* was a mission around Yuma where the Gila and the Colorado meet."

"There *was* one marked on a map drawn by Father Kino in 1702," corrected Dave. "Yet there is absolutely no trace of any such mission ever being found."

Ash laughed. "I've been all over that area. There isn't and never was a mission anywhere around there."

Jack looked up. "You're wrong."

"How the hell do you know?" demanded Ash.

Jack pointed at Jesus with his manacled hands. "*He* told me. I believe him."

"I suppose you know the name, too," sneered Ash.

Jack nodded. "I do. It was Mission San Dionysius."

Ash grinned. "Dionysius sounds like a good Irish name. In fact, this whole damned story sounds like an Irish tale of leprechauns, banshees, and pots of fairy gold. Maybe this Jesus is a leprechaun who is looking for that pot of gold." He looked at Dave, and his face changed. "What's the matter with you?" he asked.

Dave was looking over his shoulder at Jesus. Something had come back to Dave like a bolt out of the blue. He stood up and went to Jesus. He knelt to pick up the cross. Jesus opened his eyes. "I want to look at your cross, Jesus," he requested gently. Jesus nodded. He raised the silver chain over his head and handed the cross to Dave. Dave tossed some wood on the fire. "Look at this, Ash," he said quietly. He handed Ash his magnifying glass and pointed to the letters on the long upright part of the cross. "The first letter is almost illegible, but it could be an 'S,' which, joined to the next letter, which is a 't,' could be 'St,' an abbreviation for San or Saint. By adding a capital 'D' ahead of the letters we get 'Dio.' Add a 'y' after the 'n' and before the letter 's' and follow the 'i' with the letters 'u' and 's.' "

Ash looked up at Dave. "San Dionysius," he said quietly.

"I told you there was a Mission San Dionysius," said Jack.

"At Yuma," Dave reminded him.

"He didn't get the cross there," said Ash. "So where *did* he get it? He didn't have it when he left Jack. Now he comes along the Camino del Diablo naked as a jaybird wearing only this cross. *Where did he get it?*"

"Somewhere out on the Gran Desierto," put in Jack.

They all looked toward the southeast.

Dave replaced the cross chain about Jesus' neck. "Can you talk?" he asked him in Spanish.

Jesus shook his head.

"He wouldn't tell you anyway," insisted Jack.

It was very quiet. The moon was dying. The firelight was little more than a red glowing of embers peering through a layer of fine, grayish white ash.

Jack's irons rattled as he moved. "I told you that you'd be stupid to take him back to Yuma Pen. Where that cross came from might just be a hidden cache of treasure, probably Jesuit. He's the only person who probably knows right where it is. You take him back there to Yuma Pen, and he'll be sprung again and forced to show them who sprung him where it is. That'll be the end of him and me, too, if you take him and me back there."

Dave eyed him. "So, what's your proposition, Jack?"

"Keep us here until he recovers enough to travel. Then we can go back east to where I lost him, and maybe, just *maybe*, he'll lead you to the treasure."

"What's in it for you?" asked Ash.

Jack shrugged. "I want none of it. Give me a horse and a gun, and let me go free into Mexico."

"You mean because the treasure has the Jesuit curse on it?"

Jack nodded. "I don't want any of it."

Ash scratched his beard. He cocked his head to one side. "Then what about us if we share in the treasure?"

Jack laughed. "What the hell do I care? Go on! Take your share! Then some dark night when you're sleeping off a big drunk and are in bed with some damned prostitute, if a Jesuit ghost comes lookin' for you and his treasure, you'll see what I mean!"

Ash looked sideways at Dave. "You think he means it?"

Dave nodded. "He does. And I'm not too sure I don't believe him either." He paused. "He did give us some good advice. We'll stay here another few days until Jesus is ready to travel and then head back east. After that we'll play it as it comes along. Come on. I want to talk with you. Privately . . ."

They walked out beyond the tank and stood looking down the long slopes to the southeast. The moon was almost gone.

"You think Jack is telling us the truth?" asked Ash.

"*Quien sabe?* He's slick, that one. I really believe he's frightened of the legendary Jesuit curse. We still don't know who 'they' are. He knows we're manhunting to fill in the gaps between treasure hunting. He knows now that gold cross is a helluva bait for us. We'll move up the mountain and find a cave to hide out in. There are a lot of them up there. We'll have to keep a lookout twenty-four hours a day. I have a feeling someone will come here looking for Jesus. We'll have to risk that. That's the best I can do for now. Any questions?"

Ash nodded. "Just one. If that cross is marked for San Dionysius, and San Dionysius was supposed to be up near the Gila and the Colorado, how is it Jesus was probably looking for Jesuit treasure somewhere southwest of Agua Salado where Jack here lost track of him? Then he shows up *here* with that cross. How in hell can *that* be?''

''A good simple question,'' said Dave. He shook his head. ''I've heard the Jesuits had been tipped off about their forthcoming expulsion. They sealed their mines, or at least some of them. They moved their treasures from where they had kept them to some other place. I can't imagine San Dionysius being much of a mission and probably not a very wealthy one. The Jesuits might, just might, mind you, have sent a load of treasure to San Dionysius, possibly with a plan to move it somewhere else in time. Now perhaps they couldn't make it to San Dionysius and decided to cache it somewhere on the Gran Desierto de Altar. Or they might have made it to San Dionysius and then decided to move it again. They took what there was at San Dionysius and started back south. For some reason, they might have hid it out on the Gran Desierto. They made a record of it somewhere, perhaps committed their directions to memory, and left Mexico forever.''

''And Brother Jesus perhaps *knows* those directions and knows where the treasure is and comes walking out of the desert damned near dead of thirst with the cross of San Dionysius hanging around his neck and right into our hands,'' added Ash.

Dave nodded. ''You've finally gotten the idea, partner.''

''Well, it ain't really much, but it's the best we've got.''

They grinned at each other.

Somewhere out on the Mesita de los Muertos a coyote howled just once.

CHAPTER 5

"THE WALKING SANDS," THE HOARSE VOICE SAID OUT OF the midnight darkness.

Dave rolled over in his sleep. He suddenly opened his eyes. He placed his right hand on his Colt lying beside him on the blanket. He could dimly see the sleeping figures of Jack and Jesus. He sat up with the Colt in his hand and his thumb on the spur hammer. "Jack?" he queried quietly. There was no response. "Jesus?" he asked. There was no response.

Someone whistled softly beyond the boulders ringing the upper edge of the tank.

Dave stood up. "Ash?" he called out.

"The same," replied Ash. He came silently through the darkness. "It's your turn on guard."

"Did you say anything before you whistled?"

Ash looked at him queerly. "Me? No. Why?"

Dave put on his hat. He picked up his Sharps with his left hand.

"What are you doing with your Colt in hand?" asked Ash.

Dave shook his head. "I thought I heard someone speak."

"Maybe you were dreaming?"

"No. I heard it plainly."

"Maybe it was one of these two?"

"They didn't reply when I spoke to them."

Ash shrugged. "So what did the speaker, *whoever* it was, say?"

"The Walking Sands."

37

Ash stared at him. "You're sure?"

Dave nodded. "Absolutely."

Ash took a flask of Baconora from one of his saddlebags. He handed it to Dave. "Maybe you need this."

Dave drank and passed the flask back to Ash. "I needed that all right, but I *did* hear someone say The Walking Sands."

Ash drank and then tilted his head to one side and studied Dave. "I believe you, Davie." He paused. "Maybe it was your 'power' speaking." Ash wasn't joking or needling Dave. "You know well enough where The Walking Sands are."

Dave nodded. "I've been there. Somewhere on the Gran Desierto, say west-southwest from the Agua Salado area, and between it and the Gulf of California."

"Where Jesus Valencia may have wandered after he left Jack of Spades and maybe found that cross of solid gold."

Dave holstered his Colt. "I'd better get on guard. God alone knows who or what is out there on the desert maybe looking for Jesus. Jack said someone was supposed to meet him here where he was to deliver Jesus. Maybe they took off when Jack didn't show up, or maybe they never got here in the first place and may still be on the way. I think we'd better move out sometime tomorrow afternoon. Jesus has had a full day of rest. We'll see how he feels when he awakens. We'll let him rest and recuperate until late afternoon so that we can travel back to Agua Salado and the Rio Sonoyta during darkness. It'll be damned rough, but I can't see any other way to go about it. We can't stay here much longer."

Ash nodded. "I'll relieve you some time after dawn. If anything happens and you can't get back here, just fire three warning shots, and I'll be right with you."

Dave picked up his canteen and took the flask of Baconora. "Get some sleep, Ash. You're going to need it." He padded off into the darkness.

"Don't forget The Walking Sands!" Ash called after him.

Dave walked and slid down the slopes until he was just about above the top level of the Mesita de los Muertos. He could see down toward the desert floor where the Camino del Diablo passed. He sat on the ground with his back against a boulder. The Walking Sands should be somewhere to his right, to the south beyond the farthest southern tip of the Tinajas Altas Mountains in Sonora. There the furnace winds of the Gran Desierto had driven the sands into tall, crescent-shaped dunes called *barchans*. They moved across the desert surface like agonizingly slow waves of the sea. It was a place of perhaps thirty square miles. The dunes moved inexorably north and east with the strong prevailing winds. They would bury everything in their path only to unearth it again and then eventually rebury it as the wind moved them on and on in their timeless routine. The Mexicans called them *Las Andar Arenas*, The Walking Sands. It was a particularly apt name for them. There were little or no distinguishing features to the area, at least to a stranger, although few strangers ever penetrated the Sands. There was said to be no water in the area, at least in modern times. But a persistent legend, at least a hundred years old, told of a fine spring, possibly nourished by a vast underground lake, that had flourished for many years, then flowed sporadically off and on until it finally disappeared forever, buried by the shifting mounds and ridges of blowing sand. There were, too, vague tales of a ''lost mission'' somewhere in the sands whose tumbled ruins might be revealed at extremely rare intervals for a very short time only. Those inveterate seekers of myths and folk tales— hunters of lost mines and buried treasures who went by the slogan ''Gold is where you find it''—avoided the Sands like a plague.

Dave raised his field glasses and looked out into the darkness. There was really nothing to see until daylight. He stood up and continued his scanning until at last he lowered the glasses. There seemed to be an irresistible lure lingering persistently in his mind. He stood there, motionless like a pillar of salt, a gaunt lath of a man peering out into the vast desolation shrouded by darkness. Had Jesus Valencia staggered naked out of the Sands dried out to within a fraction of his life? It was a curious coincidence for Dave in that he, too, had once traversed the Sands in the days before he had become partners with Ash Mawson. He had been looking for Scalphunter's Ledge—said to be a ledge of solid silver jutting up out of the ground like the dislocated bone of a giant, stumbled upon by a group of American scalphunters thirty years past. That had been in the days when Dave and other treasure seekers had been looking for it much farther west than it was really supposed to be. Dave had lost his way and wandered into the Sands and almost into oblivion. He had never forgotten the search. Few had had the experience and lived to talk about it.

Dave slowly worked his way around the shoulder of the mountain. It was hard going through the rocks, boulders, and thorned brush that infested the slopes. He reached a point where he could see many miles across the desert west of the Tinajas Altas. The Colorado River was about fifty miles in that direction. He was about to return when something made him look back toward the west. The tiny, infinitesimal speck of light came and went so fast he wasn't sure at all that he *had* seen it. He waited. Minutes ticked past. It did not reappear. What had it been? How far from him had it occurred? Had it occurred at all? The air was incredibly clear. The light could have been anywhere from five to seven, perhaps even *more*, miles to the west.

Dave worked his way back toward the eastern face of the shoulder. He kept looking back, hoping and yet not hoping to see that mysterious speck of light. It might have been, and probably was, someone out there who had lighted a cigarette. He retrieved his canteen and the flask of Baconora. Then he slowly made his way to the western part of the shoulder, where he had been before. He saw nothing but the velvety black darkness. He sat down with his back against a boulder and sipped a little Baconora now and again.

The ruins of the lost mission were marked by the partially collapsed bell tower protruding from the rolling sand dunes like an elongated broken tooth or fang. For as far as the eye could see there was nothing but sand, sand, and more sand, on and on into infinity. The sands had been sculptured by the wind into great crescent-shaped dunes like dun-colored ocean combers held static under a full moon.

Dave stared at the ruin. There it was—the lost mission! He had found it but had no recollection of how he had gotten there. It was almost as though he was part of the scene, like a character in a painting, and yet not part of it. Smoky-looking mists began to gather slowly between Dave and the bell tower. He extended his left hand to try and dispel them. To be so near and yet so far away, and to have the mission disappear before his eyes, perhaps forever, was too much to bear. He knew that if the mists became thicker they would perhaps conceal the ruins forever. His left forefinger touched something round and hard with a hollow at the tip of it.

"Is the son of a bitch awake or not?" someone growled.

A man laughed low. "I'll find out."

Something hard poked viciously into Dave's lean belly. His eyes snapped open from his sleep. His left forefinger was resting lightly against the muzzle of a heavy-barreled rifle two feet from his face. He quickly withdrew his hand and looked into the hard eyes of the man holding the rifle, which he suddenly recognized as his Sharps. Dawn light was in the sky. He had been asleep for hours and had been dreaming of The Walking Sands and a lost mission.

The man holding the Sharps was a Mexican, short and stocky with a pendulous belly held partway in by his cartridge belt. His hair and mustache were flecked with gray. His nose had been smashed flat against his pockmarked face, causing his breathing to have a faint whistling sound to it. A slim, young, light-blue-eyed man stood to one side of him. He wore a flat-brimmed, rounded hat, a real "muley," with a band of silver conches. His hair was light blond, and he sported a thin Mexican-dandy mustache almost like a pencil line on his short upper lip. His lips were drawn back from his teeth, and they had spaces between them like wide pickets on a fence. The growing light revealed a low-slung, tied-down Mexican holster of carved leather at his left side from which protruded the ivory butt of a Colt revolver. He wore a long, funereal black coat to midthigh and skintight, black-leather gloves on his long, slim hands. A tall, broad-shouldered man stood just behind the youngster. His chest was wide and deep. His nose was large and thrust out from his sallow face like the prow of a Roman bireme, while his salt-and-pepper mustache looked like a dark sea being parted by a prowlike, aggressive nose. His eyes were flat and hard-looking, like agates. The last of the quartet seemed pure Mex—a broad-shouldered and slim-waisted vaquero type with dark and lively eyes and a set of teeth like the white keys on a piano. He wore a broad, upturned-brim sombrero. He held a nickel-plated Winchester in his gloved hands, and it was pointed directly at Dave's head.

Someone moved behind Dave. "Get his six-gun and knife, Dancy," the cold voice ordered.

Dancy was the man with the muley hat. He came to Dave. "Get up," he ordered in his rather high and toneless voice.

Dave stood up.

"Unbuckle your gun belt and let it drop," Dancy ordered.

Dave fumbled with the buckle. It had always been tight.

"I said to unbuckle it," repeated Dancy.

Dave glanced sideways at him. "I'm doing the best I can," he grunted.

Dancy's right hand shot out and the palm slapped stingingly hard against the side of Dave's face. "Goddammit! Faster!" The last word seemed jerked out of him as Dave swung from the hips and planted a vicious left hook low, just above Dancy's gunbelt buckle, then shot out a right jab that clipped him on the left side of the jaw and sent him crashing into the meaty-bellied man holding the Sharps. Dave tore the Sharps out of his hands as he went down. He leaped sideways as Dancy rolled free of the man he had knocked down. The big man who had stood behind Dancy reached down with his right hand and gripped Dancy's collar. With one powerful surge of strength he picked him up and settled him on his feet just as Dancy drew his Colt with the left hand in as fast a draw as Dave had ever seen.

Dave leaped over a low boulder and dropped just as Dancy

aimed to fire. The man who pulled Dancy to his feet slapped up his left arm. The pistol cracked flatly, driving a puff of white smoke upward. The shot echo bounced off the side of the Tinajas Altas and died, rumbling in the distance.

Dancy cursed and broke free of the man holding him. He ran lightfootedly toward Dave while thrusting out his pistol.

Dave rolled up on his feet with the Sharps at hip level. He raked back the hammer with the palm of his left hand and set the firing trigger.

"Dancy!" roared the man behind Dave. "Goddamn you! Hold it right there! He'll blow a hole right through you with that damned Sharps you could stick your hat into! Stop, goddammit!"

The Mexican thrust out a leg, and Dancy went down over it like a poleaxed steer. His left hand tightened. The Colt fired. The slug furrowed a thin line in the hard soil and then ricocheted off a nearby boulder.

Dave turned to run. About ten men stood down the slope, holding the reins and lead ropes of twelve or more horses and pack mules. Two of them raised their rifles. Dave turned. Big Belly had his pistol aimed right at Dave's gut. The other Mexican was sighting his Winchester on Dave.

"Throw down that Sharps!" ordered the man behind Dave. "I don't want you killed! Throw down that damned buffalo gun!"

Dave pointed the barrel upward and squeezed the firing trigger. The Sharps blasted off, sending out a cloud of white smoke. The rumbling, rolling report slammed against the heights of the mountain. By a quirky stroke of fate Ash had received the three warning shots.

"Drop that gunbelt and get your hands up in the air!" snapped the man, who had managed to stay behind Dave all the while.

Dave dropped the gunbelt.

Dancy broke free from the man who held him and snatched up his dropped Colt. Dave hit the sand just as the tall man clamped a big hand around Dancy's gun wrist and thrust the arm upward. He twisted the Colt from Dancy's hand and then dragged him, cursing and screaming hysterically, behind some boulders.

"You can get up now," the man said from behind Dave.

Dave stood up and gazed sideways into a cold-looking gray eye. The other eye was covered with a black patch. The nose was thin. The mouth was a tightly drawn slash turned down at the corners. The salt-and-pepper colored, heavy dragoon mustache was thick and ragged. A fearsome-looking, ridged white scar stood out in contrast to the saddle-leather-tanned skin. It ran from under the left eye patch down along the indented cheekbone to vanish into the mustache at the corner of the mouth, then reappeared running through the short beard to the tip of the chin. The skin itself was drawn tight like parchment. To Dave the impression was that the skull was trying to force its way through the skin. This man wore a dirty grayish hat stained with stale sweat around the inner side of the wide brim. The acorn-tipped hat cord was of an indeterminate neutral color. A brass wreath ornament had the letters "CS" intertwined within the wreath.

A prewar model LeMat "grapeshot" pistol was held in the man's gloved right hand. It was cocked and pointed at Dave's belly. Dave knew the LeMat. It was a nine-shot, cap-and-ball revolver of .42 caliber. Below the rifled pistol barrel was another barrel around which the nine-shot cylinder revolved. The lower barrel was a smoothbore of .63 caliber that could fire buckshot or a disintegrating ball load. The man's thumb flipped down an adjustable nose on the big spur hammer to activate the possible firing of the lower barrel. Dave remembered all too well when a mortally wounded Confederate officer in the Wilderness had fired such a fearsome weapon at one of Dave's squad mates of the 24th Michigan. The shot had taken off a part of his mate's head with a load of buckshot from the lower barrel.

The one eye held Dave's attention like the stare of a basilisk. "I'm Major Cole Ransom. You're Dave Hunter. You were sent with your partner Ash Mawson on a manhunt after two men. One of my scouts saw the two of you come in off the Camino del Diablo to the High Tanks with a prisoner. Who was that prisoner, and where were you taking him?"

Dave shrugged. "To the water here. Where else?"

"And then?"

"Back to Yuma."

"You didn't answer *all* of my question. Who was that prisoner?"

Dave looked around at the other men. They were watching him intently. "John Spade," he replied. "The Jack of Spades."

Ransom nodded. "I thought as much. Where is the man who calls himself Jesus Valencia? The one who escaped from Yuma Pen with Jack Spade?"

Jack's words came back to Dave. "There was supposed to be someone here to meet me and take charge of Valencia. Valencia himself told me that I would be killed as soon as I delivered him."

Ransom's gauntleted left hand came up rather stiffly until it was pointing at Dave's face. It was not more than a foot from his nose. "Answer me! Damn you!"

"We caught Spade in the area south of Quitabaquito Springs. We never found Valencia," Dave lied.

"You're lying!" snapped Ransom.

Dave had had enough. "You can go to hell!" he said flatly.

The hand moved so fast Dave had just time to turn his head aside. The glancing blow thudded against his right cheekbone and half stunned him. The impact was hard, metallic hard, and certainly not flesh and bone. He staggered back, his senses swimming. Blood trickled down his face.

Ransom waved his left hand. "Will you talk now?" he demanded. "Will you tell me the truth before I smash in your face like a shattered pumpkin?"

Dave was fascinated by the fact that the fingers of Ransom's left hand had remained curved and clawlike. He could see blood on the leather of the gauntlet—*his* blood.

Ransom suddenly smiled, but only with the facial muscles. The eye was as cold as that of a shark. "I see you're curious about my hand. I can make good my threat to smash in your face. I can tear a man's face from his skull with this hand. I can grab your privates and make a eunuch out of you. I can rip out your throat or your guts. Look, damn you!'' He holstered his LeMat and then stripped off the gauntlet from his left hand. The sun was up by now. The rays reflected from a polished metal claw. The tips of the fingers were sharpened to fine points. The metal hand was neatly made of steel. It was set into a sort of leather-covered cuff that fitted over the wrist stump of Ransom's missing limb. The man was a grotesque cripple with his missing eye, misshapen face, terrible ridged scar, and missing left hand. The fearsome wounds probably added more venom to Ransom's already-warped soul.

Fear was Ransom's ally, thought Dave. He glanced about at the diverse and seemingly hard-case men of Ransom's *corrida*. He knew right then, unless there was a miracle, he'd never live to talk about this wild experience. He had absolutely no hope at all. He had faced death before during the war and on the Great Plains while hunting buffalo. He had worked in death-dealing mines. During those years death had been his constant companion. Though he had accepted it, he had never gotten used to it.

''Hold out that Sharps, Cipriano,'' Ransom ordered the smiling Mexican. ''Turn the butt toward me.'' Cipriano did as he was told. Ransom stepped back a little, then lunged forward as lithe as a leaping mountain lion. His left arm shot out, and the fanged metal claw struck the hard walnut of the rifle with a dull sound. The force of the blow moved the rifle back and upset Cipriano's balance a little.

Ransom turned to look at Dave. ''Show him, Cipriano,'' he ordered.

Cipriano held out the butt toward Dave. There was a crescent-shaped dent in the hard wood.

Ransom smiled thinly. ''If that had been your face, it would have smashed your nose into pulp or broken your jaw or cheekbone.''

Dave had to play for time. Ash surely must have heard those three gun shots. He shrugged. ''All I know is that we found Spade. All he said was that Valencia had gotten away from him.''

''Which way did he say Valencia went?'' demanded Ransom.

Dave pointed vaguely toward the east and south. ''Into Sonora.''

Ransom moved closer to Dave. ''Spade was to bring Valencia here days ago. I knew the day they escaped. One of my men brought me word about it. He said they had gone east. I left some of my men here in case Spade showed up with Valencia. We rode east to the Quitabaquito Springs area. We separated and scattered to pick up Valencia's trail west of Agua Salado. Two of my men found him. Somehow he or someone *with* him managed to kill both of them. His trail led off to here, Tinajas Altas. The men I had left here had not seen him. I know Valencia would not have gone to Yuma for fear of being slammed into the Pen again. There was only *one* place he might have gone for water and safety—to the Colorado. We rode for the Colorado. No one had seen him. I figured somehow he had eluded us and was possibly still somewhere southwest or west of Agua Salado and the Rio Sonoyta.'' He smiled again. ''*And* what did we find? Dave Hunter, the mighty treasure hunter and manhunter, sound asleep on the slope of the Tinajas Altas Mountains claiming he *knows* nothing of Valencia's whereabouts!'' He looked up toward the heights, beyond which were the High Tanks. ''Now isn't it just possible that your friend Mawson is up there somewhere keeping a close eye on Valencia while you try to figure out a way to get away from us?''

Dave shrugged. ''You're doing the talking, Ransom,'' he said dryly, all the while keeping an eye on Ransom's damned metal hand.

Ransom gently waved his claw. ''That's *Major* Ransom,'' he corrected.

Dave nodded. ''*Major* Ransom.''

Dancy had returned to the scene. ''We heard you were supposed to get five hundred dollars each for Spade and Valencia, Hunter.'' He shook his head. ''You went all the way down to Mexico for Valencia and only found *Spade*? If you knew what we know about Valencia, you would have gotten rid of Spade and gone after Valencia. I . . .'' He saw the black look on Ransom's face and backed off a little, well out of range of that damnable metal hand. "Maybe we ought'a water the horses and mules," he added hastily.

Ransom nodded. He kept his one eye on the gabby young fool, like Cyclops staring malevolently at Ulysses. "Gordo," he said to the big-bellied Mexican, "you get the boys to take the horses and mules up to the High Tanks. Ben," he said to the tall man, "you and Dancy cover them in case that bastard Mawson is prowling around up there. If you see him, kill him! Don't kill Spade yet. I want to talk with him."

Dancy nodded. "I've heard Mawson is crazy as a loon, maybe even worse than this big-nosed ugly bastard here."

Dave grinned. "If you do find Mawson, little man, he'll take a helluva lot of killing, and you ain't exactly the type to do it."

Dancy's face went white. He dropped his left hand to his ever-ready Colt.

"Git, damn you!" roared Ransom.

Dancy got.

Cipriano leaned against a boulder with his nickel-plated Winchester pointed at Dave. He was smiling again. Dave wondered if he might not be a little light in the matter of gray matter. The others had taken their eyes off Dave now and again, but not Cipriano. It was as though he was analyzing Dave. Dave had the uneasy feeling that this smiling man might just be the most dangerous of them all.

The horses and the two pack mules laden with water kegs were led slowly up the steep slope. Dave didn't expect to hear any defense made by Ash. He would likely be gone with Spade and Valencia. An uneasy feeling crept through him.

Ransom turned to Dave. "Just how much do you know about Jesus Valencia? How much were you told?"

A vision of the gold cross seemed to float before Dave's eyes. Ransom and his *corrida* were after the treasure supposedly hidden in The Walking Sands. Valencia had not gotten the cross *before* he parted with Jack Spade. He did not have it when he escaped somehow from Ransom. He had it when he reached Tinajas Altas. Ergo, he must have gotten it somewhere in The Walking Sands.

"I've told you all I know," insisted Dave.

Ransom drew his LeMat pistol and pointed it at Dave's head. "Lead the way, hombre," he ordered. "Show us where you left Mawson and Spade."

Dave saw the quick, reddish-orange flash two hundred yards up the slope and away from the area where the horses and mules were being taken to be watered. The flat report of a rifle carried along the slopes and died away. A puff of white smoke hung where the shot had been fired. Ransom cursed as his hat was plucked from his head as though by an invisible hand. He whirled away just as the rifle cracked again. The bullet passed just about where he had been and not very far from Dave's head. Ransom plunged into the cover of some brush. Cipriano saw Dave jump behind the boulders and snatch up his gunbelt and Sharps rifle. He could have dropped Dave instantly with a .44/40 slug from his nickel-plated Winchester, but he did not raise the weapon.

Dave stood up to run. He glanced warily at Cipriano, who jerked his head to his left, to the north. "*Andale*, hombre!" he said. He dropped out of sight and elevated his rifle to fire a shot into the air.

Dave hurdled a low boulder. He ran at a crouch, weaving in and out of the low boulders and thick clumps of brush. He could hear faint shouting in the distance far up the slopes. The rifle was fired four or five more times at intervals as Dave made the most of his good fortune. Maybe it was the miracle for which he had hoped. Actually it was the power of the .44/40 cartridge fired from a Winchester by an expert marksman, in this case Dave's partner, Ash.

Ransom poked his head up out of the brush. A thin trickle of dark blood ran down from his scalp line. "Why the hell didn't you kill that son of a bitch!" he yelled furiously at Cipriano.

Cipriano peered from under a mesquite bush. "That bastard up the hill kept me down,'' he complained. His expression changed. "You've been hit, Major?" he asked solicitously.

"Creased!" Ransom snapped. "Just cut the skin."

The shooting had died away. It was quiet on the slopes in the windless air. Heat waves had begun to waver up from the bare sandy earth.

"We'd better get to the water, Major," Cipriano suggested. "I'll take a look at your wound up there."

Ransom shook his head. That had been first-class shooting. A fine thread of fear seemed drawn through his brain.

Cipriano ejected the spent cartridge and worked the Winchester lever to place another round in the chamber. "You want me to go look for him?" he asked.

Ransom shook his head again. "He's well away by now. If he starts shooting that damned Sharps of his, we won't be able to get within two hundred yards of him. We'll go up to the Tanks. I'll send out some of the boys to see if they can track down him and that bastard Mawson." There was grim resolution in his voice and manner as he replaced his bullet-punctured hat on his head. He strode upslope, carefully keeping the boulders between him and the last position of that damned marksman hidden among the brush and boulders.

Cipriano grinned. He looked to the north. There was no sign of Dave Hunter. Nothing moved except the newly rising and shimmering heat waves brought on by the moving sun. He shrugged and started up the slope after the hurrying Major Ransom.

CHAPTER 6

DAVE WORKED HIS WAY THROUGH A WILD TANGLE OF rocks, boulders, and brush. He looked back to see if he was being followed. He could see the distant figures of men and horses bobbing up and down behind boulders and clumps of thick brush.

A soft whistle made Dave whirl and raise his Sharps. He saw the grinning face of Ash peering around a boulder. "Jesus!" he snapped. "You ought to know better than to come up behind a man like that!"

Ash stepped out from behind the boulder. "What else could I do? I don't want a .44/40 slug through my head."

"Are any of them around here?"

Ash shook his head. "I think they're more interested in water than us right now."

"Where are Valencia and Spade?"

"When I heard the shots I got them away from the tanks and down the northern slope. Then I came back to help you. We'll have to get them back to Yuma. We can't make it to the east or the Colorado."

Dave nodded. "We'll worry about Yuma later. Let's go! We haven't much time."

They worked their way over a ridge and down the northern slope.

"Do you know anything about this Major Cole Ransom?" asked Dave.

"Steel Hand? Yeh, I sure do. Cole Ransom is one of many names of his." He looked sideways at the cut on Dave's right cheekbone. "You'll have a nice scar there in time. You're damned lucky he didn't break the cheekbone. He's been known to do that. Both sides, too."

"Is he an ex-Confederate officer?"

"He *claims* to be. Says he rode with General Jo Shelby and his Missouri Brigade fighting in the Trans-Mississippi. Hell! He was nothing but a damned bushwhacker. A guerrilla. The son of a bitch was a lieutenant under Quantrill. After the war he and his men were run to earth trying to cross the Rio Grande into Mexico. A U.S. trooper swung a helluva blow at him with a saber. Ransom threw up his left arm to ward off the blow. The saber cut clean through his wrist and hit his face. Took out the left eye and cut through his cheek down to the chin. He was said to be half-loco before that happened and now is completely loco." Ash grinned. "But I figure you learned that down the mountain side there."

Dave touched the cut on his cheek. "I owe him something," he said quietly. "He was after Jesus Valencia. He said he was supposed to meet Spade here with Valencia. He found out that Spade had gone to Quitabaquito Springs instead. He rode there. They searched for Valencia. Valencia, or maybe someone with him, managed somehow to kill two of Ransom's men. Ransom returned here to find out his men hadn't seen Spade or Valencia. Then he decided Valencia might have gone west to the Colorado. When they couldn't find him there, they returned here. Then they found *me*. . . ." Dave shook his head. "Sound asleep. You know the rest."

"It must have been Steel Hand who had Spade and Valencia sprung out of Yuma Pen. I wonder how he worked it."

"What kind of mess have we gotten ourselves into this time?"

Ash shrugged. "Not much worse than others we've been in."

Dave shook his head. "*Quien sabe?* By the way—where's the gold cross?"

Ash unbuttoned his shirt front. The sun shone on the gold

of the cross. "Valencia didn't like it when I took it away, but I figured it was safer with me. Besides, I had my doubts whether or not he'd survive a ride to Yuma, and what would happen to it if we reached Yuma and he was still wearing it?"

Ash had picketed the four horses and the pack mule in a deep arroyo. Jack was mounted on one of the horses with the chain between his wrist irons tied to the saddle horn. Ash had tied a rope from one of his ankles under the horse's belly to the other ankle. Jesus was seated on another horse and lashed upright in the saddle. Ash had dressed him in a reserve pair of jeans and an old shirt. He had fashioned a turban out of an undershirt and placed it on Jesus's head. Dave thought he looked somewhat like an Eastern potentate, albeit from a rather impoverished province.

Dave looked back toward the distant area of the Tanks. They would be cautious in approaching them because of the marksmanship of Ash and Dave. Dave turned. "Go on ahead, Ash. I'll keep behind and cover the retreat." He waited after Ash had left the arroyo. A thin veil of dust was rising from behind them. It would be visible for miles. A hot wind was beginning to make itself felt. Dave took the reins of his dun and led him from the arroyo. He could see Ash and the others far down the slope. He followed them, now and again looking back over his shoulder toward the distant Tanks. He reached the lower level of the slopes above the edge of the Lechuguilla Desert. To his left were the Tinajas Altas, tending northwest on a parallel line with the Copper Mountains across the desert. The Lechuguilla Desert was the natural pathway for the Camino del Diablo northwest to the Yuma area. Yuma itself was about thirty miles northwest. From where he now stood it was another fifteen or so miles due west to the Colorado River.

Dave reached the bottom of the slope. He looked back. A sinking feeling came to him. He had expected to see dust rising from the higher slopes, but still the sight was almost unnerving. He walked on, leading his dun. Half an hour later he stopped and turned to look back up the gently rising slopes. The sun reflected sharply from something. Dave took out his field glasses and shaded the lenses with his hat. The powerful lenses picked out a movement and something darker against the lighter-colored rocks and boulders. The wavering heat waves distorted the view, but Dave saw, at last, the tall, spare figure of Major Ransom standing on a boulder and looking in Dave's direction with his field glasses. Two men stood close to him. There were others with horses and mules nearby. Steel Hand pointed directly toward Dave. Dave looked back over his shoulder. A thin wraith of dust rose into the heated air and was raveled out by the wind. It marked the passage of Ash and his companions. It was possible that Ransom had not picked out Dave's position in a low area directly behind the clump of boulders where he had stationed himself and his dun.

The *corrida* started to move down the slope.

Dave opened the aperture in his Sharps butt plate. He tilted the rifle so that the vernier tang sight he stored there slid out into his hand. He mounted the tang sight at the small of the stock. He looked up. The range of the *corrida* was now about 325 to 350 yards. They were moving slowly while leading their horses and mules.

Dave picked up his field glasses. The sun flashed from the lenses, warning the *corrida*, who scattered into the cover of brush and boulders. Dave cursed under his breath. He had been careless. The reflection from the lenses had revealed his position.

Something flashed, a tiny needle of light next to the bottom of a tall, fat boulder. Dave focused the glasses. He saw a booted foot with a shiny spur on the heel. Dave recalled the gaudy brass-and-silver spurs Ransom wore. The steel, needle-spiked rowel had almost been as big as a silver dollar. He ruminated. They had been walking their horses to rest them. That meant walking in high-heeled boots. It was bad enough walking in such boots designed for riding, but with a heel shot off it would be a limping hell. Dave figured he'd have to kill off some of their horses to slow them down, but they were too slick for him. Not a horse or mule was in sight.

Not a man showed. There was nothing but that inviting spur rowel glinting in the sun.

The tang sight was graduated to 1300 yards. Dave loosened the cupped eyepiece sight and raised it to 325 yards. The shimmering heat waves distorted distant objects and made them seem to move in a slow rhythmic dance while uncertainly advancing and retreating. He centered the long-beaded front sight in the eyepiece. If he missed, it wouldn't matter that much in a sense; but if he made a hit, it would put the fear of God into them or at least the fear of Dave Hunter and his deadly accuracy with his Sharps Old Reliable.

Dave patted the sun-hot barrel of the rifle. ''Come on, Old Satan,'' he murmured. ''Let's show them what we can do together.''

Dave cocked the big hammer and squeezed the rear trigger to set the front firing trigger. He drew in a full breath then let out half of it. He placed the flat of his right forefinger on the firing trigger. The front sight seemed to have the bright spot sitting on top of it like a bird on a fence rail. The wind faltered a bit then seemed to die away. Dave tightened his right hand on the small of the stock. The Sharps bellowed and spat out flame and stinking white smoke. The rifle drove solidly back into Dave's shoulder. Dave raised his head from the rear sight. The bright spot was gone. The smoke began to drift as the wind picked it up. The thudding shot echo died away against the slopes of the Tinajas Altas. Dave could have sworn he had heard a hoarse scream from where the *corrida* was hidden, but he wasn't sure. It might have been a horse or mule frightened by the blasting sound of the shot.

Dave was gone from his position before the first bullet struck the boulders behind him and whined off into space. It was the first of many. He slung his field glasses case from the saddle horn, grabbed Ulysses' reins, and trotted to the north, trailing his reloaded Sharps in his right hand. He grinned a little as he heard the rapid fusillade of shots crackling and echoing behind him.

Ransom had screamed in pain and then leaped into the air and fallen sideways as the big 500-grain slug smashed cleanly through his left boot heel and neatly grooved the leather above it to within a sixteenth of an inch from his heel sole. He had felt the burning passage of the bullet, which went on to strike the hard ground, then screamed into a short and vicious ricochet and ended up by smashing full force into the head of one of the mules. The mule went down without a sound. One of the water kegs was crushed under its fall and spewed its contents onto the thirsty ground.

The white-faced men looked quickly at each other and then at their commander. He hopped around on his uninjured foot while raising his left leg upward so that he could grab it with his right hand. He yanked off the boot and hurled it into the brush. All dignity was gone. There was black rage on his gaunt face and, although his men could not see it, a growing fear in his one good eye.

Ransom sat on the hard ground rubbing his left ankle. The impact of the big bullet had sent a painful shock wave up his leg. "Get my boot, damn you!" he yelled at random.

Cipriano pulled it out of the brush. He looked at the heel and the groove in the sole leather. He shook his head. "That must have been Hunter," he said as he handed the boot to Ransom.

"It was the Devil!" shouted Gordo.

Ransom took the boot. He looked up sideways at Cipriano. "How do you know that?" he asked quietly.

Cipriano shrugged. "He was carrying that big Sharps when we surprised him. That sure as hell wasn't a Winchester that was just fired. Besides, that was at least a three-hundred-yard shot through those damned heat waves and an uphill shot at that."

"How do you know about Hunter?" asked Ransom suspiciously.

"Can you walk all right?" asked Cipriano.

Ransom nodded. "You didn't answer my question."

"I've heard about him along the border. I didn't know his name. I wasn't too sure about him until he got away from you. Then it came back to me. Besides, how many men do you know who carry a big Sharps like that? That rifle shot convinced me.''

Ransom eyed him coldly. ''He didn't get away from *me*. You were standing right there with that fancy nickel-plated Winchester of yours. You could have dropped him with a leg shot. Or maybe you were afraid, *cabron*.''

Cipriano stiffened slightly at the deadly insult of ''*cabron.*''

Dancy looked over the saddle of his horse. ''While we're standing here jawin' that son of a bitch is making tracks.''

Cipriano seized his chance to get out of the taut situation. ''We'd better get that unbroken water keg off that dead mule, Major.''

Ransom eyed him for a moment. ''All right. Go on ahead and scout. If that's Hunter alone out there, we've got him by the crotch. Now, all of you! Move! *Andale!*''

Ash was waiting for Dave a few miles along the trail. ''I was thinking of coming back for you. What was that shooting about?''

Dave shrugged. ''I think it was Ransom's boot heel. At least, I *hope* it was his. All I had to shoot at was the sun reflecting from a spur. I think I got a hit. At least I heard a scream.''

Ash nodded in appreciation. ''Must have been a helluva shot.''

Jack Spade was looking back along the trail. ''You'd better get moving! That dust is getting closer!''

Ash nodded. ''First time I knew 'ol Jack of Spades was anxious to get to Yuma.'' He looked at Dave. ''Can't you just see that ornery, one-eyed, one-handed son of a bitch Ransom limpin' along on a heelless boot and trying to keep the sun off that steel paw of his so it don't heat up too much?''

Dave and Ash grinned at each other.

''Lead out,'' said Dave. ''I'll come along behind you at about a quarter- to half-a-mile and occasionally give them a round or so of .44/90 to keep them busy.''

"Supposing they get close enough to put a round or two in *you*?" Ash asked.

Dave shook his head. "I won't let them get that close."

Jack shifted in the saddle. "They might have someone back there who's as good a shot as you, Hunter. It would only take one round to get your horse, or maybe you."

Dave shrugged. "Them's the odds," he admitted.

Dave squatted in the dubious shade of his dun until Ash and the others were a good half mile away. He sipped a mouthful of water from one of his canteens and rinsed it about in his mouth before spitting it back into the canteen. He poured some water into his hat and let the dun drink it. Dave put on the hat. It felt somewhat cool for a short time at least. Nothing could stay cool or even comfortably warm out on that heated gridiron called a desert. Everything was *hot*. Exposed metal could hardly be touched with the bare skin.

Dave looked back along the trail. Heat waves shimmered and postured. Distant objects seemed magnified and distorted, and sometimes they seemed to have risen from the ground into the shimmering air. The sun was now an incandescent ball of blazing fury. It could not even be glanced at. To stare at it too long would bring on temporary and possibly permanent blindness. It struck down in fury at travelers who looked like lice crawling across a vast dun-colored table-cloth.

The sun reflected off the ground and struck up beneath low-pulled hat brims. It did no good to look up and ahead. Nothing could be distinguished clearly because of the heat waves. Dust devils had been aroused by the hot strong wind. Caused by a mass of heated air, they whirled with the force of the wind while traversing the desert. Something passing by might set one to rising—a jackrabbit, a coyote, or perhaps a horseman. There were many back about where Ransom and his *corrida* were moving. The dust became a rising column with the inflowing air spiraling upward. Once in a while one might hit some obstruction such as a knoll, hillock, or rock formation, perhaps even a thick clump of brush. Then it would reverse its rotation and revive itself after the trauma of striking an obstruction and being stopped in its nomadic wandering. They usually zigzagged across the desert, following the topographical relief of the land, such as a ridge crest. Sometimes they would remain stationary for hours. Such was the case of several of those Dave could see somewhere near the *corrida*.

Dave stopped and uncased his field glasses. He rested his forearms against the saddle and studied the dust devils behind him. It took him awhile to figure it out, but he finally concluded one of them seemed to be traveling *into the wind* while most of the others he could see were traveling *with* the wind.

He patted the dun's neck. He was a tough one. Dave usually selected a dun horse. This animal was a *bayo coyote* with a light-colored stripe down its back. The Mexican vaqueros said in truth, "If you would lead, the riders pick the coyote dun. He is of the race that dies before tiring." Ulysses had that which the Mexicans, horsemen par excellence, called the *brio escondido*—the hidden vigor—beneath.

"We may need that *brio escondido* this day," he said to the dun.

He waited with the patience of a spider. He squatted in the shade of the horse, hat brim pulled low and eyes slitted against the cruel sunlight. Now and again he looked up toward that almost-imperceptibly moving cloud of dust. Distance was always deceptive in that country. He couldn't let them get too close or a .44/40 Winchester might get him or the dun. He remembered all too well the Mexican named Cipriano with his fine, nickel-plated Winchester '73. He felt that the man knew how to use it and yet, when he could easily have killed Dave, he had jerked his head to the north. "*Andale*, hombre!" he had said.

"What the hell was his game?" Dave muttered to himself as he shaped a cigarette. He lighted it and looked back over his shoulder. The haze and windblown dust were such that he could no longer clearly distinguish Ash and the others, just a vague shadowy something appearing and disappearing like a coin twisted between the supple fingers of a master prestidigitator.

Dave stood up. The field glasses picked out the slowly moving *corrida*. Fifteen men riding or walking through the haze and dust. They could see Dave now. He'd stand out like a fly caught in amber. Ash would be out of sight now except for the dust trailing behind the horses and mule.

The *corrida* halted a quarter of a mile from Dave. He had no concealment now. The sun reflected from his field glasses. What were they thinking? Their logical conclusion would have to be that he was the rear guard, all *one* of him alone on the burning sands.

The *corrida* moved up toward the motionless man and horse.

A gun flashed and cracked. The flat report rolled across the desert. The slug whispered past Dave's right ear. ''Son of a bitch,'' he murmured. One of those bastards *could* shoot.

The *corrida* spread out in a wide crescent, Plains-Indian fashion. Dave slid the Sharps across his saddle and sighted it on one of the horsemen on the left-hand horn of the crescent. The man spurred his horse into a dead run and raised his rifle. The Sharps roared angrily. Dave peered through the powder smoke. The horse had gone down. The rider sprang from the saddle and hit the ground on his shoulder. He flew head over heels to drop hard and lie still.

A horseman each broke from the right and left horns of the crescent. Dave fired at the horseman on the left tip. The horse was turned aside a second before Dave fired. The bullet tore through the back of the rider's shirt while raising a searing welt. He screamed and hollered all the way to the rear and the cover of the haze and dust.

Dave raised his head, then ducked. Five or six guns flashed and cracked. There was the sound of a stick being whipped into thick mud. The dun swayed as he was hit then went down with thrashing hoofs, Dave leaped backward as he reloaded. The dun was dead before he hit the ground. Dave heard the yells of triumph from the *corrida*. ''You haven't got *me* yet,'' he murmured grimly.

Dave yanked his rifle cartridge belt and field glasses from the saddle horn. He saw the stain of water spreading from one of his canteens, which had been smashed under the horse. He pulled the other one free, but it had developed a leak along a seam. He drank deeply then tore off his bandanna and wrapped it tightly about the canteen.

Rifles cracked again. Then came the staccato pounding of many hoofs on the hard-baked ground.

Dave turned and raised his heavy rifle in one fluid motion. He cocked the hammer, set the trigger, and fired all in one ,smooth movement. The lead horseman went down. Dave reloaded and fired again. Another horse went sprawling as his rider cleared leather and hit the ground running, but he ran *away* from Dave's position.

The *corrida* retreated into the dust and haze.

Dave began to walk. Now and again he looked back. All he saw was the dust and haze and what he was *almost* sure was the *corrida*.

His thirst increased. Now and again he would raise his head and look about himself. It was always the same. Nothing but sun-heated sand, wind-driven dust, and a haze which was painful to look at. There were mountains to the right and left, hardly perceptible through the haze except as leaden gray humps of rock. It was as though he had somehow wandered off the face of the earth and had been transported to the moon or some other barren satellite or planet.

''God help me,'' he husked. He was silent after that. The effort to speak was too much. He bent his head and slogged on.

CHAPTER 7

THE SUN WAS BEATING DOWN IN A DIABOLICAL EFFORT TO drive Dave Hunter to his knees and make him scrabble, broken-nailed, in the harsh soil in an effort to find water. Man was stupid, he thought dully. This type of Sonoran desert was no place for him or any man. He thought about it as he went on, one solid step at a time on his burning feet. He was probably on his way out of this world of danger, spilt blood, eternal violence, and constant woe.

The animals of the desert had adapted themselves to their environment. The sidewinder rattlesnake who struck without the honest whirring of rattles hunted in the desert night. The land by day seemed empty of animal life, yet hidden from the human eye were its nocturnal denizens. The kangaroo rat and the kit fox had tufts of bristly hair between their toes to aid them in traveling across the loose sand at night. Horned toads, which were actually lizards and not toads at all, had flattened bodies enabling them to wriggle from side to side to get under the sand, escaping the blasting heat of the day. The rattlesnakes rested in their dens during the day. They could only live a short time under the blazing sun. They hunted at night, when their prey was out gathering food of its own. The herbage, too, had become environmentalized. The thorns of some cacti interlaced and formed shade, like a lath house, to prevent overheating and drying out by the sere winds of the desert.

Dave slowly came out of his self-imposed reverie. He looked behind himself. They were still back there in the haze, monstrously misshapen and magnified. He stared at them for a time and slowly realized they were much closer. As he stood there gaping, one horseman moved swiftly toward him. Dave raised the Sharps and fired. The horseman halted his mount and sat there in the saddle looking at Dave. Dave had missed. . . .

He turned and plodded on as he reloaded. One step after another. "The journey of a thousand miles begins with a single step," he murmured. He grinned and then winced as his dry lower lip cracked.

On and on. The distance seemed limitless. His mind began to wander again. His thirst was a living torment within him. He thought back on the granite tanks of Tinajas Altas and their deep pools of rainwater sheltered from the burning sun. He thought of their clear green depths. He remembered the tracks of animals who came there to drink at night. He thought of the water skaters skimming the surface amid the floating feathers drifting across the pools.

He awoke with a start and found he was almost walking back the way he had come. As he turned back on the trail he remembered all too clearly his full canteen being smashed beneath the dead dun, and the water soaking all too quickly into the thirsty sands.

The seemingly endless afternoon dragged on. He no longer peered through slitted eyes to search for Ash. Still, Ash would be the solution for the immediate problem. He had water, and he could help Dave drive back their pursuers. "You volunteered to act as rear guard," he hoarsely accused himself.

He fired now and again when Ransom and his *corrida* got too close, although it was getting increasingly difficult to estimate the range. Still they came on. Why? The thought moiled through Dave's mind. It was not only the thought of vengeance that was the spur to Ransom's iron will and his discipline over his men. No . . . It had something, perhaps *all* to do with Jesus Valencia—that poor, dried-out relic of a man staggering out of the desert more dead than alive with the heavy gold cross suspended about his gaunt neck.

Dave had begun to be conscious of the heavy weight of

his rifle cartridge belt and his gun belt laden with many cartridges, holstered Colt and sheathed knife. His canteen was almost empty now, so that was no problem. He would not have minded the weight of water. He forced himself to concentrate on his position. He knew of thirst and its effect on humans. They would hallucinate by seeing water where there was no water. There were times when they would dig frantically into the harsh soil with their bare hands until their nails and knuckles were broken and bleeding. Then there would come a time when they became acutely aware of the itching, clinging annoyance of their clothing, even as Dave himself had become aware of the weight of his cartridge and gun belt. Once he dropped those, his clothing would be next. He still had the will power and discipline to avert that decision.

He staggered a little in his stride. It was as though he was walking barefooted across a red-hot kitchen range. He looked back. The pursuing *corrida* was a mere blob of spots like a dark and gelatinous mass of rice pudding such as his mother used to make. When he turned again, they were much closer. He opened fire with three rounds and grinned as they dropped back.

Hours must have passed. Now and again Dave fired back at his pursuers. They kept their distance for fear of the big Sharps. They were tough and hard-case to a man, but they weren't damned fools. They probably figured Dave couldn't last much longer without the smashed canteen they had seen under the side of the dun. They probably knew he had but the one canteen left, and they also knew it took at least one gallon, more likely two gallons per day, for a man to survive in the desert heat.

The sun was slanting to the west.

The Sharps was heavy and seemed to be getting heavier. Maybe he had better drop it and the rifle-cartridge belt, fill his shirt pockets with pistol cartridges, then tuck his Colt under his waist belt and dump the gun belt. He shook his head. That would be for a last-ditch defense. He wasn't ready yet to give up the fight. Still, he was carrying too much weight. Get rid of the gun belts and his shirt. The wool shirt was heavy with accumulated sweat and had become intolerably itchy, a damp and soggy annoyance. His undershirt would serve just as well.

"But for how long?" a mental voice seemed to question him.

He plodded on. The stagecoach road to Yuma should be somewhere ahead of him. The Southern Pacific railroad was building tracks from the west to Yuma with plans to carry them across the Colorado on a bridge and then on to Tucson and the east, but that would be further north, beyond the stagecoach road. The stagecoach road would not solve Dave's problem unless there was salvation there, say something like a cavalry patrol that just happened to be passing by.

He could not keep the persistent, nagging thought of water out of his tired mind. He remembered his teenage days aboard the fast sidewheel steamer *Nokomis* on lakes Superior, Huron, and Michigan. To skipper such a steamer had been Dave's ambition, but his father had talked him into going to college at the age of seventeen. He didn't think about that. He thought of the fresh, cold, gray-blue waters of the Great Lakes.

He plodded on. He began to think of water, water, and yet more water. He stripped his bandanna from the leaky canteen. It was still a little damp. He squeezed but nothing dripped from it. *"Nada,"* he mumbled. He folded the bandanna into a thick, flat roll, tied it about his head, and then perched his hat atop it.

Dave looked ahead. Through the film of dust he thought he saw something opaque perhaps half-a-mile ahead of him and something else moving toward him. He wasn't too sure of whether or not it *was* moving toward him, away from him, or really moving at all. It was a mirage.

Someone shouted behind him. He whirled and saw two riders quirting and spurring their flagging horses toward him. They were less than two hundred yards away. They were evidently risking everything on a toss of the dice, thinking and hoping that he wasn't alert and was almost at the point of exhaustion.

Dave suddenly remembered the first day at Gettysburg, when the Iron Brigade had charged into action to stop the Confederate onslaught. He had been a skirmisher for his regiment, the 24th Michigan. He raised his Sharps and somehow it seemed to him that it changed from a Model 1874 cartridge model into a Sharps New Model 1859 percussion lock .54-caliber, the type he had carried into battle that terrible day. He unslung his Sharps, cocked it, set the firing trigger, and fired all in one fluid motion. The Sharps blasted flame and smoke. The lead horse went down, hurling its riders shoulder and head against the hard desert floor.

There was no time to reload the smoking Sharps. Four more riders appeared through the dust charging toward Dave. Dave dropped his Sharps and yanked out his Colt while cocking the big spur hammer. Dave waited until the lead horseman was within twenty-five yards. The Colt cracked and cracked again until six rounds of .44/40 tore into horse and man, cutting them down into a sliding, sprawling tangle that raised a cloud of dust.

The following horsemen drew aside and slowed down. Their gamble had failed. Some of them drew their rifles from saddle holsters.

Dave flipped open the loading gate of his hot smoking Colt and filled the chambers with six fresh loads. He did not take his eyes off the horsemen, who had now halted, and were milling about, holding in their horses, who had gotten excited because of the rapid staccato fusillade from Dave's six-gun.

The powder smoke drifted off to mingle with the dust.

Dave grinned crookedly. He waved his Colt. "Come on!" he yelled. "There's a round left for each of you, you bastards!" He weaved back and forth; a tall, lean man wreathed in a film of dust that somehow seemed to increase his stature. The sun glinted as it reflected from a shiny Winchester barrel. Dave moved quickly as it flashed and cracked. The slug seemed to fan his right ear as it went past.

One of the men was pointing, seemingly in Dave's direction. Another, Ransom in fact, stood up in his stirrups and stared toward Dave. Another rifle cracked. Ransom thrust out a hand to stop the shooting just as Dave started to turn to look north. He heard a staccato beating of something like hoofs on the hard ground. Then something seemed to slap Dave hard along the left side of his skull, semi-stunning him, but he would not go down. He turned back again to face his enemies. His eyes seemed out of focus. Were the horsemen closing in on him again? Something trickled down his face from under the left side of the bandanna he had bound about his skull. He touched the finger tips of his left hand to his face and then looked at them. Blood glistened. He had been hit, more correctly "creased," by the bullet. Maybe it was worse than he thought. Maybe it was the end. . . . Better to die game, he thought dully.

The staccato beating of hoofs on the hard desert floor became louder. The sound came from *behind* Dave. The horsemen of the *corrida* were frantically turning their mounts to stampede.

Dave waved his Colt. "Come on, you sons of bitches!" he roared hoarsely. "Fill your hands, you bastards! Come on! I'm only one man, and a damned ring-tailed roarer!"

Ash pounded past him on Dearly Beloved at a dead run. He turned in his saddle. "That's it, Davie!" he yelled as he waved his Winchester. "You tell 'em who they're dealing with!" He grinned clear across his lean face.

Dave swayed loosely on his feet. He felt as though he was drunk. The pain in the side of his skull was becoming excruciating. However, he took his cue from Ash. "I hunt grizzly bears with a switch!" he howled at the blazing sky. "I bite off the necks of whiskey bottles." He poured out a creditable imitation of the fearsome Rebel yell, *"Yaaaaaiah!"*

A woman wearing a dress hiked up about her knees and riding astride a big claybank horse hammered past Dave. Her long dark hair streamed back over her shoulders. A rifle rested on her rounded thighs. She glanced sideways at Dave. "You're a real stud, amigo!" she cried. Then she was gone after Ash. Dave knew he must be hallucinating. A moment

later half-a-dozen troopers led by an officer rode past him
following Ash and the woman, if it indeed *had* been a
woman. "That's enough, Mawson!" shouted the officer in a
bellowing, parade-ground voice. "I want no killings! They're
on the run! Let the bastards go!" The *corrida* was gone out
of sight into the dust and haze. The officer pulled his bay
horse to a plunging halt, scattering sand and gravel in every
direction. "Back to the wagons!" he commanded. "Ash,
you bring along your fighting friend here." He grinned as he
turned his horse.

Ash came cantering back.

"Where the hell were you when I needed you, you big-
nosed bastard!" Dave yelled hoarsely at Ash.

The officer looked curiously at Dave and then at Ash. "Is
he always like that when someone saves his misbegotten
life?" he asked dryly.

Ash nodded. "I told you he missed me. The ugly horned
toad loves me better than any brother." Suddenly he was off
his horse, plunging with short, driving steps to catch Dave
as he started to fall.

Dave opened his eyes once thereafter in time to see a dusty
column of dismounted troopers standing ahead of three dusty
but brightly painted wagons. He could have sworn a yellow-
haired woman was descending from the rear of the first
wagon. She came quickly toward him with outstretched hands
as though to help him. Two thick reddish blond pigtails hung
in front of her shoulders. He looked away from her. "Another hallucination," he murmured. There were half-a-dozen
freight wagons behind the three wagons. Their canvas tilts
were marked U.S. There were more troopers behind them.

Dave blinked. The last thing he was aware of was the
garish green, yellow, and silver paint on the side of the first
wagon and the bold printed lettering: Colonel/Doctor
Myron T. Buscombe, and beneath it a sign—Purveyor of
Buscombe's Abyssinian Desert Companion to Her Majesty
Queen Victoria of England.

CHAPTER 8

THE SWAYING, BUMPING MOTION AND THE RUMBLING noise combined with a steady dull clopping sound fully awoke Dave at last. He had a vague, dreamlike memory of someone talking and of hands touching his head. Something had stung the side of his skull, and the astringent odor of strong carbolic had come to him. "He's got a skull as thick as a bull," Ash had said. "You can't kill a Hunter by hitting him on the head."

Dave half opened his eyes as he raised a hand to touch the bandage that was bound about his skull. Something firm and yet soft pressed against his shoulder. He put his hand over to see what it might be and touched what he knew right well had to be, from the shape and feeling of it, a woman's breast. He thoughtfully squeezed it.

"Now, now, no time for that, right *now* anyway," remonstrated a soft and pleasant female voice. A hand gently removed his hand from the breast.

He opened his eyes fully and looked dreamily into a pair of the most lovely, interesting, and immense green eyes he had ever seen. They were not the hard bottle green of Ash Mawson's eyes but rather a transparent liquid green that seemed almost unreal. They were framed in an oval face that revealed a pert nose dusted with tiny freckles, full bee-stung lips and flawless, transparent skin that was slightly reddened and freckled from the sun. Her shapely head was surmounted by reddish blond hair that had been neatly braided and wound about it. She wasn't a great beauty. Her face was too broad;

69

the mouth too wide. Still, she was a handsome baggage, as Dave's mother might have designated her.

"Can't you speak? Just what *are* you thinking?" she asked suspiciously.

Dave reached his right arm around her shoulders and felt about them.

"I *said* there was no time for that," she repeated. She didn't sound displeased.

He withdrew his arm. "Sorry," he apologized. "I was trying to find out if you had wings. I thought maybe I had died and gone to heaven and I was being ministered to by an angel."

She laughed with the trilling tone of tiny silver bells. "*Me?* No chance, Mr. Hunter!" She studied him for a moment. "But maybe you are in hell, and I'm a she-devil deceiving you with the outward appearance of an houri."

He grinned. "That would be more like it."

"How are you feeling?" she asked again.

He looked about. He was in a rather high-ceilinged wagon that was rocking and swaying on the rough, rutted road. A partition had been built across the middle of the wagon bed with a narrow door cut into the center of it. There were two bunks, one on each side of the wagon. He was lying in one of the bunks; and when he raised his head, he could see Jesus Valencia sleeping in the other bunk. There were cabinets hung over each of the beds and on the wall on each side of the door. He turned his head to look at the forward end of the wagon. That, too, was walled with ceiling-to-floor cabinets, evidently wardrobes, for one of the doors was partly open, and he could see women's dresses hanging inside. A short ladder was against the front partition between the two wardrobes. It extended up to a half door, which evidently opened to the wagon seat.

The whole assembly reminded him of some of the cabins on the steamer *Nokomis*, so well designed and compact it was. There was something else that was a clue to its occupants—the unmistakable mingled odor of perfume, face powder, and the indefinable female scent. He looked back into those great eyes of his savior. They were deep enough and enchanting enough to engulf some poor stupid male son of a bitch and make him a helpless slave or drown him forever.

"I'm Callie Sutherland," she said. "You didn't answer my question."

He nodded. "I'm all right," he replied. "Still thirsty. Helluva headache. My feet are still burning." He suddenly pushed her back a little and sat up. "Where's my Sharps rifle?" he quickly demanded.

She studied him curiously. "It's all right. Your *compañero* Ash kept it with him. Is it that important?"

He nodded. "I'm a rifleman born and bred," he replied.

"You could always get another one."

Dave shook his head. "They don't always shoot alike."

She smiled teasingly. "Dead center? I know."

It was his turn to study her. "You do? About rifles I mean?"

She nodded. "Somewhat. I was raised by my father. He was one of the great riflemen of his day."

He narrowed his eyes. "Not Gil Sutherland of Kentucky?"

She smiled again. "That was him. 'Deadshot' Sutherland."

"One of the greatest, or possibly the *greatest*, range and trick shot of his day," he agreed.

There seemed to be a sudden bond of affinity between the two of them. She quickly looked away. "You've got more luck than brains surviving that 'creasing' you got, El Buscadero."

El Buscadero—The Seeker—Dave and Ash shared that nickname.

"I'll buy that," he admitted. "How did you know my nickname? Ash Mawson tell you?"

She drew back a little from him. "He said you were Dave Hunter and that he was Ash Mawson, and we knew from that you were The Seekers. Then, of course, Colonel/Dr. Buscombe knew who you were as well."

It was then he recalled the garish lettering on the wagon side he had noticed before he passed out. He grinned. "That old charlatan? Colonel/Dr. Myron T. Buscombe—Purveyor of Buscombe's Abyssinian Desert Companion to Her Majesty Queen Victoria of England," he said sonorously.

She flipped her slender hand about. "This is one of his medicine wagons. And he's not *old*, at least in his actions."

Dave looked around the interior and shook his head as though he could not believe it. "Where the good Colonel/Dr. Buscombe dispenses magical potions, elixirs, and Buscombe's Abyssinian Companion to one and all for a considerable fee until he gets run out of town?" He grinned again. "What's your relationship with him?"

She shrugged her pretty shoulders and tilted her head to one side while holding him enthralled with those great green eyes of hers. Twin emeralds in a field of ivory, thought Dave.

She placed her hand alongside his left cheek. "I work for him. He is my uncle. My mother was his sister." Her palm was firm and surprisingly hard.

He could have swallowed his wagging tongue. "I'm sorry," he apologized. "What do you do for him?"

She half smiled. "I'm a performer."

Visions of a hootchy-kootchy dancer crept before his eyes. Perhaps she was a belly dancer; a Salome of the Southwest. She had the figure for it.

She turned her head as someone undid the outer latch on the half door at the front of the wagon box.

Colonel/Dr. Buscombe—the name brought faded memories back to Dave. Stories were told about him but were wreathed in the mists of legend, or myth, perhaps outright falsehood. Dave had originally heard of the doctor during his own service with the Army of the Potomac. There, Buscombe had originally been appointed by General McClellan, with his great flair for organization, as chief inspector of the various sutlers, who supplied necessities to the troops. Buscombe's appointment was not a military one, nor was it a government position. Sutlers were usually honorarily titled major, but Buscombe had either been appointed an honorary colonel or had assumed the title himself. He was said to have served as a medical officer during the Mexican War. That was true, but there had been some doubt about the medical degree he claimed to have. There had been no doubt about his popularity with many West Point and volunteer-army officers whom he was said to have liberally supplied with medical alcohol and fine Havana cigars. Later, during the War between the States, he had renewed his friendships with McClellan, Grant, Meade, and Hooker on the Union side and was said to still have thought kindly of Confederates such as President Jefferson Davis, a colonel of Mississippi Volunteers during the Mexican War, as well as Lee, Longstreet, Pickett, Stuart, and even the irascible Braxton Bragg. Before and after the Civil War he had been a gambler on Mississippi River steamboats, adept with cards and dice and certainly with derringer and bowie knife. He was known as an accomplished duellist; a man of quick temper when his touchy "honor" was impugned. He was known to have killed three men, and the count was quite probably somewhat higher than that. One he had shot at with a derringer under a gambling table, placing a .41-caliber ball in his belly; another he had beaten to death in a bare-knuckle knock-down-and-drag-'em-out fight in a Memphis saloon. The third was one whose violent death had become legend throughout the south— Buscombe had been challenged, thus having the choice of site and weapons. His choice had been razor-sharp bowie knives. There was nothing outright unusual about the choice of that deadly weapon. It was the site and the method of duelling that was macabre. They had dug a grave together during a moonlit night on a sandspit on the Mississippi River. Stripped to the waist and with their left wrists firmly tied together, they had fought to the death in the grave. It had been Buscombe who had climbed weakly out of the grave, covered with his own blood and that of his dead opponent. He had contemptuously kicked down the first sand to cover the body and then had collapsed. He had nearly died himself before being nursed back to health by a beautiful Haitian mulatto woman. It was said she had used voodoo rites to accomplish her purpose and dedicated her life and that of Buscombe to some bloody god.

Callie was speaking to someone who had opened the half door leading to the wagon seat. Dave turned. His eyes opened in amazement. The first thing he saw was a pair of firm, shapely, and very slightly bowed female legs clad in thin cotton hose. A petticoat and long skirt had been hiked up so as to negotiate the steep ladder. There were no drawers that Dave could see as high as midthigh. There was a shapely behind under the taut fabric of the dress.

Dave looked up to see a pair of lustrous, liquid brown eyes surveying him over a shoulder. "Seen enough, Mr. Hunter?" she asked. She smiled. "You must be feeling better." Her throaty voice had a soft tone of patois to it.

Dave smiled. "I'd have to be at death's door, and maybe not even then, to not notice *those* legs. . . . Begging your pardon, *limbs*, ma'am." By God! She was the same woman he had seen riding hell-for-leather with Ash!

She descended to the floor and turned to face him. She pulled down her dress and petticoat and smoothed the fabric over her thighs. "They're *legs*, not limbs, but I appreciate your courtesy; but then your partner Ash said you weren't like him in the respect that you're *always* the gentleman."

Callie placed her hand across her mouth and stifled a titter. Her green eyes and the brown eyes of the newcomer held each other. "This lady is Madeleine Dupree," Callie said. "My partner," she added quickly.

Madeleine held out an elegant, slender, and long-fingered hand to grasp that of Dave. "Charmed, I'm sure," she said. She was wearing a straw sunbonnet adorned with flowing ribbons. "That setting sun is beastly, Callie. Best to wear this hat when you take your stint driving the damned wagon."

Madeleine was dark in direct contrast to Callie's lightness. Her nose was slightly aquiline but flared somewhat at the nostrils. Her skin was almost a creamed coffee color. There were faint wrinkles at the corners of her huge eyes. Her mouth was almost too full, and her pearly white teeth were a little over natural size. Her lips were thick and full and rather heavily rouged. She had full breasts straining at the dress fabric, a narrow waist, probably without benefit of a corset, and full, rounded hips. Where Callie seemed like a child of the bright sunlight, open meadows, tinkling streams, powder-puff clouds, and immense beds of wild flowers nodding in the soft breeze, Madeleine was a child of the moonlight, often hidden by dark scudding clouds. There was a hint of the bayou about her—a dark, mysterious stream, a ruined plantation house, and an almost eerie midnight wind whispering through a dark grove of moss-hung trees. In any case, Dave realized he was looking at a pair of what he would have thought of as "real" women, and damned handsome to boot.

Madeleine opened a wardrobe door. "I'm going to ride for awhile. My bottom is stiff and sore from that damned wagon seat. The colonel wants you to take over for a while when he checks out El Buscadero here. Ash assured me that Davie had a skull thick enough to turn a twelve-pounder solid shot aside." She eyed Dave over her shoulder. "Is that true?" she asked.

Dave shook his head. "Not quite. One of Ash Mawson's frequent fabrications."

She shrugged. "Well, maybe he was thinking psychologically." She studied him for a moment.

He looked into those dark midnight eyes and thought of the green pools Callie had. For a moment he forgot the whacking pain in his head. What a pair of women! A man would experience a mental hell trying to decide which one of them to pick. Ah! But if a man had *both* of them! One at a time, of course. The two of them together would likely kill a man in his intense frustration and possible inability to perform.

Callie pulled up her skirts to ascend the ladder. Dave was a leg man. He nodded in approval. Her legs were straighter and more slender than those of Madeleine but just as thought-provoking.

Madeleine grinned. "You don't miss much, do you?"

Dave grinned back. "Try me," he suggested.

Their eyes met in a semi-challenge with the old competi-

tion of the sexes. She looked away. "I've got to change,"
she said, almost as though to herself. She looked back at
him. "Do you mind?"

Dave sat up and reached for his hat.

She shook her head. "You don't have to leave. I've been
an actress. I'm used to dressing and undressing backstage in
the middle of actors, stagehands, and hangers-on. It doesn't
bother me."

He swept his hat sideways. "Be my guest," he said gal-
lantly. "I'll look the other way."

She shrugged. "You're a strange one," she murmured as
though to herself.

He felt in his pocket for his tobacco canteen and lucifers.
"All right to smoke?" he asked.

She grinned. "Sure, as long as you shape one for me."

"It's Lobo Negro," he warned. "Potent stuff."

She looked at him out of the corners of her dark eyes.

"I'm used to *potent* stuff, Davie," she said dryly.

He shaped a quirly, watching her as she raised her skirt
and pulled the dress up and over her head. She did the same
with her petticoat to reveal those gorgeous long legs of hers.
She wore a pair of midthigh-length cambric drawers trimmed
with lace and a cambric brassiere. She leaned back against
the bunk opposite Dave and quickly unbuttoned the cloth
tops of her shoes and pulled them off. She slipped her feet
into fine woolen hose and rolled them up to above the knee
and gartered them in position.

"Your cigarette," Dave said thoughtfully as he offered it
to her.

She came close and placed the cigarette between her lips
while he dragged a lucifer across his belt buckle and then
lighted the cigarette. He couldn't help but look into those
dazzling eyes of hers again. She smiled faintly and returned
to her dressing leaving the impression of her perfume in his
nostrils.

Dave shaped a cigarette for himself while he watched her.

She put on a shirt tailored like a man's but with full allow-
ance for her breasts. She then drew on a midcalf-length,

serge-split skirt. She looked at Dave as she did so. "Ever see one of these before?" she asked.

Dave shook his head. "I thought all women but circus performers *always* rode sidesaddle," he admitted. "They of course always wore spangled tights."

"You're right," she said. She yanked on a pair of Mexican half boots of embossed leather and buckled on a pair of small roweled, silver-mounted spurs. "I'll be damned if I'll try to ride sidesaddle in this country," she added. She placed a flat-brimmed hat on her head. It had a rattlesnake skin band about the crown.

Dave lighted up, looking at her over the flare of the lucifer. "There's a saying here in the Southwest that anyone who wears such a hat band is warning the general public not to tangle with a real bad hombre. I mean *bad.* . . ." He fanned out the match. "Does that apply to you, Madeleine?"

She eyed him steadily. "*That*, Mr. Hunter, is none of *your* damned business." She smiled faintly, taking some of the sting out of her response.

Dave shrugged. "Each to his own."

She nodded. "Exactly."

He watched her as she opened a drawer and took out a holstered pistol and gun belt. She withdrew the pistol and spun the cylinder to check the loads. She looked at Dave. "Ever see one of these?" she asked.

Dave nodded. "It's a Colt New Line, isn't it?"

"It is. Five-shot. Centerfire .41-caliber."

He studied her. "I know better than to ask if you know how to use it and can hit anything with it."

"I'm glad you didn't," she said.

She buckled the gun belt about her slim waist then moved the pistol in and out of the holster to check the ease of draw.

"You're a caution, Madeleine," Dave said dryly.

She took a quirt from a hook on the wall and opened the door that led into the rear of the wagon. Dave stood up and walked slowly to the doorway. The rear double doors were open. A roan horse was tethered next to a blocky claybank. Madeleine untied the claybank, dropped to the ground from the moving wagon, and then mounted the horse. She waved a gloved hand to Dave and then spurred the horse to ride ahead of the wagon.

The wagon following the one Dave was in was evidently another of Buscombe's caravan. Dave recalled seeing three such wagons before he had passed out. The one following was being driven by a burly bearded man who looked like Ali Baba. There was a series of large rolls of what might be canvas and bundles of poles piled atop the wagon. Dave began to feel a little faint. He entered the rear room of the wagon. There was a double bunk on one side and a small stove beyond its foot. The chimney went up through the roof. Tin for fire protection had been nailed to the wagon side and the back of the double doors near the stove. One full side of the area was filled with a long counter with cabinets below and above it. There were three shelves just back of the counter filled with rows and rows of bottles and tin and pewter containers, all neatly labeled with their contents of chemicals, drugs, pharmaceuticals, and medicaments. Fastened to the wall between the two rooms was a rack filled with shotguns and rifles. There was a row of cases on the floor, each of them labeled ABYSSINIAN DESERT COMPANION and *Product of Colonel/Doctor Myron T. Buscombe, M.D. & PhD.*

Dave wondered idly what Buscombe was pushing now. It seemed odd that Buscombe would be traveling west, but perhaps he was carrying his magic potions, elixirs, cures, and general bullshit to the west coast, perhaps even as far as San Francisco. And where did the two women fit into his plans? Callie had said she was his niece. Madeleine had said nothing about her relationship with the good Colonel/Doctor. Ash had said Buscombe had been quite a ladies' man in his time. Perhaps he still was.

Dave rooted around in the cabinets under the counter and came up triumphant with a bottle of brandy in his hand. He helped himself to a deep draft and grunted in animal satisfaction. A second shot seemed to help the throbbing pain in his skull. So it was worth a third long, long pull at the bottle.

Dave blinked a little and grinned. *"Aha!"* he said. He hiccupped loudly.

He peered into the front compartment. There was no one there except Jesus, who was still sound asleep. Maybe he was dead. . . . Evidently the Colonel/Doctor was still up on the wagon box with the delectable Callie, his *niece*. . . .

CHAPTER 9

JESUS WAS STILL ASLEEP. DAVE PLACED HIS HEAD AGAINST the man's thin chest and detected a faint heartbeat.

The door to the driver's seat was opened. "Is he still alive, Hunter?" a sonorous voice asked. It was followed by a deep-throated coughing.

Dave looked up into a pair of cold-looking gray eyes. He nodded. "Just about, I'd say."

"I'm Dr. Buscombe," the man said as he descended the ladder.

"It used to be *Colonel* Buscombe," said Dave. "A *Kentucky* colonel."

Buscombe nodded. "Sometimes I'm called doctor and sometimes it's colonel, as well as Colonel/Dr. Buscombe. You can use any of them you like. They all fit." He cleared his throat and coughed again.

Dave eyed the man who had long been considered to be one-quarter moonbeams, one-quarter myth, one-quarter legend, and the remainder pure unadulterated bullshit. The once-handsome face was now somewhat drawn with an unnatural ruddiness about the cheeks, while the rest of the facial skin was of an off gray color. The cheeks had a hollowness to them. The eyes were exceptionally bright, and there were dark half circles beneath them. To Dave there seemed to be an almost haunted look lurking in them coming and going, as though trying to hide from the casual observer. There also seemed to be uncertainty in them. Myron T. Buscombe (that was his given name) was somewhat less than six feet tall, broad of shoulder and once narrow of waist, but now supported a somewhat rounded paunch under a brocaded silk vest. He had taken off his wide-brimmed, low-crowned southern-planter's-style hat to reveal thick and wavy gray hair, with dark and light streaks like a badger's pelt. His thick mustache was fully gray. His teeth were large and regular with rather prominent canines. It was his eyes that had always caught one's attention, or so Dave had heard. There was almost a mesmerizing quality about them. It seemed to Dave that a person with much less will power and mental discipline than he could be drawn under their power. It had been rumored that he might be a past master of that pseudo-science known as hypnotism.

Buscombe coughed. He eyed Dave. "How do you feel?"

Dave shrugged. "About as well as I could expect."

"How's your head?"

Dave grinned. "Still on my shoulders."

Buscombe studied him. "I've heard about you. You're the one they used to call El Buscadero."

"They still do, Colonel/Doctor."

Buscombe took out a moroccan-leather cigar case and opened it. Dave thought he had seen the pearl-handled butt of a hideout gun held in a shoulder holster close to the left armpit.

Buscombe offered the cigar case to Dave. Dave selected a short six and bit off the end. Buscombe took a long nine and cut off the end with a silver clipper attached to the watch chain that was strung along the front of his vest. He lighted a lucifer and held the flame to the tip of Dave's cigar. He looked into Dave's eyes over the flare of the match. "I've heard you and your partner Ash had come upon hard times and had to revert to manhunting again."

Dave puffed the cigar into life. "That so?" he asked dryly.

Buscombe nodded. "That's so. I understand the two of you were working out of Yuma Pen."

"Ash told you, of course."

"That's true. He also said you had been down southwest

of Quitabaquito Springs and had caught Jack Spade down there, and later Jesus Valencia.''

Dave shrugged. ''Anything else?''

Buscombe nodded. ''He showed me the gold cross. He said you two had found it down in that area. You may be wondering why?''

There was no reply from Dave.

Buscombe leaned closer to Dave. ''All three of us damned well know it was Jesus Valencia who had that cross when you captured him.''

''Yep. We all damned well know,'' agreed Dave. He began to speculate on why the usually close-mouthed Ash had talked so much to Buscombe. Then it came to him. Ash had probably, almost certainly been trying to work a deal with Buscombe to keep Valencia and Spade hidden until Dave and Ash could spirit the two of them out of Yuma and the hands of the law, as well as the mysterious ''they'' who had sprung them from Yuma.

Buscombe studied Dave. ''I think you know what he was trying to do.''

Dave smiled thinly. ''And that's why you are here.''

Buscombe leaned back on the bunk. ''Exactly! Ash suggested I conceal Spade and Valencia in my wagons, take them to Yuma, where I was going anyhow to put on my world-famed medicine show, keep them concealed until such time as you and Ash, or *I* . . .'' He paused and searched Dave's eyes with his own. ''Could get them out of Yuma,'' he continued. ''And then we can treat Valencia back to reasonable good health and take him back to the area of The Walking Sands to show us where the long-lost Jesuit treasure of San Dionysius is hidden. Now, Hunter, what do you think of that?''

Dave studied him in turn. He smiled a little. ''And, as the saying goes—what's in it for me, meaning *you*, of course.''

Buscombe spread out his hands. ''A fair share of the treasure.''

''And the alternatives?''

Buscombe smiled. It was a smile of the facial muscles,

but not of the eyes. "There are several. I know you had no choice but to bring Valencia and Spade back to Yuma. Back into the lion's den, so to speak. Major Cole Ransom found you there at Tinajas Altas as Ash stated. Ransom, or Steel Hand as he is better known, is at this moment somewhere back on the Yuma Road following us. He wants Valencia as you and I do, and perhaps others as well. You could take Valencia and Spade back into Yuma Pen, but that would place them into the hands of whoever sprung them from that hellhole. You would then draw your thousand dollars, the most princely sum I've ever heard of as a bounty for prisoners out of Yuma Pen." He smiled. "I know of you two men. A thousand dollars would hardly keep the pair of you going for more than a month or so at best."

"Get on with it, Buscombe," Dave dryly suggested.

"I made a proposition to Ash, and I will repeat it to you. You turn those two prisoners over to me and I'll pay the bounty money plus another thousand apiece for each of you. That's three thousand dollars. Fifteen hundred apiece. What do you say?"

Dave blew a smoke ring and poked a finger through it. "Does that include the gold cross?" he asked dryly.

Buscombe was all coolness. "Of course!"

"That alone should be worth at least double, maybe triple, what you have offered us for the two men."

Buscombe smiled. "You are a shrewd bargainer, Hunter. Well, I've been bested at my own game. I'll do it!" he cried heartily.

Dave shook his head. "Bullshit, Colonel/Doctor."

The forced smile left Buscombe's face. The eyes seemed to have a chill in them. "What the hell do you mean?" he demanded.

"The cross is the property of Jesus Valencia. The man and the cross go together. If he goes back into Yuma Pen, Ash and I keep the cross until such time as he can get out of that hellhole."

"There is another alternative," Buscombe said coldly.

"Such as?" Dave knew what was forthcoming.

"I'll keep Valencia *and* his gold cross and be damned to you."

"There's another alternative, Buscombe. What do you think your army escort commander is going to think about you taking over those prisoners and not delivering them to Yuma Pen?"

Buscombe smiled. "They're some miles ahead of us now and probably are about to ferry across the river to Fort Yuma. Besides, it's really none of their affair, is it? It's not a Federal matter." He coughed thickly then turned his head aside to wipe his mouth on a silk handkerchief. Dave was sure he saw spots of blood on the fabric.

The door to the front seat was opened. Callie thrust her head into the opening. "Ash and Madeleine were riding a mile or so ahead, Myron. They saw a party of horsemen coming from the direction of Yuma."

"Did they say who they were?" asked Buscombe.

Ash opened the door to the rear of the wagon. "Lawmen. In fact, they are led by an old friend of Dave and me. Deputy-Sheriff Daniel 'Bull' Andrews."

"Are you sure?" demanded Buscombe.

Ash nodded. "He's wearing his big white hat. I put Dave's field glasses on him. I think he's after the prisoners." As Buscombe looked up toward Callie, Ash winked at Dave. His meaning was clear to Dave. Bull Andrews was the official who had closed the deal for Ash and Dave to pursue and capture Spade and Valencia. In Ash's succinct opinion Bull Andrews was "That crooked son of a bitch!"

"There's no way you can stop him, Buscombe," Dave said quietly. "What Bull wants, Bull gets. It'll be back to the Pen for both prisoners. That takes care of any deals you have thought up, Colonel/Dr. Buscombe."

Buscombe shook his head. "I don't believe you two hard cases would give up that easy. I'll make a final offer. Let Andrews take the prisoners back to the Pen. Then all we have to do, working as a team, is spring Valencia out of the Pen and smuggle him out of Yuma and then head for The Walking Sands."

"That's all?" Dave said dryly.

Ash grinned. "He has a great sense of humor."

Buscombe studied them. "You mean to say that you've given up on the deal? That you two inveterate treasure hunters are going to let the treasure of San Dionysius slip through your hands?" He shook his head in mock despair.

"But you plan to go ahead on it?" asked Ash.

Buscombe nodded.

Dave and Ash looked at each other. "It's something to think about," suggested Ash. "Besides, what else do we have to do?"

Dave shrugged. "You've got a point there, Ash."

"After all, all we have to do is spring him out of Yuma Pen."

"Just like that."

Ash nodded. "Just like that."

Buscombe looked from one to the other of them. "I've heard about you two. I never believed much of it. I'm beginning to now. Shall we shake hands on the deal? They say your word is as good as your bond."

Ash looked at Dave. "Did we mention anything about having *him* in on the deal?"

Dave shook his head.

Buscombe started up the ladder to the driver's seat. He looked back at them. "I'll give you time to think about it." He coughed hard, and tiny flecks of blood came from his lips. He hastily covered his mouth with his handkerchief.

"We've got plenty of time," Ash reminded him. "Valencia won't be going anywhere."

Buscombe studied them over his shoulder. "Don't be too sure of that." He climbed through the door and latched it behind himself.

Dave reached under the mattress and withdrew the brandy bottle. He uncorked it and handed it to Ash. Ash drank and passed it back to Dave. Dave drank. He wiped his mouth. "You think the good Colonel/Doctor. might be the 'they' people, or person?"

Ash nodded. "Or one of them. Might be quite a few people involved."

"Such as?"

Ash shrugged. "Buscombe, Andrews, Steel Hand, and maybe a few others."

They looked at each other.

"Someone who hasn't shown his hand yet," suggested Dave.

"You're right," croaked a rusty-sounding voice from behind them.

Faster than one might say, two Colts were out of their holsters, cocked and held at hip level with one pair of icy blue eyes looking over one gun barrel and another of adamantine green looking over the other.

The sunken eyes of Jesus Valencia peered at them from his gaunt face.

"The son of a bitch is still alive," murmured Ash.

Dave let down the hammer of his Colt and holstered the weapon. "You heard everything?" he asked.

Jesus nodded. "And everything that passed between you and Colonel Buscombe."

"You know him?"

"Yes. And Bull Andrews as well. Are you going to let him take me?"

"There's not much we can do about that."

"You still have the cross?"

Ash unbuttoned his shirt and showed Jesus the cross.

Jesus nodded. "Good. Keep it in trust for me."

Dave studied him. "Do you remember where you found it?"

A slight veil seemed to pass over the man's eyes. "I don't remember. *Now*, at least."

"You trust us with it? Why?"

The blue eyes studied Dave as Dave had been studying him. "What else can I do? It would be taken from me as soon as I was moved from this wagon and returned to Yuma Pen. God alone knows where it would end up." He closed his eyes for a moment. "The cross does not belong to me. I am merely the temporary custodian. It is a holy relic."

"From *San Dionysius*?" asked Ash. He smiled.

"That name was placed upon it not much more than one hundred and ten years ago. It is much, much older than that and has traveled many leagues to come here. It does not belong to *anyone*. The Church itself has merely been its caretaker over many years. There is a 'power' within it. The cross itself is merely the custodian of that 'power.' I, too, have a power." His voice died away for a moment. After a time he spoke again in a very low voice. "Perhaps you do not believe me?"

Dave leaned close to him. "I'm not sure, Jesus. But certainly *something* brought you alive out of that desert."

Ash shrugged. "Why didn't it give him a little water to make it easier on him?"

Jesus shook his head. "That was not to be. To have a power one must be prepared to suffer."

"Well, Jesus, you certainly paid your way," Ash said dryly.

Jesus' eyes seemed to glitter. He extended a thin, curved claw of a hand. "Say what you will. You two men are inextricably mixed up with me *and* that cross of gold. If you don't know it now, you will surely know it in time."

"Is there any way we can tell if Buscombe was mixed up in getting you sprung from Yuma Pen? That he might be one of the people involved? Say with Bull Andrews?" queried Dave.

The door to the seat opened. Callie stuck in her head. "Bull Andrews is almost here. Dave, if you want to leave, take my roan. I can pick it up later when we are in Yuma." She closed the door.

"You didn't answer my question," said Dave.

Jesus smiled a little. "If Buscombe reveals the fact that you two have possession of the cross, then you will know that he is in partnership. If, on the other hand, he does not, then you will know he is not. That latter will leave you still open to his proposition of partnership with you."

"And what do *you* think of that proposition?"

Jesus closed his eyes. "He cannot make it without you two."

"Can we make it without *him*?"

Jesus opened his eyes. "That I don't know."

The wagon was stopped.

"They're here," said Ash.

Dave took the right hand of Jesus. He looked into the sunken eyes. "The best of luck, my friend. Somehow we'll get you back out of Yuma Pen. Don't lose hope. Use your *power*, amigo. *Vaya* . . ."

Jesus nodded. He did not speak.

They went to the tailgate. Ash swung down to the ground and neatly avoided a quick nip from Dearly Beloved's yellowed teeth, untethered the sorrel, and swung up into the saddle. He slammed a doubled fist down on top of the horse's head. "Damn you!" he growled. "You nearly did it, didn't you?"

Dave could have sworn the sorrel grinned. Callie's roan was also tethered to the tailgate. He mounted. Ash handed him his Sharps and cased field glasses. "Thanks for the loan," he said.

Dave nodded. "Anytime."

Bull Andrews came striding around the side of the wagon. Dave looked down into the saddle-hued face. He smiled. "Howdy, Bull," he said. "Looking for someone in your line of duty, or is this just a social call?"

Bull spat tobacco juice to one side. "Cut the bullshit, Hunter. I've come here to get the two prisoners *you* were supposed to have delivered to Yuma Pen."

Dave eyed him. "We're not in Yuma yet."

Bull nodded. "That's so. However, by the authority vested in me by Yuma County, *I'm* taking over."

Ash rested his forearms on his saddle horn and studied Bull. "Does that include the thousand dollars bounty money?"

Bull shrugged. "Well, part of it anyway. Naturally I'll collect it for you."

Ash nodded. "Naturally," he agreed.

Bull turned. "Barnes, you and Naylor get in this wagon and bring out Valencia."

Dave shook his head. "He's not fit to ride."

Bull studied him. "Who says so?"

"I do. You can ask Buscombe for his medical advice."

Bull grinned. "That charlatan? For what it's worth, of course."

Dave moved the Sharps slightly so that the muzzle was about three feet from Bull's broad chest. "He was nearly dead of thirst and exhaustion when we found him. We don't know how he survived. You'd better let him ride in the wagon until he gets to Yuma."

Bull looked along the heavy barrel into those icy blue eyes. "You're bluffing, as usual," he said slowly. Bull didn't scare easy.

Dave smiled thinly. "Try me," he suggested.

Buscombe came around the side of the wagon. His right hand was concealed just within his coat. "Now, gentlemen, let us not have any unpleasantness. Andrews, I suggest you get into the wagon and see for yourself. I think Hunter is right."

Bull thought for a moment. "All right, Doctor. I ain't promising anything. If I say he goes with us, he *goes*."

Bull clambered awkwardly up into the wagon. He looked down. "Keep an eye on those two, Barnes," he ordered. He disappeared inside the wagon. Barnes nodded. He wasn't too happy about facing those two hard-case bastards. He knew all too well of their legendary reputation.

Bull was only in the wagon a few moments. "You're right," he reluctantly admitted. "I'll leave a few of my men in the wagon with him. I'll take Spade with me now. You'll deliver Valencia to Yuma, Buscombe. I'll have an ambulance ready to take him up to the Pen."

Dave and Ash watched Spade being taken from another wagon and placed on a led horse. "Keep the irons on that son of a bitch!" barked Bull. He heaved his bulk up into his saddle. Jack Spade looked past Bull at Dave and Ash, as though he was trying to communicate mentally with them.

"You'll need the key to open those irons, Bull," said Ash. He kneed Dearly Beloved close to Bull's horse and handed him the key. Bull nodded shortly as he took the key. "If anything happens to him between here and Yuma, and anywhere else for that matter," warned Ash, "we'll come looking for you, Bull."

Bull shrugged. "I'm fearful of that," he growled.

"You'd better be," said Ash.

Their eyes met. It was Bull who looked away first. He spurred his horse away.

"Don't forget our bounty money, Bull!" Dave called out.

Bull did not look back. He merely waved a hand.

Buscombe looked over from the wagon seat. "You'll be lucky if you get a small percentage of your money from him."

Dave shrugged. "We'll get it all right. I see you know him pretty well."

Buscombe nodded. "He used to be a city marshal in El Paso until they ran him out of town. It wasn't the first, and it won't be the last place that'll do the same. Now about that gold cross. Have you changed your mind? Will you part with it?"

Dave shook his head. "You know whose property it is. We'll keep it in trust."

Buscombe smiled a little. "Well, I hope so."

Ash looked sideways at him. Their eyes met, as Bull and Ash's had before. This time it was Buscombe who looked away.

Madeleine rode up. "There's a lot of dust on the road a mile or more behind us. Quite a few men riding."

"If it's Steel Hand, they'll be after Valencia," said Dave. "Ash and I will ride with you into Yuma. Bull will be waiting for you to deliver Valencia. There's nothing we can do about that. Get these wagons moving!"

Ash and Dave let the wagons pass on, and then they waited, watching that ominous cloud of dust slowly rising into the hot air.

Ash hooked a leg around his saddle horn and shaped a

cigarette. He handed it to Dave and then shaped another for himself. He lighted both cigarettes. "We're being watched, Davie."

Dave nodded. "It'll be Steel Hand all right."

Ash grinned. "He's probably got a mortal respect for you and Old Satan."

"I think he remembers the hole you shot through his hat and the slug that passed right where his mechanical claw had been a second or so before that."

Ash looked back toward Yuma and the dust rising behind Buscombe's wagons. "You think by any chance Buscombe just *might* be mixed up with Steel Hand?"

"It's always a thought, partner."

"If he is, there's not much we can do about it."

Dave nodded. "It's getting to be quite a mess, eh?"

Ash grinned. "Well, I've always thought the only person I could ever trust was you. Lately I'm beginning to have my doubts."

"Me, too," agreed Dave. "About you, I mean."

"Salt, pepper, and gravel in the grease," opined Ash solemnly.

They grinned at each other, turned, and rode on toward Yuma. Now and again they looked back along the road. The dust had drifted off and no more had risen, but a dark mass of something could just be discerned on the road—no doubt Steel Hand and his *corrida*.

Buscombe's wagons had been halted within the outskirts of Yuma near a large adobe structure with a huge corral. A rather dilapidated U.S. Army, Rucker-type ambulance stood next to the wagon in which Valencia had been kept. The side canvas curtain was somewhat crudely lettered ARIZONA TERRITORAIL PRISON, YUMA. Dave noted the incorrect spelling of "territorial." The painting seemed fairly fresh. Bull rode off beside the departing ambulance. The medicine show wagons were moved in behind the large adobe.

Callie was standing beside the wagon she had been driving. She looked up as Dave and Ash approached. "Your prisoner is gone," she reported.

Dave nodded. "Is this where you'll be staying while your show is being put on?"

She nodded. "First performance tomorrow evening."

"You'll be needing your horse?"

She shook her head. "Take him with you. Where will you be?"

"Ash and I have quarters on the old *Topolobampo*, a stern-wheeler moored along the riverbank. She's temporarily laid up for repairs. Owned by Captain Jock Fletcher, skipper of the *Hassayampa*. Good friend of ours." He smiled. "Trying to talk us into forming a steamboat company with him. There's a corral and an old adobe up the bank from where the steamer is moored. We keep our horses there."

She smiled. "*Bueno!* I'll come and see you when I pick up the horse."

"I can always deliver him," suggested Dave.

She shook her head firmly. "No. I insist."

Dave shrugged. He tipped his hat. Ash and he rode on into town.

Ash looked sideways. "She's got a soft spot in her head for you."

"You think so?"

Ash nodded. "I rarely, if ever, miss."

"Except with your women."

"Right! But now we're talking about one of *your* women."

"She's not my woman."

"She will be. That's why she wants to come and get her horse. You're not too bright on these matters, Davie."

"But *you* are."

Ash inspected the fingernails on his right hand. "Oh, I don't know," he murmured with fine modesty.

"I'll buy you a drink at the Barrel House."

Ash smiled widely. "I was hoping you'd say that."

They rode on into Yuma.

CHAPTER 10

THE BRAWLING, SILTY, YELLOW GRAY COLORADO RIVER rushed below the bluffs on the south bank upon which Yuma sat. The Colorado flowed from the north until, within a few miles of Yuma, it turned abruptly west and then flowed about five more miles until it turned rather sharply again on a course to the south and continued about 150 miles to Mouth of the River in the Gulf of California. Across the river from Yuma on the California side was Fort Yuma. A new swing bridge crossing the river had recently been built by the Southern Pacific Railway so that the railway could continue east to Tucson and beyond.

Yuma was a windy place swept by cold blasts in the winter and furnace gusts in summer from the deserts that surrounded the town. The deserts were a vast infinity; a grim, foreboding expanse of sand, a wasteland in every direction including toward California across the river. June through September the "Big Heat" came to Yuma, when temperatures rose to 120 degrees in the summer shade. Local legend said it was difficult to determine the true heat because the mercury dried up in the thermometers. *Everything* dried up in Yuma. The carcasses of cattle were said to rattle around inside their hides. Horned frogs died of apoplexy. Mules were so dry they couldn't bray. A soldier at Fort Yuma was said to have died and returned from hell to the fort to get his blankets reissued.

Yuma was a busy river port. Oceangoing steamers and sailing craft brought their cargoes to the river mouth and transshipped them to stern-wheelers that brought them up to Yuma. Cargoes were taken further upriver to places like Fort Mohave—a ten-day trip.

The Barrel House was packed with travelers, soldiers, miners, freighters, mule skinners, and railroad workers. Then there were the human buzzards who preyed on the unwary—the hustlers and chiselers, thimble-riggers, bunco-steerers, cold-deckers, and "macs" who were pimps living grandly on the money turned over to them by their whores.

Tobacco smoke hung thickly in rifted layers in the hot air of the busy establishment. The nickelodeon banged away in tinny discord at "Mother Kiss Me In My Dreams." Ash Mawson sat next to the instrument "bucking the tiger" at a faro table. He fed one nickel after another into the brass slot to keep "Mother Kiss Me In My Dreams" playing. Ash, despite his hard-case exterior, had a deep sentimental streak within. He had lost his Sac Indian mother when he was still in short pants. As long as Ash was in the Barrel House playing the nickelodeon no one but a hopeless drunk or a damned fool would complain about the seemingly never-ending repetition of "Mother etc."

Dave stood at the long bar comforting himself with one of his "town" drinks. It was a Stone Fence, a lethal concoction of a shot of rye and a twist of lemon in a tall glass of hard cider. On the way to meet Ash in the Barrel House he had stopped at the *Topolobampo* to corral Callie's roan and Ash's Dearly Beloved. He had left his Sharps, and field glasses, and Ash's Winchester locked in the cabin he used as quarters when he was in town. Now he was trying to get Ash to quit the faro table and come back to the steamer for a bath and some much-needed rest. Ash seemed set for the night. Just above his dusty sombrero, banded with part of the skin of a deadly five-foot Mojave Green rattlesnake whose acquisition was part of their search for Maximilian's gold, was a boldly lettered sign hanging on the wall. "Don't forget to write Mother," it read. "She is thinking of you. We furnish paper and envelopes free and have the best whiskey in town."

Ash was winning. Half of his stake had come from Dave.

Dave had figured on buying a good dun horse with his share of the winnings.

Dave walked over to the faro table. "I'm going back to the *Topolobampo*, Ash. Going to bathe." He wrinkled his nose a little. "Something you should consider as well."

Ash looked up. "I think it's my lucky charm," he said.

The faro dealer winced.

Ash eyed him. "Something bothering you, friend?"

The dealer widened his eyes. "Who? *Me?* Hell no!"

Dave grinned. "Maybe you're right, Ash. I know I'd not be able to deal with you at this table anyway." He turned on a heel and walked away. He looked back. Ash's green eyes were hard on him. He hurried to the door and left.

Dave stopped at the top of the wooden steps built into the bank above the *Topolobampo*. George Welch, the caretaker of the steamer, had been testing the repaired boilers. Dave saw the flash of fire as a fire door was opened. Wooden billets were hurled into the fire, and then the door was slammed shut. Dave descended the steps and crossed to the steamer.

"That you, Dave?" George cried out.

Dave nodded. "Yep, George." He crossed the creaking gangplank to the scarred and battered main deck.

George lowered the double-barreled shotgun he held. "A woman came here not long after you left earlier. She said some men were looking for you in Yuma. She was damned serious about it." He shook the shotgun. "I figured I'd be ready for them if they came here."

"Thanks. Who was the woman?"

George hunched his shoulders. "She didn't say. Nice lookin' filly. Light complexioned. Yellowish hair with a red tint to it."

"And her eyes? Large, perhaps like twin emeralds in a field of ivory?"

George studied him curiously for a moment. "Sure as hell. You sound like a poet, Dave. But they reminded me more of the eyes of a hunting mountain lioness."

"Her name is Callie Sutherland. That roan mare up on the hill is hers. Why didn't she take it with her?"

"Maybe she was afraid to get into the corral with that ornery son of a bitch Dearly Beloved. I told her you were coming back for a bath. She said that was a good reason for her to come back later."

"To see me or take a bath?"

George grinned. "Both, I expect."

"When is Jock due back?"

"Sometime tomorrow, probably along about evening."

Dave climbed the stairs to the boiler deck and entered the long passenger cabin. He walked through the saloon to the Argand lamp in the center of it. He lighted a lucifer, drew down the lamp and lighted it, then raised it again. The pale yellowish light revealed the long saloon with the rows of passenger cabins on each side. A big tin bathtub had been installed in the center of the saloon as long as the steamer was not in service. The tub could be filled by means of a rubber hose that went through a skylight and into a large tank on the hurricane deck. The water in the tank was warmed by the daily sun. The tub could be emptied by means of a pipe that went through a hole in the deck. The pipe was fastened up under the deck and led over the side of the vessel. Dave opened the brass valve from the tank overhead and filled the bathtub. The water had a rusty tint to it and was somewhat silty, but it was clean.

Dave stripped to the buff and got a flask of Baconora from his cabin. He lowered his long, lean frame into the warm water and took a long pull from the flask. *"Ahhhh . . ."* he murmured.

He bathed leisurely and then dried himself with a large huck towel. He tied it about his middle and peered into a cracked, greenish-hued mirror on the saloon wall, looking at his saddle-hued angular features and prominent nose. A real hawk-face, as the Chiricahua Apache army scouts with whom he had once served had dubbed him.

"Admiring yourself?" the feminine voice asked from behind him.

Dave whirled and instinctively drew back his right arm to hurl the Baconora bottle. Then he slowly lowered his arm.

As he did so the huck towel came loose and dropped about his feet. Dave stood there in all his lean-scarred nakedness while staring into the great emerald green eyes of Callie Sutherland. She stood just within the forward cabin door holding a small carpetbag in her left hand. She stared back, deliberately eyed him from head to foot and then back again, before bursting into tinkling laughter.

Dave put down the bottle, snatched up the towel, and draped it about his middle, twisting the ends together to hold it in place. "I could have brained you with that God damned bottle!" he roared. "Don't you ever, *ever* come up silently behind a man like that, at least in this damned territory! If you had been an enemy you might have been dead by now!"

She turned her head and coolly eyed him. "If I *had* been an enemy, mister, *you* would have been dead before you turned around, for I would not have said anything to warn you, you damned fool! There you were, standing draped only in a towel, out of reach of your guns, admiring yourself in a mirror in a room with an open door."

She was right. Dave realized his anger was addressed more to himself for his carelessness than it was to her.

She smiled that disarming smile of hers. "By the way," she added, almost as an afterthought, "I've come for my bath. Did your friend George tell you about it?"

Dave nodded. "He did."

"So, I'm here."

"And that settles it," he said dryly.

"You don't have any objections?"

He might as well play her game. "None," he replied.

She smiled again. "I'll be damned if I'll take a whore's bath standing one leg at a time in a washbasin. Is that whiskey all for you?"

Dave shook his head. "It's Baconora brandy," he warned.

She came toward him. He handed her the bottle. He caught her scent of perfume, perspiration, and the subtle woman smell. He realized how long it had been since he had been with a woman. It had certainly not been with a woman like Callie Sutherland.

She sipped at the bottle. She suddenly lowered it. A panicky look came over her face. "Jesus!" she gasped.

He nodded. "Wait until it hits bottom," he suggested. He grinned.

She blinked hard, trying to keep her composure. She handed him the bottle, patted his cheek, then stood on her tiptoes and brushed his dry cracked lips with hers. She turned on a heel and flounced back to her carpetbag.

Son of a bitch, thought Dave. "Do you want me to leave?" he asked—rather foolishly, he realized.

She shook her head. "I'll need you to scrub my back, Davie boy."

"I'll drain and refill the tub."

Callie closed and locked the door. She turned down the Argand lamp a bit. She sat down on a chair and unlaced her shoes, then kicked them off. She hiked her dress up over her knees, then took off her garters and peeled off her hose. She stood up, and raised her arms up over her head. "Unbutton me," she requested.

Still unbelieving, he crossed the room to her and undid the little buttons from neckline to waist. He stepped back a little.

She turned her head and looked at him. "Well?" she demanded. "Pull the damned thing off!"

He gripped the material of the dress just above her rounded hips and pulled it up over her firm, full breasts and then over her head and arms. She tossed it in a heap on the floor. She turned dressed only in a thin chemise that reached to her knees and was low-cut between her breasts. Dave slid the straps off her smooth, creamy shoulders and pulled the chemise down about her slim ankles. Then he undid her brassiere. He tentatively fondled her before trying to draw her toward his cabin. The woman hunger was strong and hot within him.

She kissed him. "Wait," she said as she withdrew.

He watched her as she stepped into the tub and felt about for the soap. She sat down and smiled at him. "Surprised you, didn't I?" she asked.

Dave nodded as he reached for the bottle and uncorked it.

"Don't drink too much," she warned as she began to lather herself.

"I'll be all right," he promised. "I'd be a damned fool to drink too much." He nodded. "Yes, you did surprise me. I thought when first I met you, well, that is after talking with the good Colonel/Doctor . . . ."

She shrugged. "That Madeleine and I were members of the Lost Sisterhood?"

"Well, not exactly," Dave admitted. "If you had been, I must admit I had never seen whores anywhere who looked as you and Madeleine do."

"You were right. We're not whores. At least, not myself. Madeleine, well, she did come from New Orleans and before that time from Haiti when she was hardly more than a child. She was auctioned off in Natchez just before the war. Her owner lost her gambling with the doctor." Her voice died. She looked away.

Dave took a guess. "One of the men killed by him?"

She looked away and nodded. "She's been with him more or less ever since."

"A mistress?"

"Yes, and a partner as well, as much as he'd ever allow *anyone* to be his partner."

"Even you?"

She nodded again. "Even me."

"And, what's your status with him?"

Callie shrugged. "If it's bothering you, forget it. He's my uncle, as I told you before. He dearly loved my mother, his only sister. When my parents died within a year of each other I was just in my teens. He sent money to support me and have me taken care of. Some time after the war I left my home in Kentucky and later joined him in his business."

He drank again. "You said Madeleine was from Haiti and later New Orleans and that she had been auctioned off in Natchez. Perhaps she was a creole?"

She turned her head and looked directly at him. "She is a *quadroon*," she said.

The words of the old Southern ballad came back to him—
"My pretty quadroon. My flower that faded too soon . . ."
He recalled now the features of Madeleine: the slightly aquiline nose flared at the nostrils; the creamy, coffee-colored
skin; the full mouth and thick lips.

"So, you see, it wasn't Madeleine who came here this
evening to get a bath and her horse, but also to see you, David
Hunter. And I am not a whore, nor a fallen woman." She
smiled. "Nor am I a *virgin!*" She laughed delightedly. She
looked slyly sideways at him. "But I *was* married. Twice, in
fact. Are you interested?" she asked.

Dave shrugged.

"Fascinating, your intense curiosity," she observed.

"I'm noted for that," he responded quietly.

"My first husband married me when I was just fifteen."
She prattled. "I did it to get out of the orphanage. We parted
when I was sixteen. I heard later he was killed at Chicka-
mauga. He was a nice boy but knew *nothing* of women. Now
come wash my back. My second husband was a riverboat
gambler. Very dashing. A great lover, or so *he* thought. We
weren't together long when he was killed in a duel on a
sandspit in the Mississippi River."

Dave picked the soap out of the water and lathered her
smooth back. Then suddenly he thought of what she had
just said—"Killed in a duel on a sandspit in the Mississippi River . . ." Madeleine's owner had lost her in a
gambling debt to Colonel/Dr. Buscombe and later had
been killed in a duel by him. The legend stated that Buscombe had killed three men at least—one in a bare-knuckle
fight in a saloon, one with a derringer, *one in a knife duel
on a Mississippi River sandspit. . . .*

"By the good doctor?" Dave asked.

She turned her head and looked at him intently. "How did
you know that?" she asked quietly.

He shrugged and smiled. "Guessing, Callie. I've heard
the legends, true or not, about him."

She turned away. "They're true enough," she said softly.

"Is he the man, or is it his men who are supposedly looking for me?" he asked quietly.

She did not turn this time. "No, David."

"You're sure?"

She nodded.

"Then who?"

"Major Cole Ransom. Steel Hand. He and his men arrived in town after dark."

"They'll be after Valencia, not me."

She shook her head. "One of our men talked with one of his. His man asked about you. He wanted to know where you had gone. We assumed he was asking about you because of Steel Hand."

Dave washed the soap from her back. "Did you see the man who asked about me?"

"Only at a distance. It was getting dark."

"How was he dressed?"

She shrugged. "Long black coat, seemingly inappropriate for this place, and particularly so because of the heat."

"His hat? Flat-brimmed? Rounded top?"

She nodded.

"A 'muley' hat?"

"I don't know. Is that what they are called?"

"Yes. Stand up."

Dave got a bucket from the galley. He filled it with water from the deck-tank hose and poured it over her glistening body. He dried her as she stood there. She stepped out of the tub, and he dried down her long, smooth legs.

She drew down his head and kissed him. She looked up into his eyes. "Thanks. Do you know who that man was?"

Dave nodded. "Name of Dancy. He was probably working on his own. He's got a score to settle with me, or *thinks* he has."

"Maybe he was asking about you for Steel Hand."

"I doubt it. Certainly Steel Hand also has a score to settle with me, but he's too smart to fool around chasing after me. As I said: He's after Valencia."

"I'll have to be getting back soon," she warned.

Dave entered his cabin and pulled a blanket from his bunk. He brought it out in the saloon. "Too damned hot in there," he explained. He spread the blanket on the dusty carpeting. She lay down on the blanket and looked up at him expectantly.

He got his Sharps rifle and leaned it against the wall. She watched him curiously as he opened the loading gate of his Colt and turned the cylinder to push a fresh .44/40 cartridge into the empty chamber upon which he usually let the firing pin of the hammer rest. He placed a chair close to the blanket and laid his Colt and cartridge belt on it.

"Do you always do that before making love to a lady?" she asked.

Dave nodded. "A form of life insurance."

He locked the doors at each end of the cabin and then lowered the lamplight. She held her arms up to him. He laid down beside her and drew her close. Her arms went around his neck. Her soft, warm lips pressed his dry, cracked lips. They came together like two virgin kids experimenting for the first time. "My God," she murmured. "How long has it been for you?"

"Too long. But nothing was ever like this before." He was not exaggerating. "How long has it been for you?"

"Too damned long."

They lay lazily for a time, both well spent. Dave got up and fashioned two Lobo Negro cigarettes. He lighted them both and placed one of them between her lips. He picked up a chair and twirled it about so that the back was toward Callie. He straddled the seat and crossed his arms on the top of the back and rested his chin on them.

She sat up, got up on her knees, and then sat back on her legs, placing her hands flat behind her on the blanket. The action forced her breasts outward. The perspiration on them glistened from the lamplight. She tilted her head forward and studied him from under her brows. "I'll have to leave soon," she warned.

"Is that a threat?" he asked.

She shook her head. "You want something. What is it?"

He nodded. "Why did you really come here?"

"You don't believe I really only came here for a bath, my roan, and the possibility of a little lovemaking with you?"

"Oh, I believe that all right. But did you come here on your own? Did the good Colonel/Doctor Buscombe send you? Maybe he wants to make sure we will still have a deal with him? That's it, isn't it?"

She nodded. "I agree to that, Dave. Frankly, the Colonel is in a worse situation on this matter than anyone knows."

"Except you."

She raised her head a little. "He didn't want to send me. He's always been against me having to do things like this for his benefit."

"But you came anyway," he said dryly. "If that is why you came, you've wasted your time."

"Did you think that was so while we were making love? Truthfully, Dave!"

"The thought simply occurred to me when we were done." He smiled a little. "I have that kind of mind."

"Suspicious?"

"No. I have an *enquiring* mind. I'd *like* to think you came here simply to make love with me, but there's always that little doubt. Perhaps it's because of your relationship with Buscombe."

She sat erect and folded her hands in her lap. "Then it's time to be direct. Tell me! Are you and Ash Mawson working on your own? You are not employed by the territorial government or perhaps even Yuma County?"

Dave shook his head. "We work freelance from job to job."

"Until you can grubstake yourselves for another wild goose chase out into nowhere looking for a fairy-tale lost mine or buried treasure," she said cynically.

"By the way, although you mentioned our possibly being employed by the territorial government or Yuma County, for some reason you did not mention the fact that we just *might* be hired by other agencies who are interested in the Jesuit treasure—the Federal Government of Mexico and the local government of the State of Sonora.'' He eyed her steadily. ''And, of course,'' he added deliberately, ''the United States Government itself . . .''

''Well, I doubt if you would work for the Mexicans,'' she said.

''Possibly, but what about the United States?''

''I just didn't think you would be,'' she lied.

''That's neat,'' Dave said. ''That's *real* neat. Why don't you admit the truth, Callie? It's my thought that Buscombe could very well be working as an agent for either of the two Mexican governments, but I don't quite buy that. I wouldn't put it past him, you understand, and there's really nothing wrong with it. But, deep within myself, I'm damned well inclined to think that the good Colonel/Doctor might just possibly be working for the U.S. and that, in addition, you and perhaps the lovely Madeleine are working with him.''

She got off the blanket and began to dress herself.

Dave stood up. ''Then it *is* true? The Abyssinian Desert Companion and Buscombe's lovely ladies are merely a front, and a very good one, I might add. And all for a half-mad, possibly defrocked Jesuit priest and his dream of a vast treasure of Jesuit gold and silver hidden somewhere in one of the deadliest desert areas of the southwest.''

She did not answer. She sat down on a chair and drew on her shoes.

Dave turned away from her. He began to dress. He drew on his drawers and pulled his undershirt over his head. He heard the cocking of a weapon. He thrust his head up through the neck of the undershirt and stared into the muzzle of his own Colt. He looked into her eyes.

''You don't seem to scare easily,'' she suggested.

''It's an act. What's your purpose, or are you going to shoot without an explanation? If you do shoot and wound or kill me, how are you going to explain it?''

She smiled a little. ''If I *do* shoot, which is still debatable, I can always cry rape. You know how these frontier boobs are. The lady is *always* right.''

"What brought this on?" he asked as he reached for his trousers.

"Hold it right there!" she snapped.

He studied her, head tilted to one side. "You mean you'd shoot a man to death without him having on his trousers?"

She shrugged. "It will certainly make my cry of rape seem more effective." She grinned.

"You think of everything," he grunted sourly.

"Oh, well, put them on then. I can always yank them off again."

Dave moved like a hunting cat. He turned sideways and gripped the trousers by the bottom of the legs and then swung them full-armed toward her head. The thick leather belt and heavy U.S. buckle added weight to the slashing trousers. The belt struck her alongside the head, while the legs whipped around her face, temporarily obscuring her sight. Dave leaped forward in a crouch. She staggered sideways. The Colt cracked deafeningly while spitting out flame and thick white smoke. The bullet fanned across Dave's bent back and went right through the wall behind him. He gripped her right wrist and slammed it down against his knee. The smoking six-shooter fell from her grasp. He kicked it across the saloon and swung his right forearm across her chest and drove her backwards. Her legs struck the side of a chair, and she fell flat upon the blanket. He dropped atop her with his full weight and drove the breath out of her. It was all over in a matter of seconds.

She opened her eyes and stared into his, just a few inches away. "You son of a bitch," she husked. "I was only bluffing."

Dave grinned. "Don't ever bluff with a loaded and cocked pistol in your hand. If you aim it at a man then shoot the damned thing."

"Another of your little rules for survival?" she asked.

He nodded. "They have kept me alive." He rolled off of her and raised himself up to rest on his right elbow. She tried to get up, but he held her down with his left hand. "I'll let you leave soon. But first you've got some explaining to do. Is Buscombe working for the U.S. Government?''

She nodded. ''He meant to tell you anyway.''

''I'm *sure* he did,'' Dave said dryly. ''To try and find the San Dionysius treasure?''

''Of course.''

''Are you and Madeleine involved as U.S. agents?''

She nodded again. ''Temporarily.''

''The medicine show is just a front?''

She shook her head. ''It's his real business. It hasn't been too good for the past year or so. He wrote and asked both Madeleine and I to come west and join him. We had left him a year before that, when he was in Texas. He did not mention any deal he had made with the government at that time. His health had been failing when we were in Texas with him. It was much worse when we joined him at El Paso. You saw him.

''Then he told the two of us about his deal with the government, and we both agreed to rejoin his show and help him with it. Later we realized he might be a dying man. He had taken the deal with the government for a twenty-five percent share of the treasure if he found it.'' She paused. ''He was doing it for *us*, Dave. He *knows* he is going to die.''

''And that's another reason you came here tonight. To make sure Ash and I would help him, because without *us* his mission is hopeless.''

''He is a gambler. This is his last throw of the dice. Is helping him any different from some of the wild gambles you and Ash have undertaken hunting for lost treasures?''

Dave shrugged. ''Probably not. Do you and the good Colonel/Doctor know the odds against such a mission being successful?''

''I have an idea.''

''Then you're not very bright. If we fail in getting Valencia out of Yuma Pen, we'll likely be paid off in hot lead. However, it we succeed and *do* find the treasure, we'll be paid off in cold gold and silver.''

"You can't find one without the other. You'll have to risk the hot lead to find the cold gold and silver."

Dave stood up and reached for his trousers, being careful to stand between her and his Colt and Sharps. She was right. Damn her! Maybe it might be better to forget the whole deal and let Buscombe try to get Valencia out of Yuma Pen. Buscombe was dying anyway.

"Dave," Callie said softly.

He turned. She was standing now. The lamplight glistened on her great cat's eyes. Her scent came to him, compelling and almost irresistible. *Almost* . . .

"Dave, you'll need our help to spirit Valencia out of Yuma Pen. You'll need it, too, when and if do you get him out of there. You'll have Bull Andrews after you and Steel Hand as well. The prison officials will be after you and perhaps the soldiers from Fort Yuma. If you manage to get out of Yuma you'll have the Indian trackers on your trail."

"Damned if we do and damned if we don't," grunted Dave as he pulled on one of his boots.

She studied him. "You *will* try. Impossible as it sounds, *you will try*. If you are still interested in that lost Jesuit treasure you will try. That's really the story of your life, isn't it? You're the Buscadero, the Seeker, the man always looking for the will-o'-the-wisp of lost mines and buried treasure. I wonder if that is all you *really* want out of life?"

"I'll get your horse," he said. He picked up her small carpetbag and was surprised at the weight of it. He opened it and poked about in it under her narrowed eyes. He drew out a "stingy" gun, the little gun with the big bite—a .41-caliber, double-barreled, over-and-under derringer. He found a sheathed Mexican *cuchillo* with a thin curved blade, a real *"saca tripas"* or "gets the guts." Last of all he took out a small, corked glass tube that contained a colorless, crystalline substance. He uncorked it, sniffed the contents, wet a finger tip and touched it to the crystals, and then tasted it. He made a wry face. "Chloral hydrate," he murmured. It was a sedative and also first-class knockout drops. He looked at Callie. ''Were any or all of these for me in case I hadn't agreed with you?''

Callie gathered up her soiled undergarments and hose and threw them to Dave. ''Not really,'' she replied. ''You were stupid enough to let me get between you and your Colt.''

He stuffed the garments into the bag and shut it. He picked up his Colt and holstered it. He led the way from the saloon and down to the main deck. She followed him down the gangplank under the curious eyes of George Welch.

They climbed the stairs together. Dave brought the roan from the corral, keeping a wary eye on Dearly Beloved the while.

Callie hung the carpetbag from the saddle horn and mounted the roan. She looked down at him.

He studied her. ''Tell me something. Did you fire that Colt of mine, or was it accidental? It does have a light trigger.''

She smiled. She touched the roan with her heels. ''I'm not quite sure myself.''

He watched her. ''Will you be coming back to see me?'' he called.

She looked back over her shoulder. ''Whenever you want me to.''

Then she was gone into the shadows.

''Son of a bitch,'' breathed Dave. ''What a woman. . . .''

Somewhere close by a dog howled mournfully.

CHAPTER 11

DAVE PAUSED SHORT OF THE WELL-LIGHTED WINDOWS OF the Barrel House and stepped into the doorway of a shop that had been burned out. The moon was not yet fully illuminating Yuma. It was the day after Ash and he had returned to Yuma. Dave had bought himself a fine *bayo coyote* dun with his share of Ash's winnings of the night before. After the purchase he had stayed close to the *Topolobampo*. Ash had scoured the town with great care and caution that day and early evening looking for Steel Hand but with no success. Steel Hand, of course, probably did not know how Ash looked. On the other hand, Ash really didn't know how Dancy, Ben, Gordo, and Cipriano looked, but Dave had given him a detailed description of them. The danger here was that if they knew Ash was looking for Steel Hand and them, they would be on the alert and stay out of his way. It was a game of catch-as-catch-can. They might even ambush Ash. Dave and Ash had caught up on their much-needed rest off and on that long day. Ash had slept with his usual soundness. Dave's sleep had been restless, haunted by thoughts of how they could possibly spring Valencia from Yuma Pen. They had discussed the matter between long naps but had gained little from it. Then, too, Dave had vivid dreams of Callie that interfered mightily with the more businesslike dreams of regaining custody of Jesus Valencia.

Dave walked to the rear of the burned-out shop and stepped out into the shadowed alleyway. He kept his hand on his Colt as he walked to the rear entrance of the Barrel House. He wasn't too concerned about Steel Hand or any of his men trying to kill him; that is with one exception—*Dancy*. Steel Hand would be too shrewd to let a bit of personal vengeance stand in the way of getting his hands on Jesus Valencia. Dancy would likely forego any thoughts of Jesuit treasure to pay off the blood debt he thought Dave owed him. Dave knew the type. The future meant nothing to them; nor did the past, for that matter. *Today* was the important time. The time to enhance reputation by killing someone who had affronted their magnificent and mentally distorted egos. Furthermore, Dancy must know of Dave's almost legendary reputation in the southwest. To down Dave would add a great coup to Dancy's reputation.

Dave entered the Barrel House. The place was packed as usual. "Mother Kiss Me In My Dreams" was clanging away. Ash was seated at the faro table with a pile of nickels close to his right hand to keep on the marathon playing of the song. When Ash saw Dave he spoke to the faro dealer, who nodded and then closed the bank. The dealer headed for the men's room.

Ash sauntered over to the very end of the bar, where Dave stood with his back against the wall. He reached for the rye bottle and poured himself three fingers.

"Any luck?" asked Dave.

Ash shrugged. "No Steel Hand. I did see a big-bellied Mexican with a smashed-in *nariz*. He was evidently tailing a young fella wearing a black coat and a muley hat. That would be the one you called Gordo, and the young fella would be Dancy."

Dave nodded. "I'm sure of that. Dancy didn't seem to care much for Steel Hand's orders. He might have pulled out on him, and Gordo was sent to tail him."

Ash eyed Dave. "You think Dancy might be looking for a showdown with you?"

"He's loco enough. I'm sure Steel Hand doesn't want any attention drawn to himself or his *corrida*."

Ash downed his rye. He wiped his mouth and mustache

on the back of his hand. "We can always track down this Dancy. I saw the two of them not more than an a hour ago."

"Where did you see them?"

"Along the riverbank. Not too far from the *Topolobampo*, now that I recall." He smiled. "Naturally I wouldn't have let them board her."

"*Gracias,*" Dave said dryly.

Ash waved a hand. "*Por nada.* You buyin' again?"

Dave nodded. "Naturally."

"Where do we go now?"

"I'm going up to the Pen. I want to make sure Valencia and Spade were turned in there."

Ash eyed him closely. "You think maybe they weren't?"

Dave shrugged. "You remember seeing the ambulance that picked up Valencia?"

"The one with the misspelt word, 'territorial'?"

"That's it. You ever see one like it at Yuma Pen?"

"Not that I can recall."

"Neither can I."

Ash refilled his glass. "Let me get this coffin varnish down and collect my winnings, and I'll go with you."

Dave shook his head. "It'd be better if I went alone. When you're done here go over to where the medicine show is going to be held tonight, and keep your eyes open for Steel Hand and any of his bunch."

Ash shrugged. "If you say so. I'd rather be with you. You're going to be a target for someone tonight or I miss my guess."

"I'll be all right." Dave turned and began walking along the long bar toward the batwings.

"Hey, Dave!" called out Ash.

Dave turned. "Yes?"

"You forgot to pay for these drinks."

Dave nodded. "I know." He grinned and hurried toward the door.

Dave pushed his way through the batwings and turned to his left. He glanced across the wide street and thought he saw a shadowy movement in an alleyway between two buildings. He leaped forward with a sure instinct of impending danger. A gun flamed and cracked flatly from the alleyway. The slug bored through the saloon window six inches from Dave's right shoulder as he drew, cocked, and fired his Colt in one swift, fluid motion, aiming directly at the white powder smoke drifting out of the alleyway. He saw a dark-clad figure jump and heard a loud yelp of pain just as the weapon was fired again. Dave hit the ground full length, thrusting out his Colt and firing twice at the same time. The racketing sound of the gun reports died away. The smoke cleared. A dark figure ran down the alleyway and disappeared in the shadows. Dave got to his feet and stepped into a doorway to reload.

People had scattered away from the shooting. A woman screamed. A freight wagon ground to a dusty halt. The teamster leaped from his seat and crawled under the wagon. Dust borne on the hot desert wind drifted between Dave and the alleyway and obscured his view. He heard rapid staccato hoofbeats somewhere down the alleyway. Men poured out of the Barrel House, some with ready pistols and derringers in their hands. Ash moved swiftly toward Dave like a great lean wolf.

Ash glanced sideways at the neat hole bored through the windowpane. "Gawd damned slug went right over my head and punched a hole into the guts of the nickelodeon and put a stop to 'Mother Kiss Me In My Dreams,' " he grumbled. "Might'a ruined the nickelodeon, too."

Dave grinned. "Hopefully," he said dryly. "Get out of the light from the window. He was across the street in that alleyway between those two buildings."

Ash nodded. He licked his lips. "You want to go run him down?"

Dave shook his head. "He got out of there like a streak of lightning and eleven claps of thunder."

"You get a good look at him?"

Dave shook his head. "But I think I might have winged

him, unless he dropped his own gun on his foot. He did yelp like a kicked dog.''

Shootings were not uncommon in Yuma. The bystanders, not seeing any blood, went back about their business. The teamster crawled out from under his wagon and slapped the dust from his clothing with his hat. He grinned at Dave and Ash.

Dave eyed the teamster. ''Are you all right?'' he asked. ''Did you see who was shooting at me?''

''I damned near drove right in between you and whoever that was. Friend of yours?'' He grinned slyly. ''Anyway, about all I saw was a dark figure and some gun flashes. Come to think of it he could have been wearing a muley hat. You know—flat-topped, narrow brim sticking straight out. I think you might have hit him. I heard him yell somewhat. Damned good shooting, mister.'' He peered closer at Dave. ''By God! You're Dave Hunter, ain't you? No wonder you hit him.''

Dave waved a casual hand. ''Nothing to it, friend.''

The teamster looked at Ash. ''Listen to *him*! Getting shot at. Drawing fast and getting off a shot that hit a man standing in the shadows clear acrost this wide street.''

Ash shrugged. ''He's like that. You know. Modest as hell.''

They watched the teamster drive on.

''What now?'' asked Ash.

''Were you winning?''

Ash nodded.

''Go on back then. I'll be all right.''

''That's what you said before.''

''Don't forget to go to the medicine show later on.''

Ash walked back into the saloon. Dave turned to go on.

''I heard there was a shooting scrape going on around here,'' said Bull Andrews. He was blocking Dave's way.

Dave looked sideways. There was a man standing in a doorway watching them. Just beyond Bull another man stood half in and half out of a doorway.

''They're with me, Hunter,'' said Bull. ''Who shot at you?''

Dave shrugged. "Might have been one of your boys, Bull."

Bull chuckled. "Not likely. I do my own fighting. What did you see?"

"A shadow and some gun flashes. He got away on foot."

"Any description at all?"

Dave could have told him about the muley hat. It had been the teamster who had seen it, not Dave. "Nothing," he replied.

"Might have been an old, or maybe a *new*, enemy. You've probably got a lot of them."

Dave nodded. "About as many as ever, possibly quite a few less, at that."

Bull studied him. "Well, I've got nothing to hold you on. You can go about your business."

"Did you deliver those prisoners to the Pen?"

Bull nodded shortly.

"Then you owe Ash and me a thousand dollars."

"The superintendent is still out of town. You'll have to wait until he returns. Tough, but that's the way it goes." He smiled as though that had settled the matter. "By the way, what made you and Mawson so interested in Valencia anyway?"

"Five hundred dollars, Bull. Where is it?"

Bull acted as though he had not heard Dave. He sucked at a tooth and cocked an eye upward. "It ain't like you two hombres to agree to go chasing out to the Camino del Diablo after anyone for that lousy kind of money." He grinned. "El Buscadero, ain't that what your admirers call you? Always looking for lost mines and buried treasure."

"You owe us a thousand dollars," repeated Dave.

Bull raised his shaggy eyebrows. "Oh my! You must be in a hurry! Maybe you've got another appointment with that Callie woman."

"You've got a big nose, Bull."

Bull nodded. "Part of my business is to keep an eye on suspicious characters. Observation, they calls it. Now let's get back to your obvious interest in Jesus Valencia. Damned odd how they managed to escape from Yuma Pen. Someone made it easy for them. Maybe figuring there was a helluva profit could be made out of Valencia. I know they headed for the border at Quitabaquito Springs, and that Spade lost track of Valencia. Then, like a miracle, who suddenly finds the missing Jesus?'' He grinned and stepped back and raised his hamlike hands with spread fingers. His eyes opened wide in simulated surprise. ''Why, none other than Dave Hunter and his intrepid, big-nosed partner Ash Mawson! Two of the best treasure hunters in the Southwest wasting their time for a measly five hundred eagles apiece for them! Now you got to admit there's something downright interesting and damned suspicious about that.''

Dave smiled thinly. ''Well, Bull, as you said: You're an observer. Keep on observing, and maybe you'll learn something.''

Bull dropped his hands, stepped closer, and thrust his head forward while fixing Dave with his little, hard, almost colorless eyes—like marbles shaped from flint. ''You want I should find out right here?'' He balled his big fists and thrust them upward toward Dave's hawklike nose. ''You got a lovely beak for bustin', Mr. Hunter.''

Dave didn't move; he didn't even blink. His icy blue eyes held those of Bull.

Bull was a tough customer. He had seen the elephant, so to speak. He had a saying: He'd not be afraid of Satan himself should he come walking along the *camino* looking for one Bull Andrews. This was something different. Bull had hoped Dave Hunter would have made a play for his Colt or tried to strike back. It is the unknown that unnerves a bully like Bull. He slowly lowered his hands and eased his right hand inside his coat where he carried a hideout gun in a skeleton shoulder holster. Its entire side was open for a ripping, sideways fast draw.

Dave planned fast. If he clamped his left hand on Bull's wrist, he could land a piledriver right upward into the lower part of Bull's big belly. *If* Dave was fast enough to forestall the draw.

"You draw that hideout gun, Bull," warned Ash out of the dark doorway just to the right of Bull and slightly behind him, "and you'll be dead before you clear leather."

Bull's hand froze in position. A bead of cold sweat trickled down from under the sweatband of his hat, ran down his big nose, and hung at the end of it, shining with reflected lamplight from the saloon.

"How do you want it, Bull?" persisted Ash. "A bowie thrust up under your shoulder blade? Or maybe a chop across the kidneys? How about a slash across the side of your neck where the carotid artery hides under the fat?"

Bull stood stock-still. He well knew the notorious reputation of the green-eyed killer who stood behind him. "I've got two men with me," he warned.

Dave could almost see Ash's crooked grin as he replied, "You'll be dead before they get here. Besides, I don't think they'll try anything once they see you kicking and gurgling on the boardwalk."

"You're interfering with a law officer in the performance of his duty," blustered Bull.

Dave looked beyond Bull. Neither one of his deputies was now in sight. Evidently Bull wasn't popular enough with them for them to risk facing Ash and Dave. "Your boys have skedaddled, Bull. Now take your right hand slowly out from under your coat and bring out your wallet."

"By God, Hunter, if it wasn't for your partner standing behind me, you wouldn't have the guts to face me down!" snapped Bull.

Dave smiled faintly. "Ash," he murmured. "You take off. Bull wants to see if I can face him down without you standing behind him with that razor-sharp Arkansas toothpick of yours."

"A pleasure," responded Ash.

Christ, but Bull hated backing down from Hunter; but he knew of Hunter's well-earned reputation with gun, fist, and boot. "All right! All right!" he snarled hastily. "You win! *Now* . . ." He took out his wallet, slowly and gingerly. He held it out toward Dave.

Dave shook his head. "*You* take out the money. One thousand dollars."

Bull shrugged. "I haven't got that much. I'll give you what I've got. You can collect the rest from the superintendent when he gets back." He took out the bills from his wallet and counted out loud, "One hundred, two hundred, three hundred, four hundred . . . That's it. I don't carry all that money with me." He thrust the money savagely toward Dave. "You'll not hear the last of this!" he roared.

Dave shrugged. "So? What happened? You took the prisoners away from us. You said in front of witnesses that you'd collect the money for us."

"I'll have you up on charges!" threatened Bull.

"*What* charges?" asked Dave in mock surprise.

"You threatened me! Your partner held a knife on me!" barked Bull.

Dave looked surprised. "I never said a word," he denied.

"You see a knife in my hand?" asked Ash. "Anyone outside of you hear me say anything threatening? Your two witnesses are gone, and besides, they were too far away to hear anything or see a knife. It's your word against ours, Bull my boy. From the reputation you've got all over Arizona Territory no one, not even the judge, would believe you."

They had Bull by the crotch.

Dave peeled off Ash's share of the bills and handed them to him. "Can I buy you a drink, Mr. Mawson," he politely asked.

"In a moment, Mr. Hunter," Ash genially responded. He moved swiftly, plucked Bull's Colt from its holster, then reached inside his coat and pulled the hideout pistol from its skeleton holster. He emptied the cartridges from both guns and threw the cartridges out into the middle of the wide street. Earlier a four-horse wagon team had been standing next to the boardwalk for quite some time. The animals had all defecated and urinated copiously on the street. Mud had formed in the ruts. Ash dropped both weapons into the reeking mud. He stepped on them to sink them deeper. He looked at Dave. "I'll have that drink now, Mr. Hunter," he said.

They sauntered into the Barrel House.

Bull cursed crashing thunder and blue-streak lightning as he pawed his guns out of the ammonia-stinking mud. He hastily wiped them as clean as he could under the circumstances and then crammed fresh cartridges into the chambers. He started for the batwings with short, stiff-legged plunging steps, breathing hard the while, with a cocked pistol in either hand. His face was darkly blood-congested and distorted from his choler. Then suddenly he drew up short.

Seb Barnes came up fast from behind Bull. "For Christ's sake, Bull! You go chargin' in there with drawn guns against those two killers and you'll be dead before you hit the sawdust! Besides, you'll spoil our plan, dammit!"

"Go to hell!" roared Bull. Then slow reason prevailed. He sheathed his guns. "I need a drink."

Seb nodded. "You can always get them later. *One* at a time."

"Where the hell did that bastard Mawson come from anyway? One minute me and Hunter were alone on the street, and the next minute Mawson was right behind me with that damned bowie knife of his in his hands all ready to gut me."

"He must have come out the back door of the Barrel House, then to the street from the alleyway. But I didn't see any bowie knife in his hands."

"He threatened me with it!"

Barnes shook his head. "He was bluffing."

"No one bluffs *me*! I'm *Bull* Andrews!" roared Bull.

You sure as hell are, thought Seb. "Let's get that drink. Remember, once the medicine show starts we've got to get out of town. *Pronto!*"

Just before they reached the saloon a block down the street, Bull halted. "What bothers me is how the hell Mawson knew Hunter was in trouble with me. Last thing I knew he was still in the Barrel House when I stopped Hunter in the street."

"Maybe he saw you through the window?"

Bull shook his head. "We were out of view."

"Coincidence?"

"For Christ's sake, Seb! Suddenly, for no reason at all as

far as I could tell, he's right behind me as neat as you please just when I was aimin' to bust that big nose of Hunter's into a pulp."

"Well, it was the Mexicans who likened Dave Hunter to *leon fantasma*, the phantom mountain lion, and Mawson to a lobo wolf. I tell you, Bull, some folks think they ain't even human, like maybe ghosts, you know. Maybe Mawson had a feeling something was wrong with Hunter and came a-runnin' just in time."

Bull felt a sudden chill through his big body. He, too, had heard the eerie stories about those two sons of bitches. He knew of Hunter's legendary skill with his Sharps Old Reliable and Mawson's ability with his deadly bowie knife. Implausible, sure, but all myths and legends seem to have a basis in truth somewhere no matter how unlikely. Bull suddenly looked back over his shoulder. Two tall men, mere shadows, stood at the mouth of the alleyway where he had last seen Hunter and Mawson. He turned back and then suddenly looked in their direction again. There was no one there. There had been no time for them to vanish from his sight. *Jesus,* he thought nervously. Maybe they *are* phantoms, and killers to boot.

Cipriano watched from a doorway as Bull and Seb moved toward the saloon. He had been behind the Barrel House when Ash had come quickly out the back door and hurried through the alleyway to the street. Cipriano had followed him and stood well back in the shadows but not so far away that he could not hear the conversation between the three men. He vanished down the alleyway.

Dave leaned against the bar as Ash drank. He didn't drink himself. "I've been wondering if the prison superintendent is really out of town, Ash," he said.

"Well, if Bull is lying, he's a lot stupider than I ever gave him credit for. He'd know all we have to do is go up to the Pen and find out."

Dave nodded. "That's what makes me believe him."

"So what's the problem? We can find out when the super

is coming back and then go up and ask him about the rest of the reward money.''

''There's one catch—supposing the super was in the deal to spring Valencia and Spade from prison?''

Ash shrugged. ''Well, what do we have to lose? Maybe he'll pay us off to keep our mouths shut.''

Dave studied him thoughtfully. ''You're awfully stupid at times, and sometimes you have flashes of absolute brilliance. We both know Valencia is the key to the lost Dionysius treasure. That's why they, whoever *they* are, had them sprung. Steel Hand knows that, too. Buscombe and his 'lady' aides know it as well. Maybe Bull was in on the deal as well. Maybe not, but I suspect he's damned suspicious. But if he is and knows, why would he have taken Valencia back to the Pen? It's a possibility that he had been wondering about that escape. He was probably waiting for us to show up with Valencia for that reason. Are you following me?''

Ash studied him. He rolled his eyes upward. ''Of course, now that you've so clearly worked the whole thing out for me. My God! However, please go on.''

Dave nodded. ''I'm glad you're right with me. Now another interesting aspect is the great coincidence of Colonel/ Dr. Buscombe showing up right on time to pick us up on the Yuma Road. Then being met by Bull on that same damned road. Now did he or did he not turn in Valencia and Spade?''

''Wasn't that the reason you were going up to the Pen earlier, before Cousin Bull stopped you?''

Dave smiled. ''Exactly!''

''And if he hasn't turned them in?''

''He may have hidden them somewhere here in town while waiting for his chance to get them out of here and head for the Camino del Diablo. They would go either directly to Tinajas Altas and then to The Walking Sands, or he could take them the same way they went on their own—to Quitabaquito Springs. He'd have to go one way or the other. If he does have Valencia hidden and intends to move him, we've got to know beforehand which way it is to be. If we pick the wrong way, we can end up miles and miles away from them without a hope of ever catching up. Now I'm off to Yuma Pen. If Valencia is really there, then my theory is shot to hell. If he is not, then we've got to find *where* he is. Simple, eh?''

"For Christ's sake be careful! You're liable to end up in the Snake Den yourself if the superintendent was in on the deal. I'd never be able to get you out of *that* mess."

Ash watched Dave walk to the rear door of the saloon. He shrugged, eyed his empty rye glass for a moment, then shrugged again. "What the hell," he murmured. He filled the glass and downed the rye. He reached for the bottle, shook his head, threw down the money for the drinks, and stalked majestically out through the batwings.

Cipriano had been watching both Dave and Ash from his seat at the rear of the saloon with his sombrero tilted down to conceal the upper part of his face. He left the saloon by the rear door and hurried along to the next side street. He reached the corner in time to see Dave walking in the direction of Yuma Penitentiary, perched on its granite bluff overlooking the Colorado and Gila rivers.

Steel Hand's orders to Cipriano had been, "Keep a close eye on Hunter. If you can't find him, watch Mawson. They're usually not far away from each other, but it's Hunter I really want. Meanwhile, if you see that damned fool Dancy, send him back here. He took off on his own. I think he's tailing Hunter to kill him. I don't want anything to happen to Hunter until *I'm* through with him. If Dancy tries anything with Hunter, it'll be up to you to stop him any way you can." He had held Cipriano's attention with his one cold-looking eye, almost like a snake trying to mesmerize a chicken. "*Comprende?*" he had said in a low hard voice.

Cipriano had nodded. "*Yo comprendo,*" he had replied.

Dave was almost out of sight. Cipriano trotted after him.

CHAPTER 12

YUMA PENITENTIARY DOMINATED A TEN-ACRE TRACT ON top of Prison Hill, a sheared-off granite bluff overlooking the confluence of the Colorado and Gila rivers. The Colorado was a maelstrom of swirling, muddy, swift-flowing currents and whirlpools with treacherous, shifting quicksands along both heavily reeded banks. Somewhat less than half-a-mile wide, it could become twice that distance in times of flood. Only the most powerful of swimmers aided by a great deal of luck could cross the Colorado. Beyond Yuma Penitentiary and Yuma itself—as well as Fort Yuma across the river on the California side—was the great Sonoran-type desert, a vast, foreboding expanse of almost completely waterless sandy territory. It was a seemingly endless wasteland, where summer temperatures sometimes reached 150 degrees.

Dave strode up the rutted roadway, passing a tumbledown, abandoned shack that had a wagon resting tilted on the wheelless axle ends of its left side. Thick brush had grown up around the shack and the wagon. The clear moonlight bathed the area and the prison walls in a ghostly light. It glinted off the polished metal of a Winchester held in the hands of a guard in the corner tower closest to Dave. There was such a tower on each of the four corners, manned twenty-four hours a day. Dave knew he was being watched. He turned and looked back down the road and saw, or *thought* he saw, a furtive movement beside the shack.

"Is that you, Dave Hunter?" the guard at the gate called out.

Dave waved a hand. "Yes! Is that Mark Rocha?"

"Sure is. What are you doing up here at this time of the night?"

Dave looked back down the road. "Did you see anything down at that shack?"

"Nothing but moonbeams, Dave. You been drinking?"

Dave shook his head. "Not that much."

"Might have been a drifter. They sleep in there sometimes."

Mark was wearing the regulation uniform for a prison guard at Yuma Pen. The flat-topped, flat-visored cap was of gray material banded with black braid and fastened with gilt buttons at each side. His coat was of gray material.

"You didn't answer my question, Dave," said Mark.

"Bull Andrews took two prisoners off our hands the day before yesterday. He was supposed to have delivered them here. Names of Jesus Valencia and Jack Spade."

Mark looked quickly at him. "I heard today that they had escaped some time ago. I've been on leave for a month or so. Just came back on duty this evening. Visited my brother and his family in San Diego."

"Take a look at the gate register, Mark."

The guard turned up the round wick of the Rayo oil lamp for better light. He opened the register. "Day before yesterday. Yep, here it is. Two prisoners brought back."

"Valencia and Spade?"

Mark shook his head. "Santiago Puebla and Librado Lopez."

"No Valencia and Spade?"

"Just these two. They had escaped about a week or maybe ten or twelve days ago and were picked up down the river about four or five days ago. Brought in here."

Bull was slick. He could very well have given Valencia and Spade assumed names to conceal their true identity. "Do you know what they look like?"

Mark shrugged. "Not really. We've got about 175 prisoners in here. They're just faces and numbers to me. No names. Just numbers."

"Would you know Valencia and Spade on sight?"

"Vaguely. Valencia was a little hombre. Never saw much of him. He was kept pretty much to himself. Spade was big and ugly. It was kinda odd the way they escaped."

Mark closed the register book and walked to the door of the little shack. He looked about carefully and then came back in. "I wasn't here then, as I said. One of the guards told me about it when I came on duty this evening. Spade sometimes worked in the kitchen as a butcher. Valencia was suddenly assigned as his helper. Each Saturday the next week's supply of beef comes about noon in a covered wagon. The driver was a new man on the job. No one had ever seen him before. Most of the convicts were at mess. When Spade and Valencia unloaded the beef they got into the wagon and hid under a tarp. The wagon was driven out through the sallyport gate right outside here. The guard didn't check the wagon. Evidently Spade and Valencia got out of town under cover of darkness. I heard you and Ash Mawson had caught both of them, and Bull Andrews picked them up from you."

Dave nodded. "It's possible Bull might have registered them as Librado and Puebla."

Rocha grinned. "They do funny things around here sometimes. I myself think it's because of the heat. Can I do anything more for you?"

"Let me in the prison. I'd like to check out Librado and Puebla."

Rocha rubbed his jaw. "It's against regulations for people other than personnel to enter the prison."

"I'll make it worth your while."

Rocha shook his head. "I don't want anything from you, Dave." He thought for a moment. "What the hell! You were hired to track them down. That makes you prison personnel of a sort."

"And we never got fully paid."

Rocha took a guard's coat and cap from a hook. "These belong to the guard I relieved. Leave your hat here. Keep your head down when we enter. The wall guards won't question me, but in case they do, I'll just tell them who you are and what you are doing here.''

Rocha took a Winchester '73 from a rack and a ring of keys from a locked cabinet. He lighted a bull's-eye lantern. The lens was hemispherical, with a movable cover over it that could be pushed aside so that the light would project in a beam. He gave the lantern to Dave.

The heavily barred double sally-port gate was about twelve feet wide and about fourteen feet high to the center of the arched top. A smaller entry gate had been cut into the left-hand side of the double gate. Rocha unlocked the entry gate, and the two men passed into the passageway through the eight-foot-thick wall. Rocha then unlocked the inner gate, and they walked into the prison compound. It was very quiet as they stepped toward the main cell block. Dave knew from a previous visit that the block contained thirty-four cells with six bunks in two tiers, three bunks to a side. The block could hold 204 prisoners. Then there was the Dungeon Block, which was carved out of the solid-rock hill. The block contained twenty compartments. The "dungeon" was the notorious Snake Den for the most recalcitrant prisoners, a cave at the end of a short passageway closed off by a solid wooden door reinforced by iron straps. Nearby was the horrible Crazy Hole for the insane, a narrow cavity wherein the occupant could not stand up, sit down, or stretch out. If he wasn't truly crazy when he went in there, a prisoner would certainly be so when he was dragged out, unable to straighten, stand, or walk. On the east side of the hill were the tiny cells for incorrigibles, used as well for prisoners suffering from tuberculosis, who were always segregated from the main body of prisoners because of the terrible fear of infection.

"Where to first?" asked Mark.

"If it's Puebla and Lopez, where would they be likely locked up?" asked Dave.

"Probably the Snake Den." They walked into the dark rock passage. Mark unlocked the door. "Hold your nose," he warned as he opened it. The noisome stench flowed out of the dark rock cavity and seemed to strike like a solid force against the faces of the two men who stood peering into it. It was a combination of stale sweat, fecal matter and urine, and a number of other mingled and not readily identifiable mephitic odors.

"My God," breathed Dave as he pinched his nostrils together.

A chain clanked. "*He* can't be anywhere around Yuma Pen," a sepulchral voice croaked.

"Look fast and let's leave," pleaded Mark.

Dave opened the lantern-beam cover. The pale light fell on a white-looking face with hollow, staring eyes and thin lips drawn back from yellowish teeth. Lank black hair partially veiled the face. "Who are you?" asked Dave.

The convict slowly shook his head.

"How long have you been in here?" Dave asked.

The head was shaken again.

"A long time, mister," a voice spoke up in Spanish. "He was in the Crazy Hole, but he screamed all night. They put him in here to shut him up. He hasn't said a word since."

Dave flashed the beam on the speaker. Whoever the first man was, he certainly was not Jesus Valencia or Jack Spade. He could not be Santiago Puebla nor Librado Lopez. The speaker was a Mexican with a heavily pockmarked face. "Your name?" Dave asked.

The man smiled thinly. "I have a number of them," he replied.

"Answer him! Damn you!" barked Mark.

The Mexican bowed his head. "I have only a number," he replied. He tapped the round, saucer-sized badge fastened to the front of his dirty white, horizontally blue-banded jacket. The white number on it was 829.

"His name is Amadeo Avita," the graveyard voice husked. "He's loco."

Dave flashed the light on the speaker. He looked like an old man. His shaggy hair was pure white. His facial skin was drawn and heavily wrinkled. A hawk's beak of a nose stuck out from the parchmentlike skin. His purplish lips were drawn back from his long, yellowed teeth. His eyes stared into the light beam almost as though he could see. "I smell an oil lantern," he said. "Is it lit?"

"Yes," replied Dave.

The man nodded. "Then I have gone blind at last." His leg chain clanked as he moved. Dave shot the beam down to his feet. He sickened at the sight of the gaunt feet covered with dried fecal matter. The bands about his thin ankles covered festering flesh.

"How long have you been in here?" asked Dave.

The man shrugged. "I don't know. It has been a long time. We don't know the difference between daytime and nighttime in here." He pointed upward with a long, thin, dirty finger tipped with a long curving fingernail. "That ventilation hole up there, as they laughingly call it, only shows light when the sun is almost directly overhead."

"You are not either Santiago Puebla or Librado Lopez then?" asked Dave. He knew better than to ask.

"My name doesn't matter, but I am neither one of them about who you ask."

Dave nodded. "I am sure of that," he said quietly. "Let's get out of here."

Dave flashed the beam about the stinking cave. Piles of fecal matter and a pool of urine lay on the floor in one corner. A four-inch, biscuit-colored scorpion scuttled from behind the piles with his segmented stinger bent menacingly over his head, ready to strike. Dave leaped forward and crushed him underfoot. The acrid odor of what seemed like vinegar mingled with the stench in the cave. He wanted to do something for these poor benighted wretches, but there was nothing he could do.

"Come on, dammit!" Mark snapped. "I've got a helluva headache already!"

Dave looked back once more. *"Vaya,"* he murmured as Mark slammed the door shut and turned the key in the lock. It was little enough, but it was all Dave could do.

They walked outside into the clear night air.

"How can you work here?" Dave asked quietly.

"It's a job," Mark said resignedly. "It's all I could get."

"It's sheer hell," Dave said.

Mark nodded. "I know, but you saw those three men in there. Convicted multiple murderers, every one of them. They can't be trusted around the guards and other prisoners."

"Better the gallows than that," Dave commented.

Mark nodded. "Where to now?"

"The incorrigible cells."

There was no sight of Jesus Valencia or Jack Spade there; only a few tuberculosis patients coughing up bloody sputum. They were all Indians.

They walked to the main cell block. Mark opened the iron-barred gateway. Moonlight filtered into the gloomy passageway. "I can't open the cell doors," he explained. "Too dangerous."

The round-topped, cross-hatched, iron-barred doors closed the entire front opening of the high, dome-ceilinged cells. There was no provision to keep out the heat of the summers or the cold of the winters. The cells were about nine-by-eight feet with a three-bunk tier on each side for the usual six occupants. The bunks were exactly eighteen inches wide. There was no furniture, not even a washbowl. The only toilet facility was a galvanized bucket that was emptied once a day—each morning. The bunks were each furnished with a skimpy straw mattress and one thin blanket. This, too, in the bitter cold of winter desert nights.

"Ready?" Mark asked. "They're used to such inspections at odd hours, you know."

Dave nodded. "Shoot," he said dryly.

Mark thrust the muzzle of his Winchester between the bars of the first cell and rattled the barrel against the bars. "Wakey, wakey, wakey!" he cried. "Show yourselves, you misbegotten bastards! Inspection! Wakey, wakey, wakey!"

The convicts tumbled out of their bunks and stood at attention beside them. "Look this way!" snapped Mark. Dave flicked the lantern beam from one sullen face to the other. None of them were Jesus Valencia and Jack Spade. "Are

Santiago Puebla and Librado Lopez in here?'' he asked. Six heads shook in silent unison.

It was the same way cell after cell, until there were only two left. The lantern beam probed into the darkness of the next to the last cell. There were only two men in it chained to their bunks. ''I am Santiago Puebla,'' one answered. The other man nodded. ''I am Librado Lopez,'' he said. Neither of them looked anything like Jesus Valencia or Jack Spade.

The last cell contained only one man, who did not rise when Mark rattled the bars of the cell and shouted his usual chant. He lay on the bottom bunk, on the right-hand side, with his mouth hanging open, staring at the ceiling with eyes that could not see. His thin chest did not rise and fall with his breathing.

''Dead,'' said Dave.

Mark nodded. ''We'll get him in the morning. We bury them fast in this heat.''

The clods falling on his crude coffin would be his only requiem, thought Dave.

Dave and Mark walked to the sally port. Mark unlocked the small gate set in the large outer gate. Dave took off the prison guard cap and jacket. He could still smell the stench on them. He put on his hat and blew out the flame in the bull's-eye lantern.

Mark eyed him. ''What will you do now?''

Dave stepped outside. ''Hunt down Bull Andrews.''

Mark shook his head. ''He's a mighty dangerous man, Dave.''

Dave nodded. He walked a few steps and then turned and smiled a crooked smile. ''Why, so am *I*,'' he said quietly. ''*Vaya*, good friend.'' He strode down the start of the long slope.

Dancy stood behind the abandoned shack beside the road to the prison. He had heard the slam of the prison gate as the gate guard and Dave Hunter exited the prison compound. He heard their voices and then the crunching of the gravelly soil as Hunter came down the slope. He reached down and picked up the twelve-gauge, double-barreled Greener shotgun he had loaded with Blue Whistlers whose wads had been split. He swept back both hammers with a stroke of his gloved left hand. He had tailed Hunter from town and now meant to blow his damned, big-nosed head off at twenty-foot range. It was strictly against Cole Ransom's orders, but Dancy figured that Ransom need never know. Dancy had missed killing Hunter earlier in town, and Hunter's rapid firing had sent a hot .44/40 bullet skinning right across Dancy's skinny buttocks. Now he wasn't about to try facing down that blue-eyed killer, but he meant to kill him sure enough. No man could treat Dancy the way Hunter had treated him. The lean, big-nosed bastard didn't deserve a fair shake in any case.

Dancy eased out of the shadows of the shack and crouched behind the sagging wagon. He counted silently to himself. At ten he would rise up like a deadly jack-in-the-box and let his quarry have both barrels. *One, two, three, four, five, six, seven, eight . . .* He started to rise and level the Greener. *Nine . . .* The long-bladed knife struck him in the back just below the left ribs and drove up to transfix his heart. His mouth opened wide, but no sound came from it; just a thick gush of dark blood. The Greener tilted upward, and the trigger finger tightened spasmodically on the first trigger to fire the first barrel, and then slipped and fired the second barrel. The shotgun double-blasted flame and smoke into the night air, and the echoes of the twin shots rumbled along the hillside, crossed the river, and bounced off the bluffs on the California side, then died away along the shoreline.

Dave dived for cover, landing in a ditch at the far side of the road from where the shotgun blasts had come. His head struck a rock and half stunned him. He tried to get up but couldn't manage it. He crawled into a thicket of brush and managed to draw his Colt and cock it. His senses swam. He heard shouts coming from the vicinity of the prison and then rested his head on the harsh ground and temporarily blacked out.

Cipriano eased Dancy's body to the ground. He pulled out his knife from the death wound and wiped the blood from it on the back of Dancy's long black coat. He wasn't sure where

Hunter was, but it was no time to look for that hawk-eyed killer. He picked up the shotgun and threw it into the shack, then raised up Dancy and placed him across his shoulders. He trotted down the slope away from the road toward the river. The brush concealed him somewhat, but the moon was bright on the land. He reached the narrow bank of the river and placed the body on the ground. He looked back up the slope and saw no pursuit as yet. He went through Dancy's clothing and withdrew his wallet. He emptied it of bills and then hurled it far out into the rushing river. He drew out the fancy Colt and eyed it. Christ, but it was a beauty! A beauty, yes, but a dead giveaway if anyone was looking for Dancy. It flashed dully in the moonlight as it was flung out over the river to disappear with a dull splash. The body was next. He slid it into the knee-deep water, then waded out through the thick reeds, then pushed the body as hard as he could into the current of the river. He stood there watching it as it swirled in the current, then slowly sank. The last thing he saw was a thin black gloved hand seeming to wave farewell to him in a macabre salute.

Cipriano quickly crossed himself, waded back out of the river, sat down and emptied the water from his boots, then wiped off his pistol, pulled on his boots, and trotted off along the bank. It was then he remembered: he had not replaced his knife in its scabbard. There was no time for him to go back for it. He hurried off along the bank.

"Ye can't hurt a Hunter by hitting him on the heid," Scottish Grandfather Hunter used to say with smug satisfaction. Damned old bullshitter, thought Dave, as he sat up and took off his hat. He gingerly touched the right side of his head where it had made contact with the rock. The slight lump there was a match for the fading after effects of the creasing he had suffered out on the Lechuguilla Desert.

Dave poked his head between two bushes and eyed the shack and its environs. It seemed quiet and peaceful enough in the moonlight.

"Hey, Dave! You all right!" Mark Rocha called out from along the road.

"Yes! Keep under cover!" Dave warned sharply.

"It's all right! They've gone down to the river!"

Mark came along the ditch. His Winchester was in his hands. "Friends of yours?" he asked facetiously.

Dave shook his head. "Not likely. How many of them were there?"

"Two. One was carrying the other on his back. I heard two shots. Maybe you got one of them?"

"No. I didn't shoot. Fell and knocked myself out for a time. Did you get a good look at them?"

"Not close. Fella carrying the other had on a big sombrero. The fella being carried had on a long black coat. That's about the best I can do for you. I've got to get back to my post."

Dave drew his Colt and walked across the road. He stepped behind the wagon. Something moved underfoot. He picked up a long knife. The blade was dark with something. He touched it with a finger and tasted it. It was salty. Blood . . . He held the knife up to the moonlight. The grip was set with silver wire impressed into scratches. He made out the name Cipriano in the flowing writing. He remembered then the long-bladed knife the Mexican named Cipriano had carried. He remembered, too, how Cipriano had had the chance to wound or kill him at Tinajas Altas and instead had jerked his head toward the north, an indication for Dave to escape.

Dave searched the ground. He found a place where blood had soaked into the dry earth. A dark round spot proved to be a flat-topped, flat-brimmed black hat with a band of silver conches about it. A real muley. The man being carried was wearing a long black coat. "Dancy," murmured Dave. "*Son of a bitch. . . .*"

He slid the knife down inside his right boot and carried the hat in his left hand, with his cocked Colt in his right, as he crossed the road and the ditch and catfooted down the long, steep slope toward the river.

There was a place where the river had flowed over the shore area, probably from the wash of a steamer wake. There were boot prints in the soft soil and a shallow trough with two thinner parallel lines, one on each side, as though a body had been dragged to the river's edge through the thick reeds, which had been bent to each side. He waded partway into the water and looked out toward the main channel. No sign of a floating body. He hadn't expected to see any. It had probably been shoved out into the current and sucked under. It could be a half-mile down the river by this time.

Dave took off his hat and bowed his head a little. "Gone from this cruel earth to his reward in Heaven" he murmured. He thought for a moment. "More likely to Hell," he added. He scaled the muley hat out across the reed tops and into the river.

CHAPTER 13

DAVE APPROACHED THE SITE OF THE MEDICINE SHOW AND took cover behind a sprawling adobe with a corral attached on one side. It had been taken over as temporary quarters by the medicine show, and the corral was filled with their horses and mules. Beyond the corral were the three big van wagons of the show. They stood side by side, with their lowered tailgates resting on the rear edge of a prefabricated wooden stage. Poles had been placed in sockets on each end of the platform and along the rear of it. A rope stretched from pole to pole, and from it there hung panels or curtains of brightly painted canvas depicting garish and greatly exaggerated desert scenes of palm trees, tents, and Arabs mounted on camels. Along the top part of the rear panels was the legend: "Doctor Buscombe's Abyssinian Desert Companion Elixir." At one end of the platform was a large, circular, brightly painted wooden panel mounted on a framework. It seemed like every male in Yuma was in the crowd, pressing close to the front edge of the platform with their sweat-glistening faces lighted by the flaring torches set at each end of it. The moon was low down at this time, and darkness was creeping in from the desert surrounding Yuma.

There were four musicians on the platform playing softly. The crowd was getting restless. "Where are the girls!" yelled a hoarse-voiced man.

Dave scanned the crowd looking for Ash. Suddenly he turned, crouched a little, and reached for his Colt, drawing it and cocking it in one fluid and speedy motion. A shadowy

134

figure jumped sideways into one of the doorways of the adobe.

Dave looked along the line of the barrel of his Colt, held at waist level. "Show yourself!" he called out.

A hand was waggled out of the doorway. "It's Ash, you loco idiot! By God, I saw you just in time to get into cover!"

Dave let down the hammer of the pistol and sheathed the weapon. "Where the hell have you been?" he demanded.

Ash came out of the doorway with a half grin on his lean features. "I can ask the same of you. What'd you learn up at the Pen?"

"Valencia and Spade were never brought back there."

Ash raised his eyebrows. "So where are they? Did they spring themselves from Bull Andrews?"

Dave shook his head. "Not likely."

"So what do you think?"

"Bull is after the San Dionysius treasure. He's got Valencia at least hidden somewhere in town. It isn't likely he'd try to get out of town and risk being seen."

"You mean tonight?"

Dave shrugged. "*Quien sabe?* You see anything of Steel Hand?"

"No. But I did see that big-bellied Mex again. The one called Gordo. They were around here for a time. I didn't see the fella you called Dancy. There was another hombre with the Mexican. Tall and broad-shouldered. Mean lookin' bastard."

"Probably the one called Ben. Where are they now?"

Ash shrugged. "They seemed to be looking for someone. Maybe that Dancy fella you spoke about."

"Probably. They won't find him."

Ash studied Dave. "How so? You put him down?"

Dave shook his head. He told Ash of what had happened.

Ash scratched in his beard. "I'll be damned. The same man, too, who let you get away from Steel Hand. What's his game?"

"How the hell do I know? Always smiling. Strikes me he could be the most dangerous of Steel Hand's *corrida*."

"The smiling ones always are. Davie, it seems to me you've either got a friend in the enemy's camp, or he's saving you for his own devious purposes. Maybe he's working for himself and to hell with Steel Hand. Which maybe adds yet another one to the mixed mob hot on the trail of the San Dionysius treasure—Colonel/Dr. Buscombe and his female auxiliaries, Steel Hand and his *corrida*, Bull Andrews and whoever is behind him, and now your enemy/friend Cipriano. Anyone else, partner?"

Dave grinned. "Just us."

"Maybe we ought to forget the whole damned mess and go and look for Scalphunter's Ledge."

"It's a thought, partner. A *damned* good thought."

The sound of music from the medicine show increased.

Ash cocked his head up. "Strange," he murmured. "Sounds like the drumming is coming from *behind* us." He looked quickly back over his shoulder. "Jesus!" he yelled. "Move!" He slammed a shoulder against Dave and drove him hard, back against the wall of the adobe.

There was a pounding tattoo of hoofs on the hard-packed ground. A horseman bent forward in the saddle was coming at a run directly toward Dave and Ash. Ash leaped to get against the wall beside Dave. The horseman swerved his mount at the last possible second. It was so close that his right boot brushed against Dave's left arm as he turned to face flat against the wall. "Get the hell out of the way!" the rider shouted.

"It's a God damned woman!" yelled Ash. "It's Madeleine! By God, Davie! Here comes another!"

The second rider sped past them. Callie Sutherland looked down at them from under the upturned brim of her wide-brimmed hat. She was wearing men's clothing and held a Winchester rifle in her right hand. She looked back as she rode past. "Haven't you two drifters anything better to do!" she cried. "Come and see the show!"

The two women rode their horses along the rutted road just behind the gaping audience. Madeleine reached into a box attached to her saddle horn. She tossed something round about the size of an apple into the air. It rose high with the flaring torchlight reflected from its shining surface. Callie stood up in her stirrups, raised her rifle, and fired, then levered in another round. The glass ball shattered into tiny fragments that fell in a glittering shower. No sooner had the flat report of the shot died away when a second ball was thrown into the air. Again Callie fired, and again the ball was shattered. Madeleine had reached a point fifty yards beyond the edge of the crowd. She reined in her mount and turned him to race back the way she had come, meeting Callie halfway. The rifle cracked. Another ball was smashed. Callie whirled her mount while levering in a fresh round. She hammered back along the road just as Madeleine threw up yet another ball. That one had the same fate as the others.

Colonel/Dr. Buscombe had parted the curtains and stood in the center of the platform. "Sureshot Callie Sutherland!" he roared in his pitchman's voice.

Madeleine headed her mount directly back the way she and Callie had appeared. She held the reins in her teeth and hurled upward a ball from each hand. Callie fired twice. Both balls disintegrated. Madeleine hammered back past Dave and Ash while both were cowering hard against the adobe wall. Shards of the broken glass showered down on their hats and shoulders. Dave looked up as Callie rode past. "You don't seem to scare easily, Buscadero!" she shouted. "Or are your pants full?" She grinned as she rode off into the shadows.

"What the hell did she mean by that?" Ash asked.

"A little thing that happened between us."

"*Are* your pants full?"

Dave shrugged. "Almost were. Took a little discipline."

"Me, too."

They grinned at each other.

Buscombe paced back and forth on the platform. He wore a dove gray top hat; a vest embroidered with vines and flowers; and a long, dove gray coat with black velvet lapels. His trousers were of a finely checkered material, and his patent leather shoes reflected the glaring light of the torches. He held up his arms for attention. The musicians struck up a chord.

"He's going into his pitch," said Ash.

"Didn't you have a turn at that business once?"

Ash sucked at a tooth. "Yep. Kansas. Mixed up a batch of snake oil. Had a gypsy woman who read fortunes and drew the suckers in to hear my pitch. Did pretty well. One night a couple or so of Kansas Jayhawkers got dissatisfied. One night I got drunk. They knocked in the head of my reserve barrel of snake oil to see what was in it." His voice died away.

"So?"

Ash looked sadly at him. "Odds and ends. Cayenne pepper, gunpowder, and a coupla rattlesnake heads for bite. Some chicken guts to give it that natural amber glow to it. Mixed with 150-proof alcohol." He shrugged. "I left town in my long johns only, ridin' on the then-Dearly Beloved." He lifted the hair on the back of his neck and showed Dave the scar there. "One of them Kansas bastards threw a knife at me before I outdistanced them."

"Seems to me you had another story about that scar. Chargin' the Rebel breastworks at Vicksburg. A big Confederate whopped you with a saber, wasn't it?"

"Well, maybe. Anyway I lost my wagon, mules, and my gypsy costume and tambourine, a good Sharps rifle, and a gold watch my Daddy left me. All because of a handful of chicken guts and a few rattlesnake heads. It wasn't the ingredients so much as it was the all-curing power of the snake oil."

"What happened to the gypsy woman?"

"She inherited the whole shebang. I heard she did well in the Indian Nations. I never went back to find out. Too hostile, you understand."

The drummer was thudding his big stick against the bass drum. Buscombe raised his arms like a prophet intoning a prayer to the Supreme Being. He paused and then dramatically pointed to a parting in the curtains. The musicians struck up a chord. The curtains parted, and Callie and Madeleine strode onto the stage. Callie walked to the large circular board mounted at one end of the platform. She turned her back to it, then stepped up on two pegs inserted into the board. She reached up with her arms and gripped two other pegs. She now stood in an X position. Buscombe and an aide quickly strapped her ankles and wrists to the pegs and passed a broad belt about her slim waist. Buscombe and the aide stepped back. Madeleine was a good twenty feet away from Callie. A small table covered with a red velvet cloth stood close to her side. A row of throwing knives lay on the table. They glittered evilly from the torchlight. Madeleine poised her lithe figure and nodded briefly to Buscombe and the aide. They gripped the edge of the circular board and pulled downward with all their strength. The board, loaded with its human freight, turned and began to spin.

Madeleine picked up one of the knives. Buscombe and his aide stepped aside. Madeleine threw the knife in an overhand cast. It rotated swiftly, reflecting the ruddy glare of the torches so that it seemed that it was stained with blood.

The knife point had struck the board with a thud just to the left side of Callie's neck, and in a matter of seconds another knife stuck quivering into the wood at the right. No sooner was a knife thrown—and before it struck the board—another one was in the air, hurtling toward the woman spinning on the circular board. It was all over in less than a minute. By that time knives were stuck on each side of Callie's body at her throat, her armpits, and at her sides, thighs, and ankles.

The crowd was getting excited. Faces were flushed and chests heaved. Eyes were widened and lips parted. The circular board came to a halt. Callie was loosed from her straps and stepped from the board. Her charro jacket was pinned through at the left side by one of the knives. The knife was pulled free, and only Callie felt the thin trickle of blood running down her side from a flesh wound. When the last of the knives was pulled free, Callie and Madeleine met in the center of the platform. They smiled and raised their arms in salute to the audience. The crowd roared. The two women bowed and then ran between two of the panels.

Two aides set up a folding-legged table with a set of shelves attached to the back edge. They opened cases of The Abyssinian Desert Companion and filled the shelves with the blue-and-white-labeled bottles contained therein.

The drummer beat a steady rattling roll on his side drum, accompanied by the booming of the bass drum.

Colonel/Dr. Myron T. Buscombe turned to face the crowd. He held up his arms for attention. The drumming stopped abruptly. He stifled a cough as he reached for one of the bottles of his product. "Gentlemen," he began. He paused. "And you *are* gentlemen, I am sure." He paused again, master showman that he was. Then he continued, "Why else would you be in Yuma, the fair city of the Colorado River?" He smiled benignly.

The crowd roared.

"He knows his business," said Ash.

Dave nodded. He noted a fast-moving, bent-over figure of a woman wearing a heavy shawl over her head and shoulders come from around the front ends of the three wagons lining the platform and place herself to one side of the rear of the crowd. No one seemed to notice her, so engrossed were they with Buscombe and the bottle he held high in his hand.

"Ladies and gentlemen," proclaimed Buscombe. "We have here in this pretty blue-and-white-labeled bottle the world-renowned panacea for all the known ills, both physical and mental, of the human race. The original formula was given to me in the ancient empire of Abyssinia, now called Ethiopia, by a direct descendant of one Frumentius, a Syrian missionary who converted the Abyssinians to Christianity in the year A.D. 330. The formula has never been written down and must be committed in utter secrecy to the mind. Mind you, ladies and gentlemen, it has been passed orally from father to son for over fifteen hundred years." He paused to let the words sink in.

Dave and Ash had been scanning the crowd to see if Steel

Hand or any of his *corrida* and/or Bull Andrews might be there but with no success.

Buscombe strode back and forth, waving the bottle. "For here we have the greatest remedy of all time!"

"I wonder why it hasn't worked on that bloody cough of his," mused Ash.

Dave looked at him. "Did you ever drink any of Mawson's Snake Oil?" he asked dryly.

Ash looked annoyed. "You must think I'm loco."

Buscombe looked up at the bottle as though he was adoring a holy relic. "The Abyssinian Desert Companion is a sure cure for wind colic, flatulent colic, diarrhea, scouring, dysentery, inflammation of the bowels, bladder and kidney trouble, colds in the head, congestion, fits, mad staggers, looseness in the bowels, and inflammation of the brain—*for bots it has no equal*!" He picked up another bottle and held both bottles high above his head. He subdued another cough, and shouted, "The price for a bottle of this miracle cure is usually ten dollars, but tonight, and on this night only, before we leave for a triumphant tour of the West Coast, I have reduced the price to that of little more than the cost! Tonight for a precious bottle of this liquid magic, I will gladly take five dollars!"

The curtains parted and Callie and Madeleine came forth, this time dressed as nurses with long gray skirts, blouses, and a starched white apron from their breasts down to the hem of their skirts. Pert gray caps edged with white crinkled ribbon were on their heads. They carried baskets in which were bottles of the Abyssinian Desert Companion. They came down the stairs, one at each end of the platform, and began to work their way into the crowd. The little old woman with the shawl pushed herself close to Callie and handed her a crumpled five-dollar bill. The woman took the bottle then removed the cap and began to pour the contents down her throat.

"What are bots?" asked Dave.

"You're really ignorant, Davie. Bots are the larvae of the gadfly. Found in the intestines of horses, under the hides of cattle, and in the nostrils of sheep. In short, a belly worm or maggot. Raises hell with them, I tell you. My God, look at the old lady!''

She had emptied the bottle. She jumped up and clicked her heels together, then ran to the stairway of the platform and went up them like a jumping jack. ''Thank the good Lord for the Abyssinian Desert Companion!'' she cried hoarsely.

''Look!'' shouted Buscombe. ''Sure proof of the efficacy of the Companion!''

''That ain't nothing!'' the woman cried. She extended her arms and did a series of cartwheels along the platform. Her long skirt fell down about her thighs, revealing her legs clad in long john woolen underwear. She reached the end of the platform and jumped down to the ground and disappeared from view to the roar of the crowd.

The bottles of the Abyssinian Desert Companion were rapidly emptied from the baskets carried by Callie and Madeleine. The two women stuffed the bills into leather purses hanging from their waists, then hurried back to the platform to refill the baskets.

Buscombe turned away from the crowd and bent his shoulders in a paroxysm of coughing. It became so violent, he left the platform.

Dave and Ash walked behind the line of wagons. They saw the ''little old lady'' yanking off her waist and dress and then pulling on a pair of baggy trousers and shrugging into a desert-type of robe. He crammed a turban on his head, picked up his bass drum and stick, and returned hastily to the platform to join his fellow musicians.

Buscombe stood at the front end of one of the wagons, gripping the right front wheel as his body shook in repeated spasms. He dabbed at his mouth with a handkerchief.

''Do you need any help, Buscombe?'' asked Dave from behind him.

Buscombe turned slowly. His face was ghastly pale. His lips were bright with blood. ''With this condition? *No!* To find the treasure of San Dionysius? *Yes!* Have you located Valencia?''

"No. He's not at Yuma Pen. He was not brought back there by Andrews."

Buscombe stared at Dave. "Then where the hell is he?"

"Perhaps still here under cover in Yuma. Perhaps out on the desert somewhere with Bull Andrews heading for The Walking Sands. There's a strong possibility that Andrews might be working hand in hand with Steel Hand."

"I find that hard to believe."

"I said it was a possibility, not a probability."

Buscombe nodded. "Callie told you about my commission from the government. Do you still want to work with me?"

"For what it's worth. We may locate Andrews and Valencia. If not, we'll have to find out if they left Yuma and which way they went. If they left, we'll have to follow them. It won't be simple. There's the desert to face. Hours and hours and long days riding under the worst conditions. A damned good chance of having to fight against Bull and maybe Steel Hand. Do you think you can handle it?"

Buscombe looked at him eye-to-eye. "It's my last hope, Hunter. You know that. It's the women I've been thinking about. The damned treasure means nothing to me at this stage of the game. Will you let me go with you?"

Dave looked at Ash. Ash shrugged, then nodded.

"What do you want me to do?" asked Buscombe.

"Start getting ready. Horses saddled. A pack mule or two with filled water kegs. Some spades and a pick. A lantern. Food for a week or ten days at least. Be ready to leave as soon as we notify you."

Ash eyed Buscombe. "How many men will you bring?"

Buscombe shook his head. "None. Just the two women."

"You're loco," said Ash.

"They can ride and shoot as well as any man. If anything happens to me my share goes to the both of them. Understood?"

Dave nodded. "What about the medicine show?"

Buscombe shrugged. "I've left it in charge of one of my

men.'' He smiled. ''The little old lady of the cartwheels. If I don't get back, he'll keep it for the women.''

''And if *they* don't get back, what then?'' asked Ash.

''It's yours and Hunter's.''

Ash shook his head. ''No. But thanks. I've had my one great experience with a medicine show.'' He grinned. ''I'll tell you all about it one day.''

They walked away into the shadows. They looked back. Buscombe was back at the wagon wheel and coughing hard. ''This will be the biggest and likely the last gamble of his life,'' said Dave quietly.

CHAPTER 14

THE THREE-CHIMED WHISTLE OF THE STERN-WHEELER *Hassayampa* sounded as she approached the narrow gap in the new Southern Pacific Railroad swingspan bridge. The bell signal clanged once on the main deck to slow down the engine. She moved slowly toward her mooring place down below the *Topolobampo*. The *Hassayampa* was the belle of the Colorado River. She looked like a layer cake of a boat, with her white-painted upperworks and the lacelike tracery of her railings and fret saw work ornamentation along the edges of her two upper decks. When she passed close by the run-down, dusty, rusty, and dirty *Topolobampo* it was as though she was a majestic, well-dressed society matron passing a dowdy old scrubwoman on the street.

Dave and Ash stood beside the corral where they kept Dearly Beloved and Dave's newly bought *bayo coyote* dun. They watched the *Hassayampa* with Captain Jock Fletcher at the wheel. "Maybe we should have taken up Jock's offer to partner him in a steamship line on the river," mused Ash.

"That was when we had *some* money left over from the hassle in West Texas," said Dave.

The bucket planks of the steamer slapped slowly against the dark surface of the river and created a yeasty, foaming wake. The signal bell clanged for reverse. The paddle wheel stopped and then rotated backward to slow the steamer down just enough so that the strong current carried her inshore to her mooring place. Her mooring hawsers were cast to shore and made fast. Two Bells rang out to Stop Engine. A plume of steam rocketed upward from her escape pipes along the smokestack as boiler pressure was cut.

"I worked on some of the best sternwheelers on the Missouri," said Ash. "None of them ever looked as good as the old *Hassayampa*."

Dave looked sideways at Ash. "*You* worked on the river?"

Ash nodded. "Before the war when I was a teenage kid. Sort of an apprentice engineer. Had two steamboats blow up under me. After the war I went back on the river for a time. The packet *Hattie May*. Went hard aground in 1866. Indians on the bank shot fire arrows at us. We grasshoppered her off the bar while she was still aflame. She was taking on water. The two engineers were hit by arrows. Tried to outrun the redskins. Taking on too much water. Fire boxes redhot. I was in charge then. Flames streaming out of the stacks. I closed the drafts and choked off the safety valves for all the steam and speed we could get. Boilers blew up. Threw me clear back across the damned river. My clothes were afire and my face blackened from soot. I was yelling like a banshee as I came down. Them redskins seen me coming like a rocket all aflame and with a black face screeching like a hoot owl. Scairt the hell out of them, I tell you!" Ash grinned reminiscently.

Dave eyed him. "How did you get out of *that* one?"

Ash shrugged. "Simple. Landed in a slough beside the river. Mud broke my fall, put out the flames, and eased my burns. I was picked up three days later crawling back to reach Bismarck—maybe a couple of hundred miles or more. You see, what I hadn't known was that any steamer's name starting with the letter M was hoodooed. You know—the *Moselle*, *St. Martin*, *Missouri Belle*, *Monmouth*, *Maria*, and *Helen MacGregor*. *All* of 'em. Snagged, sunk by ice, afire, run onto rocks, into bridges, boiler explosions, sandbars, storm and wind, bank collisions, overloading, swamped in eddys, and so forth." He paused, rolled his eerie green eyes upward, and added, "*And* the old *Hattie May*!"

"Well, the best I could do was the old *Nokomis*, a sidewheeler at that and on the Great Lakes."

" 'N' is pretty damned close to 'M,' Davie."

The landscape was dark now after the passing of the moon. An occasional light could be seen coming from Yuma and Fort Yuma across the river. The *Hassayampa* and the *Topolobampo* were the only river steamers showing lights, and that of the *Topolobampo* was a single dim lantern on the main deck. Now and again George Welch, the caretaker, would open a door to reveal the glow of the fire box.

"What now?" asked Ash. "We've covered this damned town lock, stock, and barrel, and haven't seen one damned sign of Bull, Steel Hand, and Valencia. What's next?"

Dave suddenly looked down toward the *Hassayampa*. Men shouted. A horse whinnied and a mule brayed. A gun cracked flatly. The flash was close to the side of the steamer, just where the gangplank had been run out.

"Come on!" snapped Dave. He plunged down the crude wooden steps leading to the shoreline.

Men were charging up the gangplank of the *Hassayampa*. They were followed by others leading horses and two pack mules to the main deck of the steamer. Guns spat flame and smoke. Someone fell over the side into the river. Men ran forward and started up the stairs leading to the hurricane deck and the pilothouse. A burly man appeared out of the pilothouse.

"Stay where you are, Fletcher!" shouted the leading man. "We're taking over your steamer!"

"That's Bull Andrews, Ash!" Dave threw back over his shoulder.

"The hell ye are!" roared Jock. He wrenched a fire axe from its rack and stood defiantly at the top of the stairway. A pistol flashed and cracked. Jock staggered backward and dropped the axe. He struggled around to the front of the pilothouse. "Ye'll no take the *Hassayampa*!" he cried. Two more pistol shots sent him reeling to the outboard railing. He grasped for the railing and then went over the side and down into the river.

"Get that son of a bitch Spade up here!" shouted Bull. "He knows how to handle one of these steamers! Gawd dammit! *Move!* Cast off those mooring lines! Get the steam pressure up again!''

"For Christ's sake, Dave!" yelled Ash. "Don't go chargin' at 'em! There's too many!"

Dave nodded. He sprinted up the gangplank of the *Topolobampo*. "They've killed Jock, George! Bull Andrews is taking over the *Hassayampa*! Get up steam! Ash will give you a hand!" He sprinted up the stairs to the boiler deck and into the cabin. He unlocked his cabin door and grabbed his Sharps rifle and cartridge belt. He ran forward and then up the stairs to the hurricane deck, then aft on the open deck past the big smokestack. The *Hassayampa* was already drifting away from the shore with her mooring lines cut through. Flames were shooting out of her stack as the fire boxes were fed to capacity. Dave loaded his Sharps and raised it to fire. A rifle flatted off from the after end of the *Hassayampa*'s hurricane deck. The slug rapped into a stanchion not a foot away from Dave. He raised the Sharps to fire and realized there was really nothing at which he could shoot at but the big paddle wheel and the hurricane deck, open all the way to the smokestack.

The steamer moved slowly out into the main current of the river with the threshing of the paddle wheel showing whitely against the dark surface of the water. The steamer's engine was hissing and pounding. The steam coughed in measured beatings from her exhausts. She headed for a bend in the distance. The last thing Dave heard was the clanging of four bells for "Full Speed Ahead!" Fire flared up from her smokestack, and in a few moments she was gone from Dave's sight.

Dave ran down the stairs to the main deck. George Welch was bent over, energetically pitching pieces of greasewood log into the roaring blaze of the fire box. "Where's Ash?" Dave shouted.

George looked up. Sweat dripped from his bearded face. "Gone to get someone. Dr. Buscombe, he said." He stood up straight. "You aim to try and catch the *Hassayampa* with this old tub?"

"We'll blow a boiler or two trying, George."

Twenty minutes passed. "Aboard the *Topolobampo!*" hailed Ash.

Ash, Callie, and Madeleine led the horses and pack mules aboard. Buscombe was in midst of one of his coughing fits. Madeleine took him to a cabin and then returned to the main deck.

The steam pressure needle was slowing rising. Ash tapped the glass cover of the dial. "Do you think the same thing I'm thinking about Bull?" he asked back over his shoulder.

"Downriver about thirty miles," replied Dave. "Land on the east bank, from there overland fifty miles east to Tinajas Altas. Then southerly to The Walking Sands."

"How do you know that?" asked Callie.

Dave shrugged. "It's the only way he *can* go."

"We'll need a pilot," said George.

Ash pointed to Dave. "Him," he said. "Old time steamboatman from the Great Lakes. Sailed the old *Nokomis* through many a blow."

"What the hell?" blurted Dave. It had not occurred to him as to who would handle the *Topolobampo.* "What about you, Ash?"

Ash shook his head. "I was in the engineering department. I'll work with Brother George here."

"What's this about you sailing the old *Nokomis* on the Great Lakes?" asked Callie suspiciously.

Dave shrugged. "I was a teenage kid. That was before the war. I spent part of the time in the engine room learning the trade."

"And the rest of the time?"

Dave looked at her. "In the pilothouse."

She smiled. "Learning the trade?"

Dave nodded.

The lazy hiss of escaping steam overrode the sound of their voices. George worked the lever to send a blast of escape steam up the stack, blowing out any accumulated soot. He looked back at Dave. "Full pressure, skipper," he reported.

Dave looked at Callie. "I'll need help. You'll have to do."

She nodded. She took her Winchester from its saddle sheath. Dave led the way up to the pilothouse. The pilothouse, or "sky parlour," was thick with dust and cobwebs festooned with dead flies and moths. The wheel was so large it had been partially sunk into a casing set in the deck. Two kerosene lamps with frosted glass cylinders hung in gimbals, one on each side of the house. A bell hung in a bracket on top of the house. The bell cord came down through a pipe so that the end of it was close to the pilot's hand. There was a brass voice tube connected to the engine room and a brass, handled pull to send signals to the engineer.

Dave whistled into the voice tube. Ash's voice responded, "Steam's up, Davie."

Dave nodded. "Cast off then."

The current worked its way in between the starboard bow of the steamer and the shore as the mooring lines were cast loose.

A whistle sounded in the voice tube. Dave put his ear to it. "Hawsers cast loose, Dave. Gangplank run in." There was a brief pause. "Can you turn her in this damned river?" Ash added. There was no answer from Dave.

Hunter pulled the signal handle to tap three times on the engine room bell, the signal for being alert and to stand by for further signals. He hadn't thought too much at first about how to turn the steamer to head her downstream. The current was fast. The waters close to the shore were shallow and full of sand banks. The draft of the steamer was about five feet. He gripped the wheel with his left hand and jerked the bell pull twice with his right to start the paddle wheel into motion. The *Topolobampo* shuddered from stem to stern and from keel to hurricane deck, as though resentful at being in motion again after the idle and peaceful months along the shore. She moved forward slowly. The current began to work against her starboard bow, forcing her to turn toward port. Dave swung the heavy wheel to turn the four rudders.

"She's turning awful slow," said Callie quietly.

"She's old and tired." He looked sideways at her. "Can you swim?" he asked.

The steamer was almost broadside to the current. Dave pulled the bell handle hard four times for Full Speed Ahead! The engine hissed and pounded laboriously. The steam coughed steadily from the exhausts. The paddle wheel began to slap the water at full speed with her buckets. The hull groaned as the speed from the hard-thrusting pistons and the powerful current wracked it. She began to cant to port as the California shore loomed up ahead of her.

"Get on the wheel," Dave said quickly.

Callie gripped the spoke handles and thrust with all her strength while Dave "walked" the wheel by planting his feet on the spokes. The *Topolobampo* was *slow*; God but she was *slow*. . . . Angry flame streamed out of her forty-foot stack. The staccato, crackling *pop-pop-pop* of the exhaust valves sounded like a Gatling gun as it echoed back from the bluffs along the shore.

"We'll never make it!" cried Callie.

"The hell we won't!" roared Dave.

Then, as though the *Topolobampo* felt the mastery of Dave's spirit—or perhaps it was the powerful current and the full-out slapping of the buckets—she swung away from the looming shore. The wheel was hard over, holding the four rudders against their stops. She suddenly slowed, and the tug of the bottom tremored through the laboring hull. For a moment it seemed as though she would go full aground, and then she slid rather clumsily over the sandbar and back into the main channel. Dave rang for three-quarter speed and then half-speed. No use in further trying the old boilers. The muted *sssooo-hhhaaa-sssooo-hhhaaa-sssooo-hhhaaa* of the engine echoed from the bluffs. The *Topolobampo* was on her way.

Callie looked at Dave. "Can we catch them?"

Dave shook his head. "Probably not on the river, unless they run aground. They'll likely have to stop for wooding up. The *Hassayampa* was probably low on fuel after her run downriver."

"Then we'll have them!" she said.

"It won't be that easy. Bull Andrews is a fighting man, and he's got more men with him than we have here."

"You have Madeleine and I. We're both expert shots."

He adjusted the course a little by lining up the jackstaff in the bow like a rifle sight against the shoreline. "You're experts all right." He looked sideways at her. "Those bastards up ahead aren't little glass balls being peppered with bird shot. How will you feel when they're shooting *back* at you?"

There was no reply from Callie as the *Topolobampo* surged down the dark river.

Ben and Cipriano reported to Steel Hand what they had seen at the river. "We'll never catch them now," growled Ben.

Steel Hand looked quickly at him. "Not on the river, you damned fool! Andrews is only going as far south as the road that leads east to Tinajas Altas. We'll leave tonight. We'll get to the High Tanks first and wait for him. We'll ambush Bull and his men and take Valencia." He looked about at Ben, Cipriano, and Gordo. "Where is Dancy?" he asked.

Ben shook his head. Gordo looked away. Cipriano smiled. "I couldn't find him," he replied. "What about Hunter, Major?"

"He's *mine*," Steel Hand said in a low voice. "If he catches up with Bull and gets back Valencia, then we'll deal with him the same as we might with Bull." He looked about him. "But he's *mine*. . . ."

An hour later they left, riding hard for Tinajas Altas.

CHAPTER 15

A SUDDEN FLARING OF LIGHT APPEARED AHEAD OF THE *Topolobampo*. The river curved to the right, so that the light at first appeared to be on the shore. Dave instantly rang for two bells to stop the engine.

"What is it?" asked Callie. "Another steamer? Perhaps Indians on shore?"

Dave rang for reversing the paddle wheel. The steamer barely moved ahead with the current. He took his field glasses and focused them on the light. It flashed up again, and he distinctly saw the flaring iron, feather-shaped ornamentation at the top of a steamer smokestack. "It's the *Hassayampa*," he reported. She was the only steamer on the Colorado with such stack ornamentation. "She's running her engine at top speed, probably trying to work her way off a sandbank." He whistled into the voice tube and reported what he had seen. "I'm going to lightly ground the *Topolobampo* here. We'll hold her in place until we can find out what's happening. Get up forward with a pole and sound the depths. We draw about five feet."

Ash appeared on the fore deck with the sounding pole. He plunged it into the water as Dave steered the slowly drifting steamer in toward the shore. "Bottom at ten feet! Bottom at ten feet! Bottom at nine feet. Bottom at eight feet. Shallowing fast! Bottom at seven feet! Bottom at six feet!" chanted Ash.

The shoreline showed dimly through the darkness as an irregularly shaped line of thick brush and a few stunted trees.

"Bottom at six feet! Bottom at six feet!"

Dave signaled for Ahead A Quarter.

The *Topolobampo* moved ahead.

Ash glanced up at the pilothouse. "Bottom at five feet!"

There was a tug at the bottom. The bow pushed into the brush overhanging the shore. Dave rang for Stop Engine. The *Topolobampo* struck hard against the bank. There was the sound of a heavy splash and a faint cry from Ash, which was suddenly cut off.

Dave went down the stairs three at a time and ran to the point of the bow. There was no sign of Ash.

Madeleine came running forward. "Where's Ash?" she cried.

Dave knelt on the deck. "He's gone over the side."

Callie called down from the pilothouse: "We can't hold her here without the paddle wheel pushing us against the bank!"

Dave grabbed the end of the mooring hawser and jumped from the tip of the bow into the thick brush. He forced his way through it with a swarm of mosquitos rising about his face. He looped the hawser about a stunted tree. He turned to go back to find Ash.

"Stay where you are, Hunter," a vaguely familiar voice said hoarsely out of the darkness. "Don't reach for your Colt."

Dave bent his head and hunched his shoulders to peer into the darkness. "Jack Spade?" he asked.

"The same, Hunter. I've got your partner here. Pulled him unconscious from the river. I've got his Colt and bowie."

"How the devil did you get here?"

"From the *Hassayampa*. Bull took me and Jesus aboard. I'll swear the only reason he didn't kill me before that was because he knew I had worked at piloting on the river. We were getting low on firewood. I took a chance and ran her aground around the bend. They're cutting wood and brush now to keep her fires going. Weren't able to get her off the bottom. Used up a lot of fuel, and there wasn't much aboard in the first place. I knew you'd come after us on the old

Topolobampo. Bull was looking out the pilothouse door on the shore side. I booted his big ass through it and jumped over the outboard side. The current swept me down past the steamer. I got ashore and circled around the woodcutters, and about that time I saw the *Topolobampo*. I was going to stop you from going around the bend and being seen by those bastards aboard. I was right here on the shore when that stupid bastard Ash fell in.''

"Watch it, you son of a bitch," Ash growled from the ground. "Get your damned foot off my neck!"

Spade laughed. "I will in time. Hunter, Valencia is locked up in one of the cabins behind the pilothouse. Got a guard at the door. The crew of the *Hassayampa* are doing the woodcutting ashore with a couple of Bull's men guarding them. The rest of them are still on board. They ain't likely to get the *Hassayampa* off that sandbar before daylight. I'll make a deal with you, Hunter. You, me, and Mawson can board the steamer and free Valencia. We can take him downriver and then across country to Tinajas Altas, like Bull planned to do, then on south to maybe The Walking Sands.''

"What's to be in it for you?" asked Dave.

"Nothing. I wouldn't touch that goddamned treasure with a fifty-foot pole! But Jesus Valencia is a good man. He's a priest, or was one anyways. Maybe the curse won't apply to him. By rights, if the treasure is found, it should all go to him. He talked in his sleep one night. He said something about giving it all back to the poor damned Indians who had suffered enough from the white man and particularly the Spaniards. Look, you let me go along with you. When we're far enough into Mexico, I'll leave you. All I want is a horse and a gun. If you do find the treasure, you can work it out with Valencia as to shares. Sure, you could take it *all*, but remember that curse.'' His voice died off abruptly. Dropping his weapons, he suddenly raised his arms up over his head.

Dave drew and cocked his Colt.

"It's me, Dave!" Callie called out from behind Jack. "I've got my Winchester muzzle up against his spine!"

Dave cursed. "I thought it was someone from the *Hassayampa*."

"Get your goddamned foot off my neck!" growled Ash. He rose up from the ground with his bowie in his hand.

"Let him alone, Ash," ordered Callie. "He can help us get Valencia."

Ash flourished the heavy knife. "Go to hell!"

"You want a .44/40 in your belly?" she asked quietly.

"You wouldn't dare," he said coldly.

"Try me," she suggested.

He studied her. "I believe you mean it."

Dave walked forward. "She does."

"You oughta get rid of that loco bastard," said Jack.

Ash whirled toward him and raised his bowie. He took a few steps and sprawled flat on the ground. "Who tripped me!" he shouted.

"I did," replied Callie. "You want to make something out of it?"

Ash sat up. "I'll be damned. A *woman* dropped me."

"Probably ain't the first time," remarked Jack from a safe distance.

Dave peered into Ash's face as he stood up. "You all right, partner?" he asked.

Ash nodded. "One of my fits. I'm all right now."

They worked their way through the brush to the boat and boarded it. Madeleine was standing guard with her Winchester in her hands. She eyed Jack. "Where did you find him?" she asked.

"In the brush," replied Callie. "He's our new partner."

"How many men does Bull have?" asked Dave.

"Five or six," replied Jack.

"How many of the crew?"

"About the same."

"The three of us will take the yawl boat," Dave instructed. "Jack, you'll stay with the boat. Ash and I will climb the paddle wheel to the hurricane deck. I'll take the flare pistol from the pilothouse locker here. If we're successful, I'll fire a flare." He looked at Callie. "It'll be up to you to handle the *Topolobampo*. Are you up to it?"

She nodded. "I'll have to be."

"We'll just take knives and pistols," continued Dave. "Jack, get yours from Colonel Buscombe."

"No," Buscombe said quietly from behind Dave. "I'm going along. It'll take more than just the three of you to carry this off. Jack can get a knife and pistol from the women."

Dave turned and looked at him. "Are you up to it?" he asked.

Madeleine shook her head. "He's very ill. He can't go."

Buscombe had already gone aft. They could hear him coughing.

Dave shrugged. "This is the way he wants it. We'll have to take him."

No one spoke. They all knew what he meant. Buscombe had been a fighting man all his life. He would prefer to die on his feet with weapons in hand rather than coughing out his lungs in a sweat-soaked bed.

They lowered the yawl boat from the hurricane deck. Jack and Ash sat at the oars. Dave took the tiller. Buscombe stood on the deck. He gathered the two women into his arms. "My two beauties," he murmured. He squeezed them hard. "We'll be back soon. Don't worry." He dropped into the bow of the boat and smiled up at them as the boat was shoved off into the current.

Dave looked back as the yawl boat followed the bend of the river. Callie stood on the hurricane deck beside the pilothouse. She held up a hand in salute. Then the boat was swallowed up by the darkness.

CHAPTER 16

THE YAWL BOAT ROUNDED THE BEND WHILE PASSING close to the shore. The stern of the *Hassayampa* loomed ahead, rising ghostlike from the darkness of the river and the shore. A lazy scarf of smoke drifted from her smokestack. Her paddle wheel was still. The voices of men and a chopping sound carried from the shore. Ash and Jack shipped their oars and let the current bring them up beside the paddle wheel. Buscombe looped the painter over a cleat.

Dave, Ash, and Jack pulled off their boots. Dave thrust the loaded, heavy, angular flare pistol under his pistol belt. He had one spare flare cartridge in his shirt pocket.

"Good luck," Buscombe said.

Dave nodded and pulled himself up on the outrigger. He used the spokes of the paddle wheel to climb to its top. He reached up to the end of the hurricane deck and pulled himself up onto it. He lay flat on the deck. He could see no one. He turned and gave Ash a hand up onto the deck, and then the two of them heaved Jack up beside themselves.

Dave crawled to the starboard side of the deck and looked over the edge onto the boiler deck and the shore. Men were working, cutting brush and scrub trees by the light of a dim lantern. Others were hauling wood up the gangplank to the main deck. Jack had said the crew of the steamer numbered about five or six, and Bull's men numbered about the same. There were about seven men cutting and hauling wood. That should leave about three to five still aboard the steamer. He crawled back to the others. "Three to five men on board," he whispered.

"There's a man forward, by the cabins behind the pilot-house," said Jack. "The guard on *Valencia*."

The pilothouse loomed whitely in the darkness. Cabins extended behind it, and behind them was the towering smokestack. Aft of the smokestack was a framework with a canvas roof and screened sides that was used for dining by the passengers in hot weather. A yawl boat sat in chocks on the starboard side of it. Aft of it were several open skylights for the boiler-deck saloon.

"We'll go after *Valencia*," Dave said to Jack. "You cover us from back here. Use your knife if you can instead of shooting."

Dave and Ash catfooted along the port side of the deck, keeping the dining area and smokestack between themselves and the lone guard. Dave pointed to the starboard side. Ash nodded and moved behind the cabins. The cabins were four in number, divided by a short corridor from starboard to port, with a door at each end. Each cabin had a window opening on the deck. The forward window on Dave's side showed a dim light. The after window was dark. Dave tested the door. It was locked. There was a dim light in the pilot-house. Dave padded to the door and looked in. The pilot-house was unoccupied.

Dave eased the door open and crawled in. A guttering kerosene lamp threw a dim and fitful light. Dave drew his knife. He reached down inside the wheel casing and severed the tiller rope on the port side, then crawled to the starboard side and severed that rope as well. If by any chance the *Hassayampa* was freed from the sandbar and drifted out into the current, her steering wheel would be useless.

"What the hell are you doin'?" a hard voice barked. "By Christ! You're *Hunter*!"

Dave came up on his feet as though on springs and stared into the twin muzzles of a double-barreled shotgun. He looked over the barrels into the eyes of the man named Seb. A shadow moved in behind Seb. Dave dropped to the deck.

Seb gasped. His eyes went wide. The shotgun was tilted upward, both barrels blasted flame and smoke. The kerosene lamp was smashed to pieces. Burning oil from the reservoir dripped down onto the desert-dry deck and into the wheel casing. Seb fell to the deck. Ash withdrew his bowie knife, dripping blood, from Seb's back. He grinned.

Dave yanked Seb's Colt from its holster and handed it to Ash. Dave felt about in Seb's shirt pockets and drew out four shotgun cartridges. He broke the shotgun and ejected the spent casings and then reloaded the smoking chambers.

"Get Valencia!" said Ash. He darted out the door.

Dave ran aft to the outer cabin door and kicked it in. He stepped into the corridor and tried the forward cabin door. It was locked, "Jesus Valencia?" cried Dave. He heard the faint voice of Jesus.

"Is that you, Hunter?"

"Keep away from the door!" ordered Dave. He placed the muzzles of the shotgun against the lock, fired one of the cartridges, and then kicked in the door.

Jesus stood with his back against the wall. There was no fear on his thin, pale face. "Hunter," he said quietly. "I knew you would come."

There was a sudden outburst of gunfire on the starboard side of the deck. Dave swung the shotgun to cover the starboard door. The door was opened, and Ash yelled from beside it, "For Christ's sake! Don't shoot! Have you got him?"

"Yes!" shouted Dave. "Are you all right?"

"Fine! It was the other hombre that got it."

Dave hustled Valencia out of the cabin and onto the deck, then hauled him aft. He looked back. The pilothouse windows were ablaze with firelight. Smoke was pouring out of the open door. A window exploded. Fire licked through it and began to eat away at the painted canvas-roof covering. Men yelled on the shore.

Ash stood spread-legged beside the smokestack with a Colt in each hand. He fired them alternately into the smoke. He turned and ran aft. "She's burning like tinder!" he yelled.

Guns cracked from the shore. Slugs whispered over the deck.

Vague forms could be seen in the thick smoke shrouding the forward part of the deck about the pilothouse.

Jack Spade was grinning. "I'll stop them!" he yelled. He picked up a red-painted tin tank that rested in chocks behind the yawl boat. He raised it high overhead and ran forward.

"For Christ's sake, you idiot!" yelled Ash. "That's *kerosene* for the lamps!"

It was too late. Jack heaved the tank with all his great strength. It struck the smokestack casing and split open, sending a shower of kerosene over the cabins and the deck where the hungry flames instantly ignited it. The flames flared up. Burning oil ran along the painted canvas of the deck and dripped down to the boiler deck below. Sparks landed on the canvas roof of the dining shebang and ignited it.

"You've done it now, you loco bastard!" shouted Ash.

Jack grinned. "That'll hold 'em!"

A pistol cracked up forward. Jack winced and gripped his left biceps. Blood leaked through his shirt and ran between his fingers. He held up his hand, glistening with blood in the firelight. "Son of a bitch! I'm hit!" he yelled.

"The whole damned steamer is going," said Ash.

A man appeared, staggering out of the smoke and flame. Blood ran down his face. His hair was afire, and his shirt was smoldering. He gave out hoarse, animallike grunts of savage pain.

"Shoot the bastard!" shouted Ash.

The wounded man ran through the flames between the smokestack and the burning cabins. He continued running right over the unrailed port side of the deck. His legs were still churning as he dropped down toward the dark, rushing river. He hit the water and was gone out of sight.

"Help Valencia down to the boat, Jack," Dave ordered.

Jack was still gripping his biceps. He shook his head. "I can't climb down," he said calmly.

"The brush along the shoreline is burning," reported Ash.

Dave leaned over the port side of the deck. "Buscombe!"

he shouted. "Bring the boat forward to the side of the main deck!" He turned to Ash. "Get down on the boiler deck! I'll lower Valencia and Jack down to you."

Ash went over the side and landed on the boiler deck. Dave lowered Valencia until Ash could grasp his legs, then Ash eased him down to the deck. Dave turned. "You're next," he said to Jack.

"I'm too damned heavy," protested Jack.

"What the hell do you want to do?" demanded Dave. "Stay up here for a last stand?" There was no argument from Jack. "Hang on by your one good arm," ordered Dave.

Jack went over the side with Dave hanging on to his right arm. Pain contorted Jack's face, but he made no outcry. Ash eased him down to the boiler deck. Dave looked forward. The deck, pilothouse, cabins, and dining shebang were a mass of roaring flames. Flame-shot smoke towered high above the doomed *Hassayampa*. Dave went over the side, hung by his hands, and dropped to the boiler deck, where he was caught and steadied by Ash. Ash dropped down to the main deck. Dave lowered Jesus and Jack down to him.

Buscombe pulled the boat along the fore end of the paddle wheel and alongside the after end of the main deck. Ash hoisted Jesus Valencia up to the top of the solid wooden railing, got up on it himself, and then lowered Jesus down into the boat. He sat astride the railing and helped Jack get up on it and then helped him as he lowered himself on the outboard side of the railing and into the boat.

Someone shouted on the starboard side of the boiler deck. Dave turned. A man was aiming a rifle at him. There was no time for niceties. Dave snatched up the shotgun and fired from the hip. The blast of the charge caught the man in the belly and drove him backward. Dave threw down the shotgun and yanked his Colt from its holster. He ran to the starboard side and looked along the deck and then down to the shore. Men were scattering into the thick brush. There should still be some of Bull's men aboard, as well as Bull himself. Ash, Jack, and Dave had accounted for at least three of them;

perhaps more had died in the raging fire that was now engulfing the entire forward part of the steamer.

Dave ran past the after end of the boiler-deck cabins. He glanced through one of the windows and saw that the forward end of the saloon was a mass of flames.

Dave looked over the deck railing. Smoke was drifting over the yawl boat, but he could see three men in it—Ash, Jesus, and Jack. Then he saw Buscombe standing in the swirling smoke at the edge of the deck with his derringer in his left hand and his bowie knife in his right. Fire was lapping along the outer edge of the main deck. Even as Dave watched, he heard a gun report and saw Buscombe suddenly buckle slightly in the middle. He clasped his left hand against his belly. He withdrew it and looked down at his hand. It was bright with blood.

"Get back in the boat, you damned fool!" shouted Dave.

Buscombe looked up. He smiled thinly and shook his head.

Dave climbed over the railing. He jabbed his Colt at his holster, then let go of it, hung by his hands from the edge of the deck, and dropped. He landed heavily, spraddle-legged, and looked into a scene from hell on the main deck. The boiler ends were hidden by roaring flames and wreathing smoke. The brushwood and greasewood sections the men had been cutting on shore and piling on the main deck were ignited. The hungry, licking, dancing flames ran along the top of the fuel. Beyond the wood, a line of horses and mules had been tethered to the bull railing on the starboard side. The horses and mules were plunging and yanking at their tethers while neighing and braying in a frenzy. Dave ran toward them.

"Get out of here, you damned fool!" shouted Buscombe. "The deck overhead will soon collapse!"

Dave drew his knife and worked his way along the line of horses and mules, avoiding their kicking hoofs and thrashing heads. One after the other he cut the tethers.

Dave turned as he freed the last horse.

"Hunter! You son of a bitch!" roared Bull Andrews. He stood beyond the burning fuel wood with two of his men.

Dave dropped his hand to his Colt. The holster was empty. He drew the flare pistol from under his belt and cocked it.

"Drop, Hunter!" shouted Buscombe. He weaved his staggering way toward the three men. A pistol slug hit him in the left shoulder. He dropped the derringer, bent his head, and charged with his bowie knife pointing toward the first man. The pistol was fired again. Buscombe jerked. He kept on. The bowie slashed high toward the throat. The man raised his arms. The bowie was thrust underneath them and was raked three inches deep across his gut. Buscombe whirled and slashed the bloody blade full force across the throat of the second man. Buscombe dropped his bowie knife and gripped his middle with both forearms. Bull raised his shotgun. Buscombe was laughing as Bull fired. The charge set fire to his ruffled shirt as he was driven backward against a stanchion. He slid down to the deck and fell sideways. Bull turned and grinned as he leveled the shotgun at Dave across the burning fuel wood. Dave fired the flare pistol. The shotgun roared upward as the flame from the old flare pistol struck Bull full in the face and exploded in a furious display of red sparks and smoke. Bull screamed hoarsely. He dropped the shotgun and with his hands dabbled at his horribly burned face. He staggered forward right into the blazing holocaust that was the forward half of the once-beautiful and proud *Hassayampa*.

Dave plunged through the burning fuel wood. Buscombe opened his eyes as Dave knelt beside him. He smiled. "What a great way to go," he said dreamily. "A real Viking funeral on the Colorado River, of all places. Dave, take care of Madeleine and Callie." He closed his eyes and then reopened them. "Your shirt's on fire, you damned fool," he said weakly. "Abandon ship! Good luck . . ." Then he was gone.

Dave slapped out the flames on his shirt. He plunged through the smoke and licking flames to the side of the main deck. He thought he heard the sonorous whistle of a steamer but knew he must be hallucinating.

"Come on! What the hell are you waiting for?" yelled Ash.

Dave reached the edge of the deck just as he again heard that haunting steamer whistle. The yawl boat was starting to drift away from the *Hassayampa*. The whistle blasted again, this time much closer, and then the old and faded *Topolobampo* came surging around the bend and into the flaring firelight from the burning *Hassayampa*. Flame streamed from her tall and rusty stack.

"Come on, damn you, Dave! She'll run us down!" yelled Ash.

The flames roared at Dave's back. Pieces of the boiler deck were dropping down on the main deck. The heat was intense. Thick smoke shrouded everything.

The *Topolobampo* was partially obscured in the thick smoke. The yawl boat bobbed close to her. Dave dived over the side of the *Hassayampa* and struck out for the small boat. Ash pulled him aboard.

"She'll run us down!" shouted Jack.

The *Topolobampo* loomed through the smoke.

"*Jump! Jump! Jump!*" shrieked Madeleine from the fore deck of the approaching steamer.

The starboard bow struck the side of the yawl boat. There was a splintering of timbers. The shattered small boat ground and bumped alongside the steamer. Jack Spade picked up Jesus Valencia with his good right arm and literally threw him up on the main deck. Ash and Dave gave Jack a leg up. He gripped the base of a stanchion and hauled himself half-way aboard. George Welch dragged him the rest of the way. Ash and Dave stepped free of the sinking small boat and reached the deck of the steamer. The yawl was half-full of water and was soon sucked under the smashing bucket planks of the paddle wheel.

Ash and Dave ran along the decks, striking out small fires that had started up from airborne embers. Dave went alone up on the hurricane deck. He looked in at the pilothouse. Callie stood at the wheel, seemingly perfectly composed, glancing down the long dark run of the river ahead of the speeding *Topolobampo*.

Callie turned her head toward him. He looked into her

magnificent green eyes. He winked, and then he kissed her. "I'm on duty," she said primly. "No time to be fooling around."

"Were you afraid?" he asked.

She nodded. "But I wouldn't have missed it for the world."

A final bullet spanged thinly off the big bell atop the pilothouse and whined off and down into the river.

The old *Topolobampo* plowed on through the darkness.

CHAPTER 17

"DAWN," ASH MURMURED.

There was the faintest, hardly perceptible nuance of a lighter gray in the eastern sky. Dave and Ash were close to the base of the Tinajas Altas Mountains and in a line east-west with the High Tanks. They had holed up in a deep gully with their horses at the first indication of the coming dawn. They had traveled from the place they had grounded the badly leaking *Topolobampo* across the Yuma Desert with the two women, Jesus Valencia, and Jack Spade. The long hours of darkness had concealed the high, thin scarf of dust rising from the hoofs of the horses and mules. There had been little disturbance until an hour before dawn, when the wind had arisen, strongly driving dust and loose soil up from the Gran Desierto across the almost sterile land at the western base of the Gila Mountains and the wide valley between them and the Tinajas Altas. George Welch had been offered the chance to travel with them and a share of the Jesuit treasure if found. He had refused to leave the grounded *Topolobampo*. "Old Jock left her in my care," he had explained. "She's in bad shape, but I might save her yet. Remember Jock left her to you, Ash, and me. He planned to leave the *Hassayampa* as well, but she's gone forever now. Still, we might be able to salvage her engine and other fittings some day and put them in the *Topolobampo*."

"A long, long shot," Ash had suggested.

George nodded. "You're right. But it's all I've got. Besides, Jock would have wanted it that way."

Before Dave had followed the others into the darkness of the Yuma Desert, he had looked back at the ghostly-looking white shape of the old steamer. *"Vaya!"* he had called out to the lone man on her deck. *"Vaya con Dios!"* George had called back. Dave had not heard him add one word, *"acaso."* It was a familiar benediction used by those hardy souls who lived near the Gran Desierto of Altar and the Camino del Diablo. "Go with God. *Maybe* . . ."

It had been a hard-driving and murderous trip across the desert. Ash and Dave had walked much of the way, leading their horses to save them. It was Dave who had first seen the infinitesimally tiny speck of light that flickered in the distance. It had been high on the dark and far-off Tinajas Altas Mountains. After that, for a few hours as they approached the mountains, others had seen it. It was like someone shielded a small light, uncovering it now and again. "Or some damned fool smoking a cigarette," Ash had suggested. There was no question about the light—it was certainly there, but by whom and why was quite another matter. Most people in that desolate and hostile country made great efforts to travel and camp unseen. Ash and Dave had moved up close to the western base of the mountain, leaving the women and the two men several hundred yards behind them. The High Tanks were on the far or eastern side.

Dave scanned the crest of the mountain with his field glasses.

"You think it might be Steel Hand and his *corrida*?" asked Ash

Dave nodded. "It's possible. He would have known Bull had taken over the *Hassayampa* and gone down the river with Valencia and Spade. He had no way of following us on the river. What would you have done in his place?"

"Ride like hell for Tinajas Altas. He'd figure he couldn't lose. If Bull got away from us, he would head for Tinajas Altas. If we caught up with Bull and got Valencia, we'd do the same."

"That's a big problem. Another big problem is who was showing that light up there. It was likely a signal. If it was for Bull, the odds are he was possibly in with Steel Hand. If it *was* for us, who in the hell *would* be signalling to *us*?''

Ash took the field glasses and studied the crest. ''You ever think it might have been a lure?''

''I've had all kinds of thoughts about it. It's possible.''

''Maybe it was the Mex called Cipriano. You said he saved your life here at Tinajas Altas. You said he likely had killed Dancy up at Yuma Pen before Dancy could kill you.''

Dave nodded. ''True. But why would he do those things?''

The crisp sound of a repeating rifle lever being worked to load the chamber came from behind them. ''Because I am your friend,'' explained the smooth, deep voice of Cipriano. ''Don't move!'' he added sharply. ''Keep your hands away from your guns! Raise your arms!''

They both turned toward him with their hands raised in the air.

Cipriano stood twenty feet away with his nickel-plated rifle at hip level and pointing straight at Dave's belly. The Mexican was standing a few feet behind Dearly Beloved. ''You moved fast from the river,'' Cipriano said. ''I had a feeling you would outwit Bull Andrews.'' He smiled. ''Unless he's following you with blood in his eye.''

Dave shrugged. ''It's possible.''

Cipriano shook his head. ''Knowing you two killers, I'd say it was not a possibility. I know you have Jesus Valencia and that son of a bitch Jack Spade back there with your women.''

Dave studied him. ''What do you plan to do with us? Turn us over to Steel Hand?''

Dearly Beloved slowly laid back his ears.

Cipriano shook his head. ''I . . .'' he started to say. It was as far as he got.

Ash whistled shrilly. Dearly Beloved lashed out with his hind hoofs. A hoof caught Cipriano with a glancing blow on the right shoulder, which slammed him sideways. Ash freed his bowie knife from his scabbard. Dave ran forward, gripped his hat by its brim with his left hand, and threw it spinning through the air. It struck Cipriano's face just below his eyes.

He dropped his Winchester. Dave was on him in an instant.
He swung his Colt, the one he had taken from the man in the
pilothouse, and thudded the barrel against the left side of the
Mexican's head. The heavy felt of the sombrero cushioned
the blow, but it was enough to send Cipriano down on his
knees. Dave's right boot heel struck him on the point of the
jaw and sent him down sprawling. Ash closed in and pushed
his left foot down on the Mexican's throat.

"Don't kill him *yet*. . . ." warned Dave.

Ash nodded. He took his Winchester. "I'll take a look for
any of his friends." He faded into the shadows.

Dave picked up his Sharps and dusted it off.

"Afraid a little dust will spoil your aim?" asked Cipriano.

Dave held the rifle on him. "No, but if you'd like to make
a break for it, I'll check it out."

Cipriano smiled. "*Ley del fuego*, eh?"

Dave shook his head. "Not yet anyway. You've got some
questions to answer."

"Before you ask, you'd better tip off your friend Ash. I
was followed down here from the Tanks. Two men. Old ac-
quaintances of yours. Ben and Gordo."

"He's right," Ash said out of the shadows. "They're blun-
dering around between us and the others."

"They're looking for me," explained Cipriano.

"To help you?" asked Dave.

"No. They think I was signalling someone from up on the
mountain."

"The lights we saw?"

Cipriano nodded. "I took that chance. I thought you might
see them and be warned *someone* was at the Tanks."

"Maybe you were warning Bull," suggested Ash.

"No. I know you two men—the mountain lion and the
wolf. Odds were that it would be you two. I was right. Now
while you're talking there are two men out there looking for
me. If they find your women and Valencia, there will be hell
to pay, as you Americans say."

Dave nodded. "You're right. Let's go, Ash!"

"What about me?" Cipriano asked.

"Pick up your fancy Winchester."

Ash stared at Dave. "You loco?"

"He saved my life twice. That's good enough for me."

"Maybe he won't the third time around."

Dave shrugged. "I've got plenty of time. I'll take the lead. You follow *behind* Cipriano. We'll talk about my motive later. That is, *if* we survive. . . ."

The wind was strong and fitful. The sky was much lighter but large areas west of the mountain remained dark.

"They were moving west," Ash said in a low voice.

Cipriano nodded. "Then they are no longer looking for me. They'd know I would not come this way without a horse. It's a long walk to the Colorado."

Dave made his way up the side slope of a low hill, beyond which was the place where the women had waited with the horses, mules, and the two men.

A mule brayed loudly.

"Come on!" snapped Dave.

They trotted through the dimness.

A man shouted.

"That's Ben," said Cipriano.

Two shadowy figures appeared in front of them. One of them was tall and broad-shouldered. The other wore a sombrero and was shorter and rotund. Ahead of them was the dark mass of the horses and mules.

"Don't shoot yet," Dave warned over his shoulder. "We might hit the women."

"Throw down your guns!" ordered Ben.

Callie's voice came loud and clear. "You go to hell, you bastards!" She punctuated her sentence with a rifle shot. Gordo cursed as he went down. Ben raised his rifle to shoot. As he did so a dark figure rose from the brush behind him, drew back an arm, and hurled a knife. It struck between Ben's shoulder blades. He grunted, staggered, and dropped his rifle. He weaved about on his feet while feeling behind himself for the knife haft. He went down and tried to push himself back up onto his feet. Ash passed Dave in a loping run. He was almost on Ben when Callie fired again. Ash's hat seemed miraculously plucked from his head. He bent over. His bowie rose and fell.

"For Christ's sake, Callie!" screamed Madeleine. "That's Ash you shot at!"

Dave moved up. He looked down at Ben in the growing light. Ben's head lay sideways with a great gash at the base of his neck where the bowie had cut through to the spine. His staring eyes seemed to look accusingly at Dave.

Gordo was breathing his last. The bullet had struck him in the chest. His shirt and jacket were black with blood. He opened his eyes and looked up at Dave and Cipriano. *"Cabrons,"* he murmured, and then died. His eyes remained open.

Callie came up to the men. Her face was pale. "I don't like killing," she said quietly.

Ash grunted. "You're damned good at it when you have to be." He pulled the knife from Ben's back, wiped it on his shirt, and then handed it to Madeleine. "You're damned good at it, too."

Madeleine and Callie looked at Cipriano. "Who's he?" asked Callie.

Dave shrugged. "I *think* he's a friend of mine. He is, or was, one of Steel Hand's men. Saved my life twice, here at Tinajas Altas and again at Yuma. He was the one signalling to us from the heights. He warned us about these two men. That's all we really know about him."

Callie eyed the Mexican. "Well, who *are* you?" she asked.

Cipriano looked at the taut, hard faces about him. A bit of a chill went through his body. He had known the two *gringos* were hard-case. Now he felt the same way about the two *gringas*. "I am Capitan Cipriano Ortega, Regimento Fronteras Fusilieros of the Mexican Army, here on special duty along the border of Sonora and Arizona Territory."

"*What* special duty?" asked Ash.

"Perhaps the same as our undercover agents in the U.S. have informed us Colonel Buscombe is doing for the United States—looking for the key to finding the Lost Jesuit Treasure of The Walking Sands. We knew Major Cole Ransom, better known as Steel Hand, was looking for it and was after Jesus Valencia. That is why I joined up with Steel Hand. We had heard Steel Hand was in some kind of plot to spring Jesus Valencia from Yuma Pen with the aid of Jack Spade. That is why we came to Tinajas Altas. Steel Hand had caught Valencia and was planning to force him to show us the treasure site in The Walking Sands. However, Valencia managed to escape.'' His voice died away.

Dave studied him. ''Then *you* were the one who helped him do so.'' He paused. ''And killed two of Steel Hand's men.''

Cipriano nodded. ''Steel Hand figured Valencia might head for Tinajas Altas. He was right. We came here and found you, Hunter. You and your partner Ash Mawson managed the almost impossible in getting Valencia away from the High Tanks and to Yuma.''

Ash nodded. ''And then we ran into Buscombe, who wanted Valencia for the treasure. And, to cap it all, along comes Bull Andrews and takes Valencia from Buscombe. Was it Bull who was in partnership with Steel Hand?''

''Yes. A rare pair, Steel Hand and Bull Andrews.'' Cipriano smiled. ''And what is still more rare is the fact that two of the most well-known and avid treasure hunters of the United States didn't know a damned thing about the Jesuit treasure. Nor did they know they might have the key to its location in the person of Jesus Valencia when they found him staggering out of the desert at Tinajas Altas.''

Ash eyed him. ''And the gold cross, amigo? Did he find that after he escaped, and were you with him at the time?''

Cipriano narrowed his eyes. ''I know nothing of any gold cross.'' His expression changed. ''*Madre de Dios!* Do you mean to tell me he found such a cross somewhere in The Walking Sands?''

Ash grinned. He opened his shirt to reveal the gold cross.

''While you three are trading reminiscences, we're standing here like damned fools out of water and with the nearest water holes probably well guarded by Steel Hand and his *corrida*," Callie said sarcastically.

"First things first," added Madeleine.

"They're right," put in Jack Spade.

Jesus Valencia's eyes were fixed on the gold cross.

"They're right," agreed Cipriano. He pointed to the east. The sun had risen in a vast, silent explosion of intense light. Anyone looking down from the heights would easily be able to pick them out against the light-colored earth.

"How many men does he have?" asked Dave.

"With Ben, Gordo, and myself gone he has seven counting the muleteer Tomaso who he hired in Mexico and is only with Ransom because he's scared to death of the man's damned hand."

"What about the rest of them?" asked Dave.

"My countrymen," Cipriano replied a little ruefully. "What you Americans would call border scum. They are a superstitious lot. They joined up with Steel Hand because they thought that hand of his gave him supernatural powers. Remember the shot you made out on the Lechuguilla Desert? It neatly removed Ransom's left boot heel as cleanly as though done by a meat axe and then ricocheted from the hard ground and killed one of the water mules. To the men this was as supernatural as Steel Hand's metal claw. They had never seen anything like that. Now they think of you as they think of him—a *brujo*, a witch. Some of them had heard eerie stories of you and Ash—the demonic rifleman and his deadly partner with his razor-edged bowie knife. There are legends about you two along the border. Those men *believe* them. . . ." He paused for effect. "Further, I saw fear in the eye of Steel Hand when you shot off his heel. I had not seen it before, nor had any of his men."

"He's still holding the water holes," put in Callie. "I'll bet you he'll try to make a trade with you—Valencia for the water."

Madeleine nodded. "And when he gets Valencia you can go to hell for your water."

"I agree," said Cipriano.

"What's your suggestion?" asked Ash. "That is, if you have one."

Cipriano looked down at the two dead men. "He's lost his three best men—myself and these two. You'll have to let him know that. Maybe it won't frighten Steel Hand, but it sure as hell will frighten the others. They're scared enough as it is about the Camino del Diablo and the Gran Desierto. He's kept them with him because of his steel hand and the promise of treasure. I think we can outweigh their loyalty to him, if you want to call it that." He smiled thinly. "We can show them Ben and Gordo have been killed."

"You mean drag those bodies to where they can be seen?" asked Callie.

Cipriano shook his head. "Just the *heads*," he said quietly.

"Jesus Christ," Ash murmured.

Cipriano looked quickly at him. "Does it bother you?"

Ash grinned. "I think it's a brilliant thought!"

Ash's bowie rose and fell twice. The heads were swathed in their owner's bloody shirts. Their bodies were stripped of their weapons and cartridges. Cipriano and Ash dragged the bodies to a gully and rolled them down into it. There would be no time for burial.

Cipriano glanced south. "Look," he said quietly.

High in the sky was what looked like a scrap of charred paper floating on the strong wind. They all knew what it was—a *zopilote*, the great Sonoran land buzzard. It would miss nothing. It was a scout. By noon at least there would be others, naked-headed, raw-necked, and with iron-hard beaks. By dusk there would be little left for nocturnal prowlers except rags and leather torn into scraps by beaks and claws and scattered bones of yellow-white held together by gristle.

CHAPTER 18

THE STRONG FURNACE WIND WAS SWEEPING FROM THE south. It drove clouds of dust and sandy grit from the vast waterless wastes of the Gran Desierto de Altar. During this time of year such dust storms would virtually stop all traffic on the Camino del Diablo. The wind would change the ever-shifting surface of the desert by gathering dust and sand, piling it into hollows, and raising *barchans*, crescent-shaped dunes.

Dave lay in a hell-hot crevice between two great tip-tilted boulders at the foot of a rock-strewn slope situated below the jagged skyline of the Tinajas Altas Mountains. To the right and left of Dave's position were *bajada arenosos*, wide V-shaped areas of coarse and gritty sand that flowed out onto the flat surface of the desert. Heat waves shimmered up from the sunbaked slopes and the areas south and west of the mountain.

Something flashed high on the crest like a split-second shard of lightning. "You think that's Steel Hand?" Ash asked from behind a boulder to Dave's right.

"He has a pair of shiny, brass-covered field glasses," said Cipriano from behind the boulder to Dave's left.

A rifle flatted from the crest near where the flash of light had been seen. The bullet caromed off the boulder behind which Ash was standing and whined thinly off into the air. The shot echo died off across the desert. It was silent again except for the dry husking of the sand-laden wind against the

176

rocks and boulders and the insistent buzzing of the flies hovering around the shirt-wrapped heads of Ben and Gordo.

"The son of a bitch can shoot," Ash growled. "That was two feet from my *cabeza*. He's got us spotted for sure."

The dry, nasal voice of Steel Hand was carried down to them on the wind. "I know where you are! I know you have Jesus Valencia! I know you must need water! Turn him over to me, and I'll let you have all the water you want!"

Dave scanned the line of crest. He saw a rifle barrel poking between two large rocks. There was another one beyond where he had seen the light reflection. He saw the crown of a dusty sombrero moving partway down the slope. It vanished.

"How many up there, do you think?" asked Cipriano.

"Four at least, counting Steel Hand, if that's him with the glasses. One of them is moving down the slope. The rest of his *corrida* are either hidden up there, moving down toward us, or perhaps are at the Tanks on the other side of the mountain."

"Maybe it's time to show him and his boys what happened to Ben and Gordo," suggested Ash. "We can't stay around here much longer without water."

Dave nodded. "Go ahead. Be careful! They've got our range."

Cipriano unwrapped Ben's head and placed it on top of the boulder behind which he was standing. Ash quickly placed Gordo's head on top of the boulder in front of him, ducked down, and then, as an afterthought, popped up to clap Gordo's big sombrero on the head. A rifle cracked instantly. "Jesus!" barked Ash. He dropped down behind the boulder and flattened his right hand against his ear. He withdrew the hand and saw the streak of blood on it. "The son of a bitch put a nick in my God damned ear!" he roared. He reached for his Winchester.

"No!" shouted Dave. "You pop up again, and this time he'll put a slug right between your eyes and win the turkey!"

Ash reluctantly nodded. He dabbed at his bleeding ear with a corner of his bandanna.

"There he is!" cried Cipriano.

Dave focused the field glasses on the head that showed from behind a rock ledge. There was no mistake. There, in remarkable clarity, was the faded hat; the patch-covered left eye; the fearsome ridge of the white scar standing out against the tightly drawn, parchmentlike skin; the thin, aquiline nose; and the down-curved slash of the mouth underlining the thick, grayish, dragoon mustache.

"Is it him?" queried Cipriano.

"Him or the Devil."

"They could be one and the same."

The head was gone as suddenly as it had appeared.

"Maybe he was trying to draw our fire to see exactly where we are," said Ash.

Dave placed his hand on the barrel of his Sharps, lying close beside him. He saw the crown of the sombrero again, but this time it was moving faster, backward at an angle toward the crest. Then the man jumped to his feet and ran awkwardly for cover behind a tall boulder. A .44/40 slug from Ash's Winchester bounced off the side of the boulder. Another of the men on the high slope got to his feet and plunged partway down the slope into a thicket of glistening cholla cactus surrounding a group of boulders. They could hear his intense scream of pain as the needles slapped viciously at his legs. Cipriano sent a slug winging over his head. "That was Bernardo," he said as he reloaded. "Gordo was his amigo. He won't be back."

Steel Hand stood up in his rage. "Get back here, you greaser son of a bitch!" he yelled. He aimed and fired his rifle. While he was looking at Bernardo, yet another of his men scuttled to the right of Steel Hand and vanished into the clutter of rocks, boulders, and brush.

"I think that was Jaime," said Cipriano. "He's about three-quarters *Yaqui*. Superstitious as all hell."

"You think they're deserting?" asked Ash.

Cipriano shrugged. "They don't like the sight of those heads grinning at them."

It was quiet again. The flies buzzed energetically about the sun-swollen heads. Now and again one of the mules brayed loudly.

"Maybe we can outflank him," suggested Ash.

"He still has men somewhere up there and at the Tanks," Dave said.

The mules brayed in unison.

"Your mules are thirsty!" shouted Steel Hand. "They're smarter than you are! At least *they're* admitting it! How long do you think that little man Valencia will live without water? If you don't deal with me, you'll have to go back to the Colorado, and I'll be on your tails waiting for you to drop! Come! Make it easy on yourselves! All the water you want for one skinny little man! Look!" He jumped up with a large canteen in his hand and swung it around so that a silvery stream of water poured from the canteen and splashed on the rocks.

"Don't shoot!" warned Dave. "He'll spot our positions!"

The moment Dave spoke Steel Hand sank quickly behind the rock ledge.

It was quiet again.

Dave scanned the crest with his field glasses. He recalled what Cipriano had said, "Now they think of you as they think of him—a *brujo*, a witch. . . ." Dave closed his eyes for a moment. Ransom's men thought of that deadly steel talon of his as something with powers of its own, wielded by a man whom they thought of as something not quite human, almost a supernatural being. The symbol of that supernaturalness was his metal hand. Maybe, if Dave could get a good clean shot at that hand of his and shoot it off, then maybe, just *maybe*, they would desert him *en masse*.

Ash whistled softly. "If we can lure him out of cover, maybe you can get a shot in at him, Davie."

It was almost as though Ash had read Dave's mind.

"It may be our only chance," agreed Cipriano.

Dave looked from one to the other of them. "We've got to get him to show himself. It's an uphill shot, maybe 250 yards more or less. The wind is blowing like hell across the slope. Half the time he's obscured by that damned dust.''

Ash nodded. ''You need a lure. I'll go.''

''I'll go, too,'' volunteered Cipriano.

''Dave and me work as a team,'' objected Ash.

''You're liable to get a bullet through your thick head!'' said Cipriano.

''So is Dave!'' snapped Ash.

Dave shook his head. ''Listen to you two stupid bastards! *Both* of you go! Ash, go to the right. Cipriano, go to the left.''

Dave opened the aperture in the butt plate of his Sharps and took out the vernier tang sight. He set it up on its base on the tang and tightened the holding screw. He raised the cupped eyepiece to 250 yards.

''You three are all loco,'' said Callie from behind them.

''Have you got any better ideas?'' asked Ash.

She shrugged. ''Happens I haven't. Can you do it, Dave?''

Dave patted the butt stock of his rifle. ''Old Satan can.''

''*You're* doing the shooting,'' she reminded him.

Dave looked down at the crescent-shaped dent in the hard walnut of the butt stock. He remembered the blow on his right cheekbone from the metallic hand. ''That I am,'' he quietly agreed.

''I'll keep you covered,'' she offered. She held up her Winchester.

Dave nodded. ''Keep your head down, Callie.'' He smiled.

He found a place where he could slide the heavy rifle between boulders whose tops rested together, forming a narrow trough that widened at the outer end. It would have to be a snap shot. *Jesus*, he thought, a 250-yard uphill shot through shimmering heat waves and blowing dust at a target not much larger than an outspread hand. He took two cartridges from his rifle cartridge belt and held them loosely between the first and second and second and third fingers of his left hand— for faster reloading if necessary. He looked to the right and left at Cipriano and Ash. ''*Andale*,'' he said.

They vanished into the labyrinth of brush, cacti, crevices and hollows, rocks and huge boulders.

Dave leaned the Sharps against one of the boulders in front of him, stepped to one side, and leveled the field glasses. There was no sign of Steel Hand. Minutes ticked past.

"Maybe he's gone," Callie suggested.

Dave shook his head. He looked to his right and caught a glimpse of Cipriano's sombrero showing between two boulders. The sun reflected on the barrel of Steel Hand's rifle. All Dave could see was the barrel protruding past a large rock and part of the crown of Steel Hand's grayish hat. Steel Hand fired. Cipriano had already vanished. The gun report died away. The gunsmoke was torn to tatters by the wind. There was no further sign of Steel Hand.

"Bastard," shouted Ash. He rose from his cover and ran across an open space, then dived to safety just as Steel Hand's rifle cracked. Dave had kept the glasses on Steel Hand's position. This time Steel Hand had been forced to move to his right, and in firing he had exposed his head, left arm, and shoulder as he raised up to fire at an angle downhill at Ash. The sun shone on his metallic left hand holding the fore stock.

Next time, thought Dave. If he fires again from that position, Dave would have about as good a shot as he could expect. There would probably be *one* such chance.

"*Cabron!*" shouted Cipriano. He was much farther to the right now.

Steel Hand did not show himself. He was probably moving to another firing position, as any veteran sharpshooter would have done.

Dave slid his rifle into the rock trough. He set the firing trigger. Steel Hand rose up and then went down again. He was in the same position, looking toward the slope where Ash had been. Dave sighted on Steel Hand's position. He drew in a full breath, then let out half of it and rested his finger on the firing trigger.

Ash shouted, "You one-eyed son of a bitch! You couldn't hit a bull in the ass with a bass fiddle!"

Steel Hand came up like a jack-in-the-box. He thrust out his rifle, cupped under the fore stock by his shining metallic left hand. Dave and Steel Hand fired at exactly the same instant. Old Satan drove back hard against Dave's shoulder. White smoke plumed from the muzzle. The heavy report thundered off along the slope, accompanied by the flatter sound of Steel Hand's Winchester.

A hoarse screaming broke out on the heights as Dave reloaded. He set the firing trigger and looked up. Steel Hand had leaped to his feet without his rifle. He waved his left arm. Dave snatched up his field glasses and focused them on Steel Hand's left arm. The metallic hand was missing. Bright blood shone in the dusty sunlight as it flew from what remained of his left wrist. Steel Hand was still howling with intense pain as he gripped his wrist with his right hand to stop the flow of blood. The big 500-grain slug had smashed through the leather-and-metal wrist cuff and then had evidently driven his rifle from his right hand.

"Shoot, Davie! Shoot!" howled Ash.

Dave watched Steel Hand scuttle up and over the crest. There was no one left on the heights. The sun shone on the metal hand lying twenty feet from where Steel Hand had been shooting.

Ash came running back. "Why didn't you finish him off?"

Dave shook his head. "He'll likely bleed to death."

Cipriano came up behind Dave. "The man is a murderous animal," he said quietly. "It would have been better to kill him."

Dave held him eye to eye. "Then *you* go up and kill him."

"We've got to get over to the water," warned Ash.

"There may be some of his men still at the Tanks," added Cipriano.

Dave nodded. "Let's put it this way—whoever sees him first will have to kill him." He looked at Callie. "Stay here until we signal to you to come to the Tanks."

The three men fanned out on the rugged slope, drifting

like ghosts through the driving dust. Now and again one of them would work ahead of the two others, covered by their rifles, until they reached the crest.

"Look!" said Cipriano.

Beyond the lower slopes trending down to the flat surface of the Lechuguilla Desert a cloud of dust rose to be frayed out and scattered by the wind. Dave put the field glasses on the rising dust. "Five or six mounted men," he reported. "Moving fast. The last of Steel Hand's *corrida*."

Ash nodded. "Without Steel Hand."

"He could not have reached them in time," agreed Dave.

"Which means he's gone to ground somewhere around the Tanks."

"Maybe to die," said Cipriano.

They worked their way down the steep, rocky slope above the eight tanks. Ash signalled to the others. He pointed to the ground. They gathered at a place where telltale spots of blood led off into a maze of boulders and brush above one of the larger tanks.

They stood there, silently scanning the terrain to the right and left and below them. Steel Hand had abandoned his rifle on the reverse slope of the crest, but he likely still had his lethal LeMat "grapeshot" revolver.

"He'll be heading for water," said Dave. Wounding always brought on intense thirst.

They scattered again: Dave in the center, Cipriano to the left, and Ash to the right. Dave entered a series of narrow, natural passageways between huge boulders. An occasional blood spot led him on. He neared the upper rim of one of the largest tanks. The thought of the cool water made him realize just how thirsty he was. He got down on his belly and worked his way by using his elbows and knees to the very rim, but could not see down over a place where the tank wall bulged out. He placed his hands on the rounded bulge and moved forward until he could see down into the pool area and also right into the two muzzles of a LeMat. Over the top barrel he saw the one cold eye of Steel Hand looking at him. He was about twenty feet away, half lying on a rock shelf just above the water level at the foot of the tank with his back against the tank wall. His maimed left wrist was held tight against the upper arm. A rag had been bound about the elbow, evidently to keep a stone or something against the pressure point in the hollow of the joint. He had lost a lot of blood. His face was pale beneath the tan. The heavy LeMat shook slightly as he steadied it while aiming at Dave. That fistful of firepower made Dave sick.

"You thought you had beaten me, you son of a bitch," grated Steel Hand.

Dave had made the mistake of leaning too far over the rim, so that his outspread hands held most of his weight on the rock bulge. If he raised his hands to push himself backward, he might very well slide down into the pool, a perfect target for Steel Hand. His Sharps lay ten feet behind him. He could not reach for his Colt without falling.

"You'll die down there unless you get help," Dave bluffed.

Steel Hand nodded. "And I'll take you with me."

There was a movement on the rim fifteen feet above Steel Hand's head. Ash pointed downward. His meaning was plain enough. It would be better for Dave to let himself slide and fall into the pool rather than try the dangerous and slow maneuver of backing up.

"Now!" yelled Ash. He dropped over the rim with bowie in hand.

Dave raised his hands and used his knees to propel himself forward and down. The LeMat's lower barrel spat flame and smoke. The charge ripped over Dave's back, tearing his shirt as it did so. Dave hit the water at the same time Ash landed with both feet on top of Steel Hand's head. Dave curved his arms upward to rise. His belly scraped the bottom of the tank. His head broke the surface at the same time Ash's head appeared ten feet from him.

Ash held up the bloodied bowie knife. The two of them struck out for the ledge where Steel Hand had been lying.

"What the hell is going on down there!" Cipriano called from the rim.

Dave looked up. "We found Steel Hand."

"Where is he?"

Ash pointed down into the pool. He waggled the bowie at Cipriano.

"I'll get the others," Cipriano said. He left the rim.

"We'll have to pull him out," Dave said.

Ash shrugged. "Why?"

"You want to drink that water with *him* down there?"

"There's seven other tanks."

Dave studied him. "Don't you ever think of others beside yourself? They might be a little more fastidious."

Ash thought for a moment. "That's you, all right—the humanitarian."

Dave and Ash grinned at each other.

They pulled the body out of the pool and dragged it up to the rim. They hauled it off to one side and dumped it into a cleft where the runoff water wouldn't drain into the pool. They covered the body with loose rock. Just another unmarked grave in the vicinity of Tinajas Altas.

Dave and Ash scouted throughout the area of the tanks. They found three horses and a pack mule picketed near the lowest tanks. Dave studied the distant dust rising from the direction in which Steel Hand's men were traveling.

Cipriano, Callie, and Madeleine, along with Jesus and Jack, came to the tanks, where Ash and Dave awaited them. Cipriano threw Ransom's metal hand on the ground. "Maybe he'll need this wherever he's gone," he suggested.

Ash shrugged. "You can mark his grave with it."

Cipriano nodded. He picked it up and took it to the grave.

Later, after they had eaten, Dave spoke to them. "Get some rest and sleep. Ash, Cipriano, and I will take turns on guard. We'll leave about dusk." He looked at Jesus

Valencia. "The Walking Sands are due south of here, are they not?" He was almost certain about the direction, but not the distance. He looked at Jesus, who was resting on a blanket.

Jesus glanced up. He nodded.

"How far from here?"

Jesus shrugged. "I'm not sure."

"Are they any roads or trails into there?"

"No roads. There are trails at times. But the wind, such as we have here today, will wipe them out. They never last long. In fact, the wind will wipe them out almost as fast as you make them, so that you cannot follow them back the way you came."

All of them with the exception of Jesus looked at each other out of the corners of their eyes.

"Can you get to the place where you found the cross?" asked Ash.

"Perhaps," Jesus returned quietly.

Cipriano eyed him. "You mean you came all this way and that is all you can say?"

Jesus studied him. "I did not *come*, mister. I was *brought* here."

"Yes, but will you show us where you found it?" asked Callie.

Jesus slowly surveyed them—the two hard-case Americans, the two women, the smiling Mexican with the steely glint in his dark eyes, and the Jack of Spades. "Perhaps," he said at last.

"We saved your life here. Remember?" said Ash.

Jesus waved a thin hand. "I would have survived."

Ash shook his head. "I'll be damned if you would have!"

Dave had a vivid memory of the night Jesus had appeared out of the desert to stand before him, mute except for a faint gutteral sound followed by a subdued roaring. Dave had recognized the obvious signs of thirst to an almost absolute extremity. It seemed impossible that Valencia could have survived, and yet there he had been, a grotesque caricature of a human being; almost, but not quite, destroyed by the deadly Desierto de Altar.

"Dave?" Ash appealed.

"After all, he *was* alive," Dave reminded his friend.

Jack Spade came closer to Jesus. "I was there, too. I saw him. Have you ever heard of anyone living without water as long as he did on the Gran Desierto?" He paused. "*And* on The Walking Sands."

"All we have is his story about that," countered Ash. He didn't sound very certain of himself.

Dave shook his head. "He never said a word about that."

"And, if it hadn't been for us, he would have been caught and perhaps killed by Steel Hand!"

Jesus smiled. It was the first time Dave had ever seen him do so. "But I *wasn't* caught by Steel Hand. And he would not have killed me. He knew, or *thought* he knew, I would show him where the treasure was hidden in the Sands."

Ash shook his head in anger. "He would have killed you then!"

"No," said Jesus. "You see, my friend, I have the 'power.' "

Jack Spade hastily crossed himself.

Callie knelt beside Jesus. "What is it you want from us?" she asked quietly. "Yes, we brought you here, but 'power' or not, you could not have done so yourself. Perhaps *we* are part of that 'power.' Did you ever think of that?"

Jesus looked about at the others. "You people will go on against any odds, even unto death, in your search for riches. Perhaps this lady is right. In any case, we must go on together. In time the puzzle will be solved." He smiled. "There is a saying: *God will sort the souls.*" He laid his head back and covered his eyes with his arms. In a few moments he was sound asleep.

Ash shook his head. "Well, I'll be damned."

Jack nodded. "You will be if you try to cross Jesus Valencia."

Dave scratched in his beard. "Jesus is probably right. Another thing, my friends—he has taken *charge* of this expedition.''

''It is the power,'' added Jack.

Dave looked at the five of them. ''There is no water in The Walking Sands from all accounts I've heard. I, myself, found none.'' His voice died away. Old memories came back to momentarily haunt him. ''We'll have to ration our water,'' he continued. ''We'll have to survive on what we can take with us. There is nothing to the west and the south of The Walking Sands except the Gulf of California. To the east is the rest of the Gran Desierto. The closest water in that direction will be at Agua Salado, about sixty miles across the Gran Desierto.''

Cipriano nodded. ''And the last thirty or so miles of that will be across the *malpais*, the lava beds that can cut your boot soles to ribbons.''

Callie looked at the sleeping Jesus. ''Then how did that fragile man survive to reach Tinajas Altas?''

No one replied.

Dave pointed at each one of them in turn. ''If there are any of you who want to hold back and not go with those that are planning to leave here at dusk, now is the time to speak out.''

No one spoke.

They left the High Tanks shortly before dusk. They struck out to the southeast, then turned due south to pass between the Lechuguilla Mountains and the southern tip of the Tinajas Altas. Then they went westerly, to clear the southern tip of the Lechuguillas, and continued due south out on the Gran Desierto proper. The wind had died down somewhat in the later afternoon, but with the coming of darkness it surged up with renewed power. Gusts drove stinging grit and bitter dust against the party as they rode toward their elusive goal of The Walking Sands and the legendary, perhaps nonexistent, Lost Jesuit Treasure of Mission San Dionysius.

CHAPTER 19

THE MOON WAS LOW IN THE WEST, A BLOOD-RED ORB AS seen through the haze of high rising clouds of dust and fine sandy grit blown by the powerful wind. The flying debris rattled like dry rain on the hard desert surface. The thudding of hooves, creaking of saddle leather, gurgling of water in the kegs, and an occasional cough mingled with the low moaning of the wind. No one spoke through the bandanna covering their nose and mouth.

Dave stopped walking. Before the rising of the full moon he had relied on his old brass army compass. Now that the moon was almost gone he would need it again. He took it out of his shirt pocket. He turned and looked back, raising his arm in the signal to halt. The horses and mules were brought to a standstill.

Ash came up alongside Dave. He pulled down the bandanna from about his mouth. "How many miles do you think we've come?" he asked.

"Twenty. Twenty-five at the most."

"I still think we should have traveled farther to the east."

Cipriano joined them. He shook his head. "We're still almost paralleling the Sierra del Viejo. If we travel east once we pass them, we'll strike the lava beds. It's much too far east. The Walking Sands are southerly from where we are now."

Dave looked past them to where Jesus sat on a pack mule with his legs between the ends of a pair of water kegs carried on each side of the animal. "I'll ask him," he said.

"He's asleep or maybe in a trance," said Jack. "You think we're still in a line with The Walking Sands?"

Dave shrugged. "He came to Tinajas Altas from the southeast. He must have come from the south past the Sierra del Viejo the same way we are heading now. He would have had to go around the southern tip of the Tinajas Altas Mountains and then southeast to the High Tanks, where he showed up that night."

Dave walked to where Jesus sat on the mule. "Well? We've brought you this far by compass. You said you might know the way to The Walking Sands, and in particular the place where you found the gold cross. What do you say now?"

Jesus looked down at Dave with the eyes of a sleepwalker. He might be there in the flesh, but in his mind he could be many miles away, and God alone might know where he was.

"Jesus?" Dave queried sharply.

Jesus looked away to the south. "I'll need the cross. The cross has the power."

It was quiet except for the low dirgelike moaning of the wind and the hissing of the windswept gravel across the hard ground.

Ash took the cross from around his neck and handed it to Jesus. Jesus kissed it. Jack quickly crossed himself. "Lead the mule on," Jesus said to Jack. Jack tied the reins of his horse to the mule and then led the mule onward.

Dave watched them. He snapped open the lid of his compass. The needle was spinning erratically back and forth. He showed the compass to Ash and Cipriano.

"It might be from iron deposits," suggested Ash.

"There are none around here," said Cipriano. "Maybe it's the power of the cross that's doing it."

"Shit!" exclaimed Ash. "It wasn't doing that when I had the cross about my neck."

"It wasn't doing that when I was using it before the moon rose," said Dave. "It held a steady and true bearing on south-southwest."

"Maybe it's because Jesus and the cross share that power between them," explained Cipriano.

Ash looked at him. "Do you believe that?"

Cipriano shrugged. "The Gran Desierto and particularly The Walking Sands have a reputation for strange happenings. Have you any other explanation?"

Dave smiled. "He's got you there, Ash. Let's follow Brother Jesus before we lose track of him."

They plodded on, leading the animals. They were buffeted by the wind in a sandy void as though somehow they had wandered off the face of the earth and into some ghostly dimension.

Hours passed. It was well after midnight.

Jack stopped leading the mule at Jesus' command. Jesus slid stiffly from the mule with Jack's aid. "Rest here," he murmured.

Dave had taken the last guard, relieving Cipriano. Dave's shift would end at dawn. What enemies would be out on the Gran Desierto at night and in such a windstorm? "None but damned fools," he murmured. "And us," he added. He walked toward the south, perhaps a hundred yards from the camp. He turned to go back, when he heard the faintest of sounds mingled with the moaning of the wind. The sound faded away. It had been so subtle he was not even sure he had heard it at all. The noise came again—seemingly the faint sound of a bell.

He walked slowly to the south. Suddenly he realized he was traveling on a sandy slope. He began to struggle up a steeper grade. He used the butt of his Sharps to aid him in his climb, until at last he reached the top of the slope and met again the full blast of the wind. He walked forward and found himself sliding down the other side. He struggled back to the crest. The sound of the bell came again, slightly louder and clearer. An uneasy feeling came over him. There were no habitations on the Gran Desierto. There were no *bells* in that part of the country.

The wind seemed to abate somewhat. He looked to the east and saw the first faint gray traces of the false dawn. He waited. The light grew. He found himself standing on the crest of a large, crescent-shaped dune. Below him was the concave side of the dune, which faced the wind. Beyond a large hollow was a steep convex slope, the leeward side of another great dune. The wind was still driving a fine profusion of sand from the crest to the leeward slope in the slow and deliberate process of moving the dune ahead of the prevailing winds. There would be another dune beyond that one, and another, and yet another, continuing on and on seemingly into infinity. *The Walking Sands*.

There should be about one hundred square miles of those dunes, or *barchans*. Somewhere in that vast expanse of emptiness and wind-driven sand might be the lost treasure of the Jesuits. Somewhere in there Jesus had found the gold cross of San Dionysius.

Dave slid down the lee side of the dune. Ash met him at the foot of it. "What were you doing up there?" he asked.

"I heard the sound of a bell carried on the wind."

"Maybe it's the Lost Ysabel Mission."

Dave shrugged. "It's said to be in half-a-dozen different places. A legend exists that Jesuit treasures were collected over on the Baja side of the Gulf of California. They were brought to Santa Ysabel some time before the Jesuit Expulsion of 1767. San Dionysius went out of existence long before that time. The cross Jesus found might have been brought to a mission on Baja quite some time before the Expulsion. It might have been brought to Santa Ysabel with the other Jesuit treasures."

"So how could it have gotten over on this side of the Gulf?"

"The bells of the Mission Santa Ysabel disappeared some time before the Expulsion and were never seen again. Think about that for a moment or two, Ash."

A slow light dawned in Ash's mind. "Maybe the Jesuit treasure and the bells of Santa Ysabel, as well as the cross of San Dionysius, were ferried across the Gulf and then hidden there in the Sands."

Dave nodded. "Or perhaps they got this far and could go no further. Perhaps they buried the treasure and went on to be expelled. Possibly they died in the Sands."

"And Jesus Valencia found a record of what they had done and came here to locate the treasure. He found the cross. The treasure was too much for him to carry out of here by himself. He took the cross and came to Tinajas Altas. Do you think maybe he knew *we* were there?"

Dave shook his head. "He knew there was water there. He needed that worse than any treasure." He looked sideways at Ash. "Keep your mouth shut about me hearing those bells."

They walked on. Ash looked sideways at Dave. "Davie," he said quietly. "I don't doubt you heard those bells, but *who* was ringing them?"

"The wind."

"You believe that?"

Dave looked at him. "I *have* to," he quietly replied.

The party rode along the base of the first dune until they found a low saddle of sand connecting it to the next dune. They led the horses and mules across the saddle. When the sun rose they could see dunes to the right and left and ahead. At times they had to struggle up the leeward sides of dune after dune, slipping and sliding in the sand while dragging on the halters of the animals, who had to buck-jump up the slopes.

The wind had died with the coming of the dawn. The atmosphere trembled with the heat waves rising shimmering from the sand. The dunes in the distance seemed to writhe in a tortuous rhythm of their own. There was nothing but sand, and yet more sand. . . . There was no vegetation. There were no signs of man. Not a bird flew through the sky. No one spoke.

It would be that way for hours to come.

It was the darkness before the rising of the moon. Dave had left the party to follow a compass course of south-southwest. All of them, with the exception of Ash and himself, were dozing and sleeping after the exhausting march they had made that day. Jesus' leadership with the "aid" of the cross had begun to develop into the typical symptom of the lost desert traveler. Time and time again he would veer off the compass course by which Dave was keeping a check on him. Jesus would lead off in long, gradual curves to either side of the compass course that would in time develop into a wide sweeping circle. It seemed as though the "power" of Jesus and the cross had failed. Dave had made up his mind after consulting with Ash that it would be up to the two of them to try to find the treasure site. All they really had to go on was the sound of the mysterious bell.

The night wind was fitful, sometimes blowing quite strongly, and at other times fading out almost completely. Dave paused at the top of a large dune. He leaned on his Sharps and waited. He closed his eyes. The bell sounded faintly, carried on a strong gust of wind. Dave opened his eyes. Had he been asleep? Had he imagined hearing the bell?

The wind gusted. The bell sound was carried on it.

Dave peered closely at his compass. The sound had come from the south southwest. He slid down the windward side of the dune, crossed a wide hollow, and slogged up the leeward side of the next dune until he reached the crest. He paused. The bell sound came again.

Dave went on topping a dune, sliding down the windward side, crossing the hollow, and climbing the next dune. Every now and then, when the wind gusted, he heard the sound of the bell.

The moon tinted the sky to the east. As it rose the wind began to abate and then ceased altogether. The clear bright light of the moon shone down on a still landscape. The only moving thing was a gaunt lath of a man carrying a heavy rifle and peering now and again into the brass compass he held in his left hand.

Dave remembered the dream. *The ruins of the lost mission were marked by the partially collapsed bell tower protruding from the rolling sand dune like an elongated broken tooth or fang. For as far as the eye could see there was nothing but sand, sand, and more sand, on and on into infinity. The sands had been sculptured by the wind into great crescent-*

shaped dunes like dun-colored ocean combers held static under a full moon.

He had crested another hill and looked down the other side into a deep, wide hollow between two great dunes. There, set into the bottom side of the opposing dune, was a low broken tower with two bells of different sizes hanging in the belfry. Here and there on the sandy ground he could see the faint rectangular traces of what must have been building foundations. It was his dream, *exactly as he had dreamt it*.

The bell sounded softly. There was no wind.

Dave stood there wondering. An eerie feeling crept through him. It had not been Jesus and his cross that had found the lost mission this time. It had been Dave Hunter and his battered brass compass who had discovered it, guided by the soft wind-borne sound of a bell. Now the bell had rung again, but there was no wind. . . .

Dave slung his Sharps and drew his Colt. It was foolish of him to do so, for he strongly felt that he might be facing the supernatural. He didn't really believe in it, but he had never closed his mind to the thought. He had experienced a number of unexplained occurrences in his life, during the war and on the Great Plains and the mountains and deserts of the southwest and Mexico. He knew well enough that powder and bullet fired from Doctor Colt would have no effect whatsoever on any phantom he might run across in this lost area of mystery and legend. But he didn't know what to expect from the mysterious remains of a religious installation.

Dave worked his way down the dune side until he reached the bottom of the wide hollow. Suddenly he turned, thrusting out his Colt and cocking it at the same time. He narrowed his eyes. The wind was gone. Nothing moved. There was no one to see. Still, *something* had seemed to warn him. He turned and looked west down the great length of the hollow. There was nothing except the sandy sides of the dunes. He let down the hammer of his Colt to half-cock.

He walked close to the bell tower. It stood as a buttress against the inexorable down flow of the dune. Sand piled up on either side of it and had flowed into the interior from the windows opening on the back side of the tower. He walked around and saw the rounded side of a large bell lying on the ground and almost completely covered with sand. Dave knelt beside it. He read the part of an inscription cast into the metal just above the heavy curve of the rim: ABEL*1729. He holstered his Colt and pushed away the sand until he cleared the first part of the lettering: SANTA YS.

"Santa Ysabel 1729," he read aloud.

From the size of the bell he estimated that it might weigh as much as two hundred pounds, more or less. He looked up at the tower. The low side of the belfry had been broken away, evidently when the bell had either been thrown down from the tower or perhaps had broken loose from its hanging and took part of the tower side with it in its fall. He could see some hanging shreds, probably of rawhide, which had bound the top of the bell to the beam next to the other two smaller bells.

Dave looked about the area. Where had Jesus found the gold cross of San Dionysius? Why had the Jesuits, if indeed it had been Jesuits, brought the bells there and built a mission or whatever it had been in such a heat-ridden and waterless area? That had been more than a hundred years ago.

Dave suddenly turned, reaching instinctively for his Colt. He paused. It was always this way when one was alone in remote areas. It was as though someone or *something* was watching just out of sight. Legend had it that they were evil spirits, demons perhaps, who were waiting for the person they were watching to crack and panic, then temporarily lose their sanity and run screaming into the wilderness. Dave had long past disciplined himself to overcome that creeping fear, which he had experienced several times.

He put the thought out of his mind. He walked about the area. "They would have to have had water," he mused. There was a legend that there was a vast underground lake somewhere in the area of The Walking Sands that had once fed an ever-flowing spring. If that had been so at the time of the formation of the mission, they would have had to have food as well. If there had been plentiful water, they would have crops of some kind. He looked at the great towering dunes, knowing that there were many square miles of them in every cardinal direction of the compass.

"They might have stayed here for a time until forced to leave," he said. "But what would have forced them to leave? The Spanish authorities? Lack of food and water?" He scratched in his beard. "Besides, who was there to come and worship in such a place as this?"

He walked about the area. He looked at the faint traces of former building foundations. The tower had been built of rocks. Therefore the buildings must have been built of the same material. Where were the fallen walls of the buildings? The sand covering the area of some of the buildings was not deep enough to obscure them. He looked up at the dune to watch the sand's slow process of flowing down to engulf the ruins and the tower as it had been periodically doing for more than a hundred years. How long would it take to bury them, and how long would it be before they saw the light of day again as the dune was moved on by the wind? If there was a treasure here, where would it have been buried? The cross of San Dionysius must surely indicate that treasure existed, or *had* existed, somewhere in the area. On the other hand, perhaps it was the *only* treasure that had been left there.

Some impulse made Dave climb the side of the dune by which he had entered the hollow. He looked to the east, beyond the ruins, but saw nothing but sand covering the ground with here and there a place swept clear by the wind to expose the hard-packed soil. He looked to the west. That part of the hollow extended almost in a straight line for quite a distance. The ground had been swept clear of sand. He took out his field glasses and focused them on the farthest reach of the hollow. He scanned the bottom and thought he saw something on the bare ground.

Dave slogged along the side of the dune until he was about where he had seen what seemed like a disturbance on the surface. He descended to the bottom of the dune. There, plainly to be seen, was a design made of stones embedded in the soil. It was a rough blunt arrowhead shape about three feet in length and about eighteen inches wide. The base was toward the west, and stemming from it was the unmistakable design of a Greek cross whose shaft and crosspiece were equal in length from top to bottom and from side to side. He looked to the east, in the direction the arrowhead was pointing, directly at the distant tower. Dave was well versed in the early Spanish and Mexican treasure signs and symbols. These two signs, the arrowhead and the cross, were simple enough. The arrowhead pointed in the direction of the next sign or to the treasure itself. The cross indicated that the treasure was the property of the Church.

He studied the ground between where he stood beside the stone design and the tower in the distance. The clear moonlight brought out every minor detail of the soil. He walked slowly toward the tower. Now and again he would squat and peer along the surface of the ground. The third time he did so he seemed to feel rather than see a small area minutely lower than the surrounding soil. He went to it. It was almost impossible to distinguish it from its surroundings. He drew his knife and scraped lines across the area. He climbed the side of the dune and looked down at the marks he had made. Then he noticed the difference. It was a roughly rectangular patch of lighter soil about ten-by-five feet in dimensions and very slightly depressed, as though the surface had subsided into a hollow or an excavation.

Dave walked and slid down the dune's side. "Maybe an old latrine," he said. He grinned. "Or a burial place for one of the Jesuits."

He returned to the tower and looked back toward the depression. "Or the burial place, or one of the burial places, for the Lost Treasure of the Jesuits."

He rested his Sharps rifle against the wall and then sat down, placing his back against the tower wall. The big bell was a yard or so away from him. He drank sparingly from his canteen and then rolled a Lobo Negro cigarette and lighted it. He rested his head back against the wall and sat there with a thin wreath of tobacco smoke hanging in the still air about him. He'd have to wait until dawn to retrace his trail back to the party. Right at that moment he was quite content to sit there. A feeling of peace and calmness came over him. He wondered idly if it was from his presence at the mission. He flipped away the cigarette and closed his eyes.

CHAPTER 20

"HUNTER, RAISE YOUR HANDS ABOVE YOUR HEAD," THE hoarse voice said.

Dave opened his eyes. The moon was low in the west. Jack Spade stood just beyond the half-buried bell. He held a nickel-plated Winchester in his hands. Beyond him was Jesus Valencia, seated on a mule. He held the gold cross in both hands in front of him. His eyes looked as they had once looked before—like those of a sleepwalker.

"Get up! Keep your hands up!" ordered Jack.

Dave glanced sideways as he stood up. His rifle was gone. He could not feel the accustomed weight of his holstered Colt.

"Throw your knife on the ground," said Jack.

Dave did as he was told. He raised his hands again. He looked into the eyes of Jack and thought perhaps there might be a hint of madness in them.

"Looking for your *compañero* Ash?" asked Jack. "Look around the corner."

Dave looked. Ash stood with his hands behind his back. A reata had been looped around his neck. "Caught me asleep like you, Dave," explained Ash. "Led me here like a dog with this damned rope around my neck."

Dave looked beyond Ash to where the horses and mules stood. Callie sat one of the horses with her hands bound to the saddle horn. She had been gagged.

Dave turned to face Jack. "What the hell is this?" he demanded. "Where are Madeleine and Cipriano?"

"You did your job, Hunter," replied Jack. "You found the mission when Jesus couldn't find his way back here with the cross."

Dave nodded. "I know that. But what about Madeleine and Cipriano?"

There was no reply from Jack.

"He stabbed Cipriano to death in his sleep," said Ash quietly. "Madeleine heard him. She fought with Jack. He killed her."

Dave studied Jack. "Why?" he asked. He felt in his mind that it was a foolish and useless question.

Jack hunched his powerful shoulders and bent his head forward. "I don't trust *any* of you. If we find the treasure, it belongs to Jesus. Cipriano would have claimed it for Mexico. Those two women wanted it for themselves. I can say the same for you and that big-nosed partner of yours."

"Bastard," growled Ash.

Jack looked at him. "You're going to look funny with the butt of this fancy Winchester stickin' in your big mouth."

"What did you find here, Hunter?" asked Jack.

Dave shrugged. "Some ruins. Three bells. Two in the tower and the other on the ground in front of you. Sand and more sand."

Jack never took his eyes off Dave. They were unblinking, like the stare of a basilisk ready to peddle sudden death with lethal breath and a glance. "You're lying, Hunter," he said accusingly.

Dave held out his hands with palms upwards. "What did you expect me to find? Piles and piles of Jesuit gold and silver for the taking? Even if I had found it, how could I get it out of here? You had the horses and mules and all the water."

"Why did you come on alone?"

"Your *patron* Jesus seemed to have lost the way. I didn't want the rest of you and myself to end up out on the desert like he did. You saw him at Tinajas Altas. Did you want to end up that way?"

Jack looked aside as though uncertain of himself.

Jesus slid from the back of his mule. "You *have* found

something," he said. "Your compass didn't bring you here, Hunter. It was something else. Tell us."

Dave shrugged. "What do you want from me? Did I hear a voice from the clouds, or perhaps the voice from the burning bush? Did the spectre of a long-dead Jesuit priest lead me here?"

"Wouldn't surprise me none," put in Ash.

Jack was puzzled. He was getting out of his depth. "What do you mean—it was *something else* that brought him here?" he suspiciously asked Jesus.

Jesus pointed at Dave. "Ask him. If he won't tell you, then you can kill one of his two companions there. That should jog his memory. And I think he *has* found something. Ask him!"

Jack looked at Callie and Ash. "Yes," he said thoughtfully. "Which one first?"

Jesus shrugged. "The choice is yours."

Jack looked at Dave. "Talk," he ordered.

"I think he means it, Davie," Ash warned.

Dave looked questioningly at him. Ash nodded. It was a gamble. What Dave had found was only a slightly subsided patch of earth. He smiled a little. Supposing it *had* been a latrine? Maybe it was the grave of a long-dead priest. Perhaps it was truly the hiding place of the treasure.

"What's so funny?" demanded Jack.

Dave looked beyond him to Jesus—the little man who had survived an escape from Yuma prison and later from Steel Hand. The little man who had found the cross of San Dionysius and then had survived the almost impossible feat of walking out of The Walking Sands and the Gran Desierto without water.

Jesus studied Dave in return. "You *will* tell us," he said firmly.

Jack looked at Ash. "Get over here," he ordered.

Ash walked to Jack. Jack pointed the rifle at the base of Ash's neck. He full cocked the Winchester. He looked at Dave.

"Tell them to go to hell, Davie," said Ash.

Jack looked at Dave. "Well? Is that what you want me to do?"

Dave shrugged. "I heard a bell during the night. I followed it here." He looked up at the tower. "The wind must have blown it so that it rang."

Jack spat to one side. "That's loco! No one else heard any bell!" He poked the gun muzzle hard against Ash's neck.

Jesus came closer. "I believe him. I think he has a 'power.' Yes, it must be so. I believe he heard a bell." He paused. He held Dave's eyes with his. "You did find something, didn't you?"

Dave looked at Ash, standing there with a reata tight about his neck and with the muzzle of a rifle close against it as well. No damned treasure in the world was worth his life. At last he nodded. "I *did* find something. It's not a treasure. Come, I'll show you." He walked away from the tower.

"Where the hell are you going?" challenged Jack.

Dave turned slowly. "You wanted to know what I found."

"Follow him," ordered Jesus.

Jack picked up the reata and led Ash after Dave, with Jesus following close behind Ash. Dave stopped where he had marked the area of subsidence. He pointed down. "Here," he said. He pointed west. "Down there is a sign made of stones embedded in the soil. A blunt arrowhead pointing east directly in line with the tower. There is a Greek cross of stones behind the arrowhead, that is, to the west. It's likely been there a hundred years or more."

Jack eyed him. "What the hell does that mean?"

Jesus looked at Dave. "Tell him," he ordered.

"It's likely a Spanish or Mexican mining symbol. The arrowhead usually points in the direction of treasure. The cross means that the treasure is the property of the Church."

"Is that true, Father?" Jack asked of Jesus.

Jesus nodded. "Do *not* call me 'Father'! Hunter is right."

Ash spat dryly. "Helluva priest you are, Jesus. Letting this son of a bitch murder two people to get them out of your way."

Jesus shook his head. "I knew nothing of that. He did it on his own."

Jack shook the rifle. "That damned Mexican would have turned the treasure over to the Mexican government or kept it for himself. That crazy woman attacked me."

Dave eyed Jesus. "What do you think of all that, eh?"

Jesus reached for Jack's rifle. "What's done is done. Jack, go and get the pick and the spades. Bring the lantern as well."

"What about the woman?" asked Jack.

There was a long pause. Dave readied himself for a leap at Jesus to get his hand on the rifle. "Bring her along," said Jesus at last. "She can dig as well as these two men." He smiled a little. "If either or both of these two men attack me, kill the woman at once. You understand?"

So it was. Jack brought two spades and a pick from one of the pack mules. He lighted the lantern and placed it on the ground so that it cast light on the subsided area. Callie was freed from her wrist bonds, but instead her ankles were bound together.

"Take the gag out of her mouth," said Dave.

"Go to hell," snapped Jack.

Dave hefted the pick. "Either you take out the gag or we don't dig up this damned ground."

Jack went into his hunched-shoulder, head-thrust-forward act. He swung the Winchester he had taken from Ash's horse and aimed it at Dave.

"You shoot that goddamned Winchester, and you'll end up with this spade half buried in that thick head of yours," warned Ash. "You can't shoot both of us at the same time."

Jesus held Cipriano's nickel-plated Winchester in his thin hands. "I can shoot," he said quietly.

Dave smiled a little. "No, you won't. You've got to find that treasure. If it *really* exists. You can't do it without help from Ash and me. When and if it is found, you've got to get it out of here, and you can't do it alone. So, shoot and be damned to you!"

Jesus studied Dave's hard-set features and cold blue eyes.

Finally he nodded. ''Take out the gag, Hunter, then start digging again.''

''You damned near did it just then,'' murmured Ash out of the side of his mouth.

Dave shrugged. ''You were the one who told Jack both of us can't be shot at the same time.''

Ash eyed him for a moment. ''Start digging,'' he said.

Dave drove the point of the pick into the hard ground. Surprisingly enough it seemed as though a layer of hard-packed soil lay on top of the hole that had been dug. Once it was broken through and the pieces were shoveled aside by Ash, the digging became easier. Dave looked at Callie. Her expression showed no emotion. Dave knew she had been very close to Madeleine. Now Madeleine was lying some-where in the empty vastness of The Walking Sands, bereft of even a simple burial.

The moon was gone. The lantern cast a pool of yellowish light about itself, beyond which was deep darkness. The tower and the horses and mules were hidden in the darkness. The huge dunes on either side were nothing but dark mounds rising up to meet the dark blue of the night sky. It was quiet except for the steady rise and fall of the pick thudding into the earth and the scraping of the spade into the harsh soil. Now and again Dave would glance toward either Jesus or Ash. They both stood well back from the lamplight with only their legs and feet fully visible.

They were four feet down in the hole when Dave threw the pick on top of the mounded earth. He scrambled up and out of the hole. He had discarded his shirt. His undershirt was soaked with sweat.

''You find anything?'' called Jack. He came into the lamp-light.

Dave shook his head.

''Get back in the hole then!'' ordered Jack.

Ash climbed out to stand beside Dave. ''Water,'' he said.

Jack shook his head. ''We don't have any to spare.''

''You thickheaded jackass!'' roared Ash. ''We can't do this heavy work without water!''

Jack smiled thinly. "Try," he suggested.

Jesus came out of the shadows. "Give them water," he said.

"Son of a bitch!" snapped Jack. He stalked off into the darkness.

Dave eyed Jesus. "You know he's loco, don't you?"

"Maybe. Probably so. But I need him now, as I need you."

"And when we find your treasure, if we do, what then?"

Jesus smiled a little. "You'll help me get it out of here."

"And if we don't find treasure?"

There was no reply from Jesus.

"You'll die," put in Callie. "You and Ash and me as well. He'll have no further use for you." She smiled a little. "So, my buckos, you had better find that damned treasure."

Jack came back with two canteens. He handed one each to Dave and Ash. Dave handed his back. "There's a lady present," he said.

Jack looked at Jesus. Jesus shook his head. "She's of no use to us. We've hardly enough water as it is."

Dave started walking toward Callie. Jack came forward with his rifle half raised. Dave walked partway past him, reached down with his left hand, and slapped the rifle aside. Jack cursed and swung at Dave with his free arm. Dave slapped the heavy canteen full across Jack's face and then brought up a knee into his groin. When Jack bent over in agony, Dave slammed the canteen down on the back of his neck and drove him face downward on the hard ground.

"Stop!" shouted Jesus.

"Go to hell!" roared Dave.

The rifle detonation was instantaneous. Dave heard the sibilant hiss of the bullet as it flew just past his left ear. The sound of the shot sounded hollowly within the confines of the two great dunes. It died away, and weighted silence returned.

Dave turned slowly. Jack started to get up. Dave placed a foot on his neck and drove him down again and kept him there. Dave looked at Jesus. The little man worked the lever of the repeater to reload. The spent cartridge tinkled on the hard ground. The two men, so different in size, strength, weight, and intention, stood there facing each other.

"Did you aim to kill me?" asked Dave.

Jesus shook his head. "It would have been easy to do so. That was just a warning. The next time I shoot to kill."

Dave nodded. "I thought so." He took his foot off Jack's neck.

Jack got up on his knees. He tilted his head up and sideways and fixed Dave with a killing stare. It was as if his whole face had changed. He reached slowly for his rifle. Dave kicked it out of his reach. "Get up, you son of a bitch," he said thinly. "Get up and I'll cave in your goddamned stupid face."

"I oughta kill you," mouthed Jack.

"Try," said Ash. He balanced the pick in his hands.

Dave walked to Callie. He unstoppered the canteen. "Drink," he said.

"You're all crazy, the four of you," Callie accused.

Dave shrugged. "Probably. Why the hell else would we be out here in this godforsaken place looking for a treasure that doesn't exist except in that crazy little man's mind?"

She drank and then handed back the canteen. "Always the gentleman." She smiled. "Ladies first. First, last, and always."

He nodded. "You've got it right, Callie." He walked back to the pit. He drank a mouthful, ignoring the glaring Jack and his ready rifle. He knew damned well that if anyone was going to kill him it would not be Jack but rather Jesus.

Dave got down in the pit beside Ash.

Ash whistled softly. "She was right about the three of you being crazy," he said out of the side of his mouth.

"She said the *four* of us."

"Well, I have been wondering about you for some time."

Dave glanced sideways at him. "Is that why you're in this goddamned hole with me? You ever think of that?"

Ash nodded. "She's right. It's the *four* of us."

When they got down to five feet there wasn't enough room

for the two of them to work, so they took turns. At six feet Dave raised the pick to break up a heavy clod of earth. The pick struck deep into the earth, and when he tried to remove it, he found that it was stuck in something. He took the spade and dug around the point of the pick. He tested the hardness of the soil with the edge of the spade. It sounded faintly hollow. There was another rounded clod of earth under the surface. He struck at it with the spade. It moved. He got down on his knees and dug with his hands. His right hand closed on something shaped like a stick. He pulled it free from the soil. He held it close to his eyes. It was the upper arm bone of a human skeleton. He placed it to one side and dug about the rounded object. He picked it up and held it close. *"Christamighty,"* he whispered. It was a dirt-encrusted human skull.

"What's going on down there?" Ash called.

Dave stood. Lamplight flooded the excavation. He looked up into the suspicious face of Jack Spade, who was standing on top of the two-foot mound of earth beside the hole.

"What the hell are you doing down there?" he demanded.

Dave grinned. "Here, Spade," he said. "Catch!" He tossed the skull upward.

Jack screamed hoarsely. He dropped the lantern into the hole and sprinted off into the enveloping darkness. Dave caught the lantern and swore as it burned his fingers. He hastily set it down on the bottom of the hole. Maybe he had been right. It might be a grave.

"Get into that hole," Jesus ordered Ash.

The little man was taking no chances. Ash dropped down beside Dave. "You're as big a damned fool as ever. You could have given that superstitious son of a bitch a heart attack."

"Might have been what I had in mind."

"I wasn't feeling too well myself when I saw that grinning thing come flying up out'a this damned grave."

Dave looked up at the spare figure of Jesus standing on the mound of earth. The lamplight shone on the barrel of his rifle. "Keep digging," Jesus ordered.

Dave pulled the pick free from whatever it was stuck into. Ash cleared the earth from around the place where it had been stuck. Pieces of bones showed up in quantity. He thrust the spade down hard. The hollow sound came again. He looked at Dave.

"Wood?" he asked.

Dave nodded. They scraped away more bones and earth. A dark level surface showed. A flat metal plate was centered on one side of it. Ash dug around it.

"A heavy hasp and a big padlock," he reported. They looked at each other in the wavering lamplight.

"Maybe a coffin," suggested Ash.

"With a *padlock* on it?" asked Dave.

Ash shrugged. "Maybe they had grave robbers around here," he suggested.

"The damned box is only four feet long," said Dave.

"Could have been a midget or a dwarf," argued Ash.

Dave shook his head. "Oh, for Christ's sake! Shut up!"

"Break it open," ordered Jesus.

Jack had slowly returned. "Maybe there's a skeleton in it, too. Maybe there's a curse on it like my mother's people claim! Maybe, if we open it, the curse will be in effect, and we'll all die."

"Hopefully, you anyway, Jack," said Dave. "Remember the curse was for the Indians not to tell anyone about the hiding place of Jesuit treasures. I never heard any white man was covered by that curse."

Ash nodded wisely. "That makes us safe enough." He looked up at Jack. "Ain't you half-*Yaqui*, Jack?"

The lamplight shone on the set face of Jesus Valencia. Gone was his usual composure. It seemed as though his eyes were lit by blue fire from within. "Break open the box!" he snapped.

Ash struck the pick at an angle deep into the wood just to one side of the hasp, then pried upward with all his might. It took Dave's added strength to move the thick metal up half an inch. The next blow of the pick went all the way under the hasp. They strained together to pry it up high. The third try broke the hasp completely loose. They dug around the sides of the box to free it from the earth, then forced a spade between the lid and the front side and pried it up high enough so that they could grip it with their hands and force it back. A layer of books covered the top. They were evidently missals, hymnals, and other books of the Catholic Church.

"Lift them out," ordered Jesus.

"If we find treasure under them, we're dead men," whispered Ash.

Dave looked at him. "We may be dead men anyway."

They removed the books and then what appeared to be some hind of garment worn by priests in the execution of their duties. Ash removed the garment from the box, while Dave held the lantern up high. As the last folds of the garment were taken from the box, the lamplight shone on row upon row of what appeared to be small rolls shaped like bread loaves, which glittered in the lamplight as only gold and silver could do.

Dave looked up into the faces of Jesus and Jack. "Your Jesuit treasure," he said.

Jesus was puzzled. "Lift them out," he ordered. "Pass them up here."

They pried them out and began to pass them up to the four greedy, grasping hands. Beneath the small ingots there was nothing but bare wood.

"Is that *all*?" demanded Jesus. He did not wait for an obvious reply. "Mother of God," he screamed. *"Is that all?"*

They pried the heavy box out of the ground. There was nothing below it but undisturbed earth. They looked at each other and then leaned the box at the hole's side.

"Dig around it!" ordered Jesus. His voice trembled as he spoke.

Dave shook his head. "We've reached the bottom of the hole. That box and the skeleton, or *patron*, if you prefer to call it that, are the only things that were buried here."

Jesus gripped his hair with his right hand. His hand shook with tension. "But that cannot be! This you have found is only a pittance of the real wealth to be buried here! It was said to be equivalent to the wealth of Croesus! It *has* to be here! It *must* be here!''

Jack was confused. ''What you have is plenty! Don't defy God, I beg you! Take what you have here and be satisfied! I want none of it for myself!''

Jesus dropped his rifle and looked down into the hole. ''Dig, damn you! Dig! Dig!''

''Time to move,'' said Dave out of the side of his mouth. ''Give me a leg out of this hole when I yell!''

Jack looked down into the hole. He full cocked the nickel-plated Winchester. ''You'll die here,'' he said.

Callie screamed.

Jack turned quickly toward her.

Dave gripped the bail of the lantern and swung it upward, full-armed. ''Now!'' he yelled. Ash linked his hands together and bent his knees. Dave placed his left foot in Ash's hands and his right on the box. Ash lifted up on his hands, boosting Dave up and out of the hole. Jack screamed hoarsely as the lantern struck the side of his head and shattered the glass cylinder. Flaming oil splattered against Jack's face and set his hair on fire. He dropped his rifle. Dave caught it as he rose up out of the hole. He thrust an arm over the side and gripped one of Jesus' legs, then pulled himself out onto the mounded earth. Jesus fell backward and struck his head hard on the pile of ingots. Dave got to his feet and raised the Winchester. Jack was running off into the darkness with his hair all aflame. His screams resounded and echoed throughout the great hollow between the dunes.

''Kill him!'' Callie shouted.

Dave dropped the Winchester beside her. She grabbed it and fired from her sitting position. The slug struck Jack in the back and drove him forward. He fell flat on his face. His powerful hands clawed at the hard-packed earth while his booted feet rapped out a wild tattoo on the ground. Suddenly he twisted, writhed, and then stiffened and lay still. His hair burned awhile in the darkness like a distant beacon and then flickered out.

Dave looked down at Callie.

"He would have died a horrible death anyway," she murmured.

He nodded. "That's one way of looking at it," he said dryly.

"Cut out the goddamned conversation and get me out of this goddamned hole!" yelled Ash.

Dave gave him a hand up. Ash looked down at Jesus. "Well, he got his gold," he commented.

Dave knelt beside Jesus. The little man did not move. He looked close. The eyes were wide and staring. They saw nothing. Dave glanced at Ash and Callie. "He's gone." He stood up and touched the little pile of ingots with his boot toe. "I guess this is ours now." He looked about through the darkness. "Unless you want to look for the rest of it."

"Maybe that's all there really was," said Ash.

Callie shook her head. "He said it was equivalent to the wealth of Croesus."

"Hardly," said Dave.

"How much do you think is here?" asked Ash.

"*Quien sabe?* No less than fifty thousand dollars at least."

"More likely one hundred thousand," corrected Callie.

Ash shrugged. "So we'll strike a value of perhaps seventy-five thousand. Twenty-five thousand apiece."

Dave looked down at Jesus and then off into the darkness, where Jack lay quiet and still. "Ironic," he murmured. "We'll never know what Jesus planned to do with the treasure. Jack wanted none of it. Now both of them are dead because of it."

Ash nodded. "We'll have to get moving. We're low on water. We haven't got enough for all the horses and mules. We can't stay here."

They placed the two bodies in the treasure hole.

"Where's the cross?" asked Dave. He looked at Callie and Ash. Both of them shook their heads. They searched the ground in the darkness, but it was not to be found. Ash got down in the burial hole and searched the bodies. He looked up at Callie and Dave and shook his head.

"Where did Jesus find it?" asked Callie.

Dave shook his head. "He never told us."

"It has to be around here somewhere," said Ash, as Dave helped him from the hole.

"But where?" asked Callie.

They looked about themselves in the darkness.

"I'm not about to go searching for it," Ash said after a time.

"Wherever it is," said Dave. "It *belongs* here."

They rapidly filled in the grave.

"We can only take three horses and one pack mule," said Dave. "We can turn the others loose to find water or kill them off to save them the tortures of dying of thirst."

"Turn them loose," pleaded Callie.

Dave looked at Ash. Ash shook his head.

They led the extra horses and the pack mule up the hollow. Pistol shots finished them off. They loaded part of the ingots into their saddlebags and the remainder onto the last pack mule. The wind began to blow some hours before dawn. It moaned softly across the top of the wide hollow.

They rode north, at times dismounting to lead the horses and the pack mule over the more difficult of the dunes. Ash and Dave were tired. Callie was near to complete exhaustion. They could not stop to rest. They kept on, up, over, and down the dunes blocking their passage until the hills began to lessen in size and the first faint gray light of the false dawn shone in the eastern sky. The wind was at their backs and was gaining in velocity.

"What do we do with our shares?" asked Ash. He was the first one to speak since they had left the ruins.

Dave shrugged. *"Quien sabe?"*

"Yuma?"

Dave shook his head. "Hell no!"

"I've always had a hankering to see Denver again. Heard it's grown considerable in the past twenty years. Knew a nice little redheaded filly there. Her name was Cordelia. Young and pretty. She liked me."

Dave looked sideways at him. "You figure she's still there?

Twenty years old? Young and pretty? She'd be around forty years old now, Ash, if she was damned fool enough to wait for you.''

''I'm here, too,'' put in Callie.

They looked at her. ''Where do you want to go?'' asked Ash. ''You've still got the medicine show waiting for you in Yuma.''

Callie looked at Dave. ''Are you going to Denver, too?''

Dave shrugged. ''I sure as hell ain't going back to Yuma.''

They rode on for a time.

''Maybe I'll go to Denver, too,'' said Callie.

There was no comment from Ash or Dave.

Just before the sun showed itself beyond the eastern mountains, Dave suddenly drew rein, placed a hand on the cantle pack of his saddle, and looked back toward the south.

Ash and Callie halted their mounts. ''What is it, Dave?'' asked Callie.

Dave looked at them. ''I heard that bell again.''

''I heard nothing,'' she said.

Ash shook his head. ''Can't be from the mission.''

''How so?'' asked Dave.

Ash hesitated a moment, then he looked squarely at Dave. ''Because I looked closely at them two bells in the belfry. Neither one had clappers in them. Besides, that belfry was too far below the dune crest for the wind to blow through.''

Dave shook his head. ''That can't be. The wind made one of them ring.''

''Even if they had clappers, that wind isn't ever strong enough to swing them big heavy bells.''

Ash was right. Dave had never thought of that, but he *had* heard the sound of a bell coming from the direction of the ruins. ''Are you sure neither one of you just heard that bell?''

They both nodded. ''You heard a *ghost* bell, Dave,'' said Ash.

They rode on. They could not return to the mission now. Water must be their top priority if they wanted to live.

Dave heard the bell again, but he did not halt or mention it to the others. He thought about the curious placing of the mission in such a remote and deadly area so far from water. Why? Jesus had been positive that the ingots were only a small part of the treasure he believed was buried or hidden there. Buried or hidden? The thought stayed with Dave. Perhaps the cache of ingots had been a decoy to lure treasure seekers away from the real cache of the mass of treasure. But where? The arrow had pointed directly in a straight line to the treasure hole. Where else? *"Jesus!"* he cried aloud as he drew the dun to a halt.

Callie and Ash halted their horses again. "Another ghost bell?" asked Ash dryly.

"I think I know where the treasure was hidden. Concealed would be a better word to describe it," explained Dave. "There was no real reason to build a mission in such a god-forsaken place. No real reason except one. To hide the treasure."

"We know that," said Ash.

Dave half smiled. "Wait! The treasure cache we found was a decoy. The Jesuits were hopeful it would lure treasure seekers away from the real place where the treasure was concealed."

"Such as?" asked Callie.

Dave pointed upward. "The belfry."

Ash shook his head. "No room up there for anything but those two bells, Davie. I . . ." His face changed. "Jesus! The *bells*!"

Callie looked from one to the other of them. She had an uneasy feeling within her. These two men were no doubt absolutely loco.

Dave noted her expression. "They could have gathered all their Church treasures from Baja, both gold and silver, and melted them down, then recast them into bells. They built what we took to be a mission to look like old ruins. They hung the bells in the tower and buried a small part of the treasure in the hole we found as a decoy to lure us or any other treasure seekers away from the real mass of the treasure hanging in the belfry disguised as bells."

"What about the big bell lying on the ground?" asked Ash.

"Perhaps a real bell made to look like it had fallen from the belfry."

"My God," murmured Ash. "If that big bell was solid gold or silver . . ."

Dave shook his head. "Not likely. Besides, if those two bells in the tower are gold and silver, there would be a mighty fortune in them alone."

"So what do we do about it?" asked Callie.

"We can't go back. Now, anyway," replied Ash.

She looked at Dave. "Later, perhaps."

"The wind will cover those ruins with sand within a matter of months. Maybe it's just as well. I don't think I'd ever want to go back there again."

She smiled a little. "Afraid of the curse?" she asked.

He didn't speak for a moment or two. He looked to the south. "Perhaps, Callie. Something within me tells me to leave it alone."

She looked at Ash.

Ash shrugged. "I feel the same way."

They rode on. Just as the sun rose, Dave heard the bell once more. He did not look back.

When they had ridden most of the way to Tinajas Altas, the bell rang again. There was no one to hear it.

Vaya con Dios. Vaya con Dios. . . . acaso . . .

EPILOGUE

THERE HAVE BEEN RUMOURS OF A "LOST MISSION" SOME-where on the Gran Desierto de Altar for many years. It has never been found. Some think it is a pure fabrication. How-ever, beginning in 1936, the railroad from Mexicali to Riitos on the Colorado River was extended to Punta Penasco on the Gulf of California, crossing the barren western and southern limits of the Gran Desierto. A group of tracklayers found two bells, a large iron one and a small bronze one, lying out in the windblown sand. No one knows how the bells got there or from where they came. At least thirty years or so ago the iron bell rested on the porch of a church in San Luis near the Colorado River and just across the border from the United States. It may still be there.

Vaya con Dios. . . . acaso . . .

Gordon D. Shirreffs
Granada Hills, California

ABOUT THE AUTHOR

GORDON D. SHIRREFFS'S fascination with the American West began in 1940, when he was stationed with the army 39th Artillery Brigade at Fort Bliss, Texas. In World War II he served as a captain of anti-aircraft artillery in the Aleutian Campaign, then as a ship transport commander in the European Theatre, concluding his service as a military historian. After the war he took up writing. His eighty-two novels to date include the Lee Kershaw, Manhunter western series; THE UNTAMED BREED, BOLD LEGEND and GLORIETA PASS, which chronicle the adventures of mountain man Quint Kershaw, and THE GHOST DANCERS, which features Major Alec Kershaw. Dave Hunter appeared in *Hell's Forty Acres* and *Maximilian's Gold*. Mr. Shirreffs is also the author of many short stories, several television plays, one T.V. series, and four films. He lives in Granada Hills, California, with his wife, Alice.